T H E

HORSE
LATITUDES

"A GOOD READ—IN SPADES . . .
Imaginatively rendered . . .
Quick, chilling, often humorous . . .
Violence as nasty as it can be . . .
Ferrigno's is a voice we'll be hearing
more of in the future."
Chicago Tribune

"Sexy, funny and sharp . . . A PLEASURE"
Robert B. Parker

"A striking California-cool thriller . . .
MARVELOUSLY MENACING . . .
Ferrigno grabs from page one . . .
An extraordinarily vivid trash-barrel version
of the American dream."
Kirkus Reviews

THE
HORSE
LATITUDES

ROBERT FERRIGNO

AVON BOOKS ◆ NEW YORK

Grateful acknowledgment is made for permission to use the following:

"Tell It Like It Is," by Lee Diamond and George Davis. Copyright ©
1966 by Conrad Music, a division of Arc Music Corporation and Olrap
Publishing. All rights reserved. Reprinted by permission.

"A Ghost of a Chance (with You)," by Bing Crosby, Ned Washington,
and Victor Young. Copyright © 1932 by Mills Music, Inc. Copyright
renewed. All rights reserved. Used by permission.

AVON BOOKS
A division of
The Hearst Corporation
105 Madison Avenue
New York, New York 10016

Published in hardcover by William Morrow and Company, Inc.; for
information address Permissions Department, William Morrow and
Company, Inc., 105 Madison Avenue, New York, New York 10016.

First Avon Books Printing: May 1991
First Avon Books International Printing: February 1991
First Avon Books Special Printing: December 1990

AVON TRADEMARK REG. U.S. PAT. OFF. AND IN OTHER COUNTRIES,
MARCA REGISTRADA, HECHO EN U.S.A.

Printed in the U.S.A.

RA 10 9 8 7 6 5 4 3 2 1

To Jody and Jake,
who are not surprised

ACKNOWLEDGMENTS

My deep appreciation to William Ungerman for answering my endless questions about police procedure and points of law, and for showing me how to clear a Mac-10

To Jack Voigt for sharing his experiences boar hunting in the Channel Islands

To Ron Tellez, who talked me through the mysteries of a new computer

To my agent, Sandra Dijkstra, for her creativity and unflagging energy, and to her assistants, Katherine Goodwin and Laurie Fox

To my editor, Doug Stumpf, who knows that the best editing is done from the inside out, and to his assistant, Jared Stamm; and to Howard Kaminsky, President of Hearst Trade Books, for his enthusiastic support.

The HORSE LATITUDES was an area of the Atlantic Ocean where the trade winds died, becalming sailing ships on their journey to the New World.

To get under way, it was necessary for the sailors to lighten ship by throwing part of their load overboard—furniture, bolts of cloth, crates of china, even the cannon. The most severe and profound doldrums could be escaped only by abandoning their most precious cargo—horses.

Once the frightened animals were pushed over the side, the sails began to fill. The horses swam after the ships for miles before they drowned. Their screams haunted the superstitious sailors for the rest of the voyage.

CHAPTER 1

IT DIDN'T TAKE MUCH to set him off these days—
laughter from the apartment below, a flash of blond
hair out of the corner of his eye. Or, late at night,
the sound of two car doors slamming in quick succession. Especially that. He imagined them walking
to his place or her place, both of them eager but
trying not to let it show, holding hands, tentatively
at first, then the man slipping his arm around her
waist while she smiled and laid her head on his
shoulder.

There were nights when Danny missed Lauren
so bad that he wanted to take a fat man and
throw him through a plate-glass window. Just for
the sound of it. Instead, he went swimming in
the bay.

The water was cold and dark and empty and
he hadn't missed a swim in the four months and
ten days since the divorce became final. He was
going to drown one of these nights, or he was going

to get over her—it was too early to tell which.

He swam out past the marker buoys, head raised just enough so the water broke over his goggles. He pulled himself toward the dim lights on the other side, swimming with a steady, economical stroke that barely disturbed the surface.

Somewhere toward the middle of the bay he stopped, pushed up his goggles, and floated on his back. The lights and sounds onshore were muted in the distance, and he looked up at the stars until the cold seeped in and forced a decision. By the time he turned back, his body shook with the cold and his diaphragm was clenched so hard it hurt to breathe—he had to take short little breaths, grunting with every stroke. If there had been someone on the beach to hear him, they'd have thought he was wrestling with someone in the water.

He crawled up onshore, exhausted, teeth chattering as he toweled off, his skin already beginning to burn with blood. He looked back across the water. His mind was as blank and clear as an amphibian's, aware only of the sharpness of the stars and the smell of the sea. It was as good as he was going to feel until the next swim, and he knew it.

He took his time walking the two blocks home, stretching it out, listening to the quiet streets. It was just a little before midnight, but Tuesday was slow in Belmont Shore, everyone hunkered down, waiting for the weekend, when the bars offered two-for-one tequila shooters and dirty-dancing contests. Every night was the same for him: a long swim, a couple of beers, then fall asleep to Larry King or the Chicano evangelist who prayed, "Heavenly Father, man."

His building was pink stucco—what the classifieds called mission-style—two stories of wrought-iron grill-work and decorative brick, rounded archways, and a red barrel-tile roof. It looked more like a Taco Bell than the Alamo.

Halfway up the stairs to his apartment, he stopped and looked out at the stacks of tiny four-plexes and condominiums with no closet space. The Shore was a jumble of ambition, filled with salesgirls who took acting classes at night and bartenders who wrote screenplays during the day, part-time waitresses and substitute teachers, single and anonymous and overextended. People got a SAG card or a sugar daddy and moved out overnight, leaving their furniture and their damage deposit behind. It was a perfect place to get lost in.

He stayed on the steps, listening to the waves chopping up the bay and Ed McMahon's hearty laugh from Eilene's apartment. She was a buyer at Nordstroms, with perfect skin and a sullen teenage boyfriend who modeled sportswear once or twice a month and talked incessantly of "the business." The boyfriend had walked out a few weeks ago with her cash and charge cards but had left half the Quaaludes. Now she kept her curtains open and the TV on—a strobe lullaby rocking her to sleep.

Danny leaned against the banister in his soggy sweats, leaned back and looked in on her.

She was curled up on the couch, in a man's striped dress shirt and white bikini briefs, eyes closed, mouth slightly open. Her hair fell across her face in a wave of curls. He shivered as she twisted a strand back and forth between her fingers. She rolled onto her back, one hand nestled against her hip, gently stroking her belly. Her fingertips made small circles as they dipped below the waistband of her panties.

He watched his reflection in the window superimposed on her, then slowly unzipped his sweatshirt so they were skin to skin. Her hand now seemed to caress the flat, defined muscles of his torso. He found himself breathing in tandem with her. The intimacy of it made him think of Lauren.

One night, near the end, still stuck to him after making love, Lauren had said that his profile belonged on a Roman coin—it was fierce with the confidence that came from winning for a thousand years straight.

She had stayed there on top, tickling the top of his thighs, and said it was only at times like this, with him inside her in the darkness, that she still believed he couldn't lose. Soon he'd be just like everyone else, afraid to make his own rules. "People die every day." She caressed the scar on his abdomen where the bullet had torn through him. "That's no reason to quit dealing."

"They didn't die," he said, the room so taut there was barely room for the words. "They were killed." She shrugged. "They were my friends," he said, "and you didn't see their faces."

He felt her grip on him tighten as she leaned forward. "God hates a coward," she whispered in his ear, the sadness spreading slowly across the bed. He made a joke, but she felt a tear slide down his cheek, suddenly cupped his face in her hands, and kissed him so hard he cried out. She said maybe making love again would help. He said he didn't think so, but it was worth a try.

Smiling back at him was his own reflection. Eilene sighed, turned over again, and tucked her long legs up.

He started up the stairs and froze, head cocked. The palm trees rustled and stirred in the breeze, rubbing their dead fronds against each other. The stairs needed another light.

The two of them stepped out of the shadows on the landing.

He jerked backward, reached for the banister.

"Daniel DiMedici? Police officers." Badges glinted.

Danny froze halfway over, landed noiselessly back on the steps. He didn't need to see their badges. They had the voice, the cop voice, slightly contemptuous and utterly assured, the verbal equivalent of a twirled nightstick.

"Still got the felony moves." The stocky one nodded approvingly to his partner. "What'd I tell you." A wink for Danny. "Once a pro, always a pro."

"I'm Detective Holt," the tall woman said in a bored monotone, "and this is Detective Steiner, Newport PD." She kept her hands on her hips as she looked down the steps at Danny. "Are you expecting someone, Mr. DiMedici, or just hyperactive?"

"You scared me," Danny said, crowding onto the
landing.

"See, Karl"—her mouth twisted with disdain—
"and you were wondering where all the heroes had
gone."

"What's that supposed to mean?" said Danny.

"I thought you said he was smart, Karl."

"Look, lady . . . " Too loud. A light went on downstairs.

"Easy, easy now . . . " The rumpled gray suit
made Steiner look slow and slack, a big old walrus
past his prime—but he had positioned himself so
that his bulk blocked the path back down the stairs.
"It's your missus," he sniffed as he lightly laid his
hand on Danny's shoulder.

Danny looked at the hand. "Ex-missus."

"Right," said Steiner. He took his hand away.
"Lauren Kiel—"

"I know her name."

"Right. Mind if we come in and talk, son? It's
important."

"Gee, Dad, you got a warrant? Or some charges?"
A yellow moth buzzed insistently against the overhead light.

Steiner looked hurt.

"It's late, Karl. Why bother?" She stepped in
close to Danny, right there, an inch from his chest.
He could smell her perfume. "Be a wise guy, Mr.
DiMedici, see where it gets you."

Steiner shrugged at Danny. "She's got a point,
son. You want the letter of the law, we'll take a drive

to Newport. It's a nice night, we'll even put the siren on if you want."

The moth charged the bulb, the sound of its wings getting louder each time it hit the glass.

"The Shore's a little out of your jurisdiction," Danny said evenly. "You want to be careful."

"Gee, thanks," said Steiner, "but you don't have to worry about us. Detective Holt took care of all the paperwork." He grabbed the moth out of the air, threw it down, and stepped on it. "She's a real stickler for details, yes siree." He looked up to see Danny and Holt staring at him. "Ate up a sport coat of mine once," Steiner explained. He dragged his shoe on the landing, looked at the bottom, and scraped it some more. "What are you two, the SPCA?" he snapped, his face getting even redder.

Danny slipped his key into the deadbolt. What the hell. They couldn't touch him. He wasn't a player anymore; he was retired. The decision had cost him plenty, but at least he didn't have to sweat a roust. Besides, if they knew something about Lauren, he wanted to hear it. "Wipe your feet," he said.

CHAPTER 2

DANNY SLOUCHED IN THE LIGHT of the open refrigerator, calmly drinking Evian from the bottle. Steiner
headed straight for the black leather armchair and
settled himself in with a hiss of the cushions. Holt
stayed in the doorway, hands on hips, her hard
green eyes surveying the room with distaste.

She was the best dressed cop Danny had ever
seen, and wore a tailored gray suit too clingy for
Sunday mass and too conservative for a good table
at Trumps. Her thick red hair was bound by an
ornate antique gold clip. She looked like old money,
the kind that got a Yale law degree but felt it was
her civic duty to spend a few years with a good PD
on the way to a federal judgeship.

She finally stepped in, but kept to the edges of
the room, as though wanting to avoid walking on
the Oriental carpet. It was a cramped studio apartment with the dining area turned into a bedroom
nook. Against one wall was a battered wooden desk

piled with books and papers. Overlooking the desk was a map of the dark side of the moon and a velvet painting of the young Elvis. Shirts hung off the doorknobs; towels were piled in the corner. No TV. No plants. No pets.

Danny sat down in the rattan lawn chair next to Steiner, both of them looking into a fake terra-cotta fireplace with a photo of a roaring campfire taped inside.

"This here's real leather, isn't it?"—Steiner beamed, patting the armchair—"The real McCoy." The pockets of his suit bagged from years of shoving sandwiches and arrest reports into them. His tie had a yellow "I Love Grandpa" pattern on a black background. "Got a La-Z-Boy myself, just Naugahyde, though. Always wanted one of these leather jobs . . ." He leaned forward and sniffed the arm of the chair. "Yep. You can always tell."

"What do you want, Detective?" asked Danny.

"Okay, okay." Steiner fumbled in his jacket, brought out a slim brown notebook. "I talk too much, I admit it." The notebook looked lost in his meaty hands, but his fingers moved gracefully through the pages, barely touching them. "I don't know, son." He shook his head. "You spent all that time in college, but a little ROTC might have done you a world of good." He sighed. "Instead, you end up with three busts tossed on technicalities, some real weight, too . . . subject of a criminal investigation, DEA, another dry hole . . . then two arrests for assault in a month." He wagged a finger at Danny.

Danny wagged back. "No wonder you moved out of Newport."

"Moved out and moved down, from the looks of it, Karl." Holt trailed a finger over the dresser, rubbing off dust.

These two almost made him miss the motherfucker narcs, the ones who kicked in your door at 3 A.M., guns everywhere, screaming, "Freeze, motherfucker!" and "Where is it, motherfucker?" and "Don't lie to me, motherfucker!" At least *they* were direct.

"I thought you were here to talk about Lauren."

"Oh, we are." Steiner's head bobbed. He turned to Holt. "See, Detective, you can always tell a pro. They got no time, never have any time."

"He's no pro, he's a jitterbug, Karl." She was there, right behind Danny. "He peeks in windows, he jumps off stairs, he's unraveling right before our eyes."

Danny found himself shifting his attention back and forth between them, twisting around in his chair to follow her. "Let's get to the point, okay?"

"Now, don't go getting prima donna." Steiner held up his thick hands, the knuckles humped with scar tissue. "I've been called a few names in my time, too."

"What did they call you, Karl? You don't mind I call you Karl?"

"You got a way about you, son." Steiner chuckled. "I like that. But I'm trying to figure out these assault beefs of yours. I'm no college boy, but even I know there's no money in assault."

"Do you find it difficult to control your temper, Mr. DiMedici?" Holt was down on one knee now, looking into the wastebasket next to the desk, the hem of her skirt riding up her thigh. She wanted something incriminating, something in plain sight, something that would hold up in court. "Perhaps you get migraines? Or blackouts, sudden rages . . . "

"Gee," said Danny, "this is just like a physical. Please, Karl, can she be the one who asks me to cough?"

"Steady." Steiner's face reddened, then returned to its bland passivity. "I don't know if you realize it, but you're not listed as the tenant for this apartment."

"Well, you know how it is, Karl—tell people your address, and the next thing they're dropping by unannounced, all times of night, and you can't get rid of them."

Holt smiled in spite of herself, revealed a slight overbite. Smooth and white, too. Signal Mars with that smile. His grandfather had had teeth like that, said the secret was to rub them down every night with a clove of garlic. She probably had a different method.

"That could be a problem." Steiner nodded. "Still, no friends and all. . . . You got any kids, Danny?"

Danny stretched out his legs, pretending to warm them by the magazine-photo fire. "Why don't you check your notebook, Karl?" he said, wriggling his toes. They were going to take their time telling him about Lauren, teasing him, hoping he'd make a mistake. The gramps-and-the-debutante routine was a little obvious, but it probably tied small-time coke dealers up in knots.

"Oh, sometimes we miss things"—Steiner shrugged—"but that's why we're here." He pulled on his ear, winked at Danny. "You know, answers."

"Karl, I'll tell you the truth, I could use a few of those myself."

"Bet you could." Steiner glanced around the apartment. "This looks like a lonely place—no family pictures on the walls, clothes everywhere . . . too many books, if you ask me. I see you as kind of quiet, keep a lot bottled in, a guy who never really lays out the welcome mat, am I right?"

"You got me pegged, Karl," Danny mocked. "I can't fool you."

"Just a hobby. I get impressions about people, that's all. I bet your wife had your number—but then, that's her job. I caught her on radio when she took over for Dr. Toni Grant, and she made a lot of sense. I don't think much of your everyday headshrinker, but she was one sharp cookie."

Holt checked out the trophies on the mantelpiece, hefted the largest one, the all-around diving trophy, second place, put it back. Every time she shifted her weight, there was a warm rustle. Silk. Definitely. She reached for the small stone head next to it, Mayan corn god, classic period.

"Careful," said Danny.

"This is very valuable," she said, surprised, holding it with both hands. "Very valuable." The solemn god stared back, the white limestone lightly pocked with the centuries.

"I'd prefer you didn't touch that," said Danny.

"They don't allow these into the States anymore." She sounded annoyed. "Not without an antiquities-export license from the country of origin. This should be in a museum."

"Put it back, Detective," said Danny.

"Please?" said Steiner.

"Please."

Holt carefully set the statue back into place.

"Served with divorce papers from Lauren Kiel on December seventeenth, 1987," Steiner read. "Missus must have really been fed up, giving you the gaff right before Christmas. What difference would it make to wait a couple of weeks?" He looked up at Danny. "You can tell me to button my lip, but did you ever think that maybe it was your dope dealing?"

"You could button it," said Danny. "I wouldn't stop you."

"All the lies and lawyers . . . no offense, son, but a woman like her, big success and a looker to boot— let's face it, she could do better."

"Mr. DiMedici has a temper, Karl. He probably threw a tantrum if she didn't have a hot meal waiting when he came home from a hard day selling narcotics."

Yeah, right. They had been living in the new condo for over a year before Lauren discovered that the oven didn't work.

"And when all her hard work started paying off and she didn't need him anymore, I imagine he resented it." Holt picked through the stacks of library books on the desk: "*Agriculture of Pre-Columbian Yucatán, Meso-American Geology, The Drowned World*— some of these are overdue, Mr. DiMedici." She scowled. "Years overdue."

She was actually serious. She had never cut in line in her life, never raced down a dark country road with the lights off.

"Do you work, Mr. DiMedici? You pay taxes?"

"Is she like this all the time, Karl, or this a PMS thing?"

"Take care now." Steiner patted Danny's knee. "It's important to know where to draw the line, where to call it quits."

"Where is your wife, Mr. DiMedici?"

"Is that what this is about? Karl?"

"We ran a check of her phone records"—Steiner's fingers glided through the notebook—"and the little woman was all business, just little two-and three-minute calls. Except for one number. Yours. She calls once or twice a week, calls late and likes to talk, just racking up those toll charges, ding-ding, ding-ding . . . " He checked the notebook. "November twenty-third, 1:31 A.M. to 2:52 A.M.; November thirtieth, 2:08 A.M. to 3:45 A.M. You get the idea."

"What do narcs do on vacation," Danny snapped, "bug your own phone or go through the neighbor's garbage?"

"You tell him we're narcs?" Steiner asked Holt.

"Not me, Karl."

"Me neither. This here's a homicide investigation, son."

*   *   *

Danny looked from one to the other. He tried to speak, but there was a hole in his chest and his voice had poured out. He saw Lauren's face through a clear-plastic body bag, caught in the glare of an overhead light. A dead tear in her eye, cracked blue glass. Too late for I'm sorry, too late for Please come back. Too late.

"You don't look so good, son."

"Is she dead?" Danny said softly.

"Don't you know, Mr. DiMedici?"

"Is she?"

"Yesterday morning"—Steiner riffed through the pages—"approximately 6:45 A.M., Mr. Thomas Burkett, seventy-eight, was walking the beach with his metal detector when he saw the sliding-glass door at three-twenty-three Via Geneva was shattered. Closer inspection revealed blood sprayed across the walls. Blood everywhere." He closed the notebook and looked up at Danny. "Terrible thing for an old man to find. I seen slaughterhouses looked better than that room."

"I don't understand," said Danny.

Steiner pursed his lips. "Three-twenty-three Via Geneva, Lido Isle . . . she *lives* there. We look stupid to you?"

"I didn't know," whispered Danny. "I saw the house once in a magazine, but it didn't say where she lived . . . "

"But she had your number, is that right, Mr. DiMedici?" Holt said. "The new one not under your name, not in the phone book?"

"I-I called her office," Danny stammered. "You can ask her secretary."

"Oh, we have, Mr. DiMedici," she said, circling in, "but that still doesn't explain why she never gave you her home phone number or her address. Why do you think that was, Mr. DiMedici?"

"It wasn't like that," said Danny. "She called. I answered. She wouldn't tell me where she lived. Said I'd just make trouble for her."

"Would you make trouble for her, Mr. DiMedici?"

"Is she dead?" Danny repeated, turning from one to the other. Neither of the detectives betrayed the slightest emotion.

"Well," Steiner said finally. "We didn't find any bodies . . . "

Danny laid his face in his hands. She was alive. Nothing else mattered.

"But there was enough blood to call it a probable homicide," continued Steiner. "Got us some semen, too. Little bitty puddle on the glass coffee table and some on the rug. . . . You okay, son? Anyway, the M.E. said it matched the blood in the room. We figure it was her boyfriend, Mr. B-positive, that bled all over. Like maybe they were caught in the act by somebody that wanted to make a point."

"I think a lot of people could understand how something like that could happen, Mr. DiMedici," Holt said smoothly. "Maybe you were watching from the beach, saw them making love and . . . went a little crazy."

"No!"

"Why don't you tell us where she is, Mr. Di-Medici?" she said. "You'll feel better."

"I told you—"

"Ruined the rug." Steiner shook his head. "Nice one too, like the one you got here—tell right off it's quality. I wonder sometimes where all the money comes from for leather chairs and Persian carpets . . . "

"What did you and your ex-wife talk about, Mr. DiMedici?" Holt looked down on him. "Did you ever threaten her?"

"She couldn't sleep," said Danny. He held on to the arms of the chair and tried to keep his voice steady. "She never could. When it got bad, she'd call me up and I'd tell her a story. She didn't want to talk, she just wanted me to tell her a story."

"What kind of story?" grinned Steiner. "Horny stuff?"

"Just stories I made up," said Danny. "Her own private fairy tales, like you'd tell a kid. I'd be half asleep most of the time. When we were married, I used to tell her stories every night."

"Didn't you ever feel angry at your former wife?" said Holt. "Maybe she wasn't alone when she called you up. Maybe she and her boyfriend would lie in bed with the phone in between on the pillow . . . she might have enjoyed that, Mr. DiMedici. Some women would."

"Would you enjoy that, Detective?"

"She has a career and a beach house," said Holt. "You've got a rap sheet and a gym locker with a fake fireplace. Did you resent that, Mr. DiMedici?"

"I think you two should leave. Now."

"You're going to need a good alibi for Sunday night, Mr. DiMedici," said Holt. "You may want to call your lawyer before we proceed any further."

"I was with you, Detective," Danny said. "I've got the toothmarks to prove it."

Steiner jabbed Danny in the shoulder with a rigid index finger. "I like you, son," he said, "but it's important to remember you're addressing two officers of the law." He leaned toward Danny, poking the same spot, emphasizing each word. "Respect. Respect the law."

"Down, boy," said Danny. They were so close that he could see every pore in Steiner's broken nose, the burst capillaries in his eyes, and the small patches of gray stubble he had missed shaving.

"I retire in five and a half months," Steiner kept up the attack as Danny tried to squirm away. "Thirty years on the job, and I remember every case. First week I make detective, a millwright named Boguski loses his job, takes the bus home, has a couple of Buds, and sucks on the barrel of a Jap rifle he picked up during the war. Pulls the trigger with his big toe. Maybe it's getting fired, maybe it's something else. You'd be surprised how little it takes sometimes."

Danny swatted the finger aside, but Steiner continued to bore in, his body positioned so that Danny couldn't get up.

"I'm the new kid on the block, see"—Steiner was breathing heavily now, Danny could feel it warm and moist against his cheeks—"so I get to clean up after the wagon's come and gone. It's like an initiation—lets the other grades know you've got sand. Bald-headed sergeant tugs a clump of hair off the wall and says to me, 'Naturally curly, and this dumb bastard blows it away. Go figure.' You gotta understand, this was the old days, before we had sensitivity training or civilian review boards. Just cops 'n' robbers." His finger tattooed Danny's shoulder, tap-tap-tap. "So I'm the one has to wade on in, I'm the one ends up with brains all over his nice new Florsheims. Fifty-dollar wingtips, too."

"You got my attention, Karl." Danny refused to allow himself to flinch. "You can knock it off now."

There was no heat in Steiner's eyes, just a watery sadness. He looked like a librarian who catalogued books in a language no one spoke or read anymore but who did his job just the same.

"Afterwards, I go home and sit on my sofa," said Steiner. "Patti Page is on the radio, singing, 'Shrimp boats are comin' and it's Saturday night,' and I'm throwing back a few Buds myself and poking this poor guy's brains out of those wingtips with a tooth-pick. Took me over an hour, and I still couldn't get it all. Ended up giving those shoes to Salvation Army. What they don't know won't hurt em."

"I said knock it off, Karl," Danny hit him in the chest with the heel of his hand. Again, harder. Steiner grunted but kept right on.

"They call the brain gray matter, but it's yellow," said Steiner. "Like cottage cheese left too long at the back of the icebox." His finger was poised between them. "Funny the things that stick with you. Thirty years. . . . A cop needs a good memory, but it's a curse, like flat feet or a vivid imagination. They don't tell you that coming in the door. I'm not complaining. Don't get me wrong." He slumped like a punctured balloon, his hands falling to his sides. "It's late," he said, staring at the floor. "It's late and I'm tired."

Holt helped him to his feet while Danny sat there, watching.

"Detective Holt's a real go-getter." Steiner's face was impenetrable. "I was the same way once. She thinks you're a hot-blooded I-talian, thinks every time you close your eyes, you see home movies of your wife grunting with the USC marching band. Me, I think you're somebody who had it all handed to him on a silver platter. And still managed to dump the whole business in his lap."

"I'm disappointed in you, Karl." Danny tried to rub the feeling back into his shoulder. "I thought you were the nice cop and she was the tough cop."

Steiner turned at the top of the stairs. "No such thing as a nice cop, son, you know that." He started down, taking the steps one at a time.

"You want to file a complaint, it's up to you," Holt said from the doorway. "I'll testify that you struck him in the performance of his duty."

"Just what duty was that, Detective?"

"You're not as smart as you think," she said.

"Who is?"

"Maybe you forgot something"—she bit off the words with those fine white teeth—"a fingerprint, a fiber sample, a skin flake . . . it doesn't take much. A loose end's enough to strangle on. You think about that, Mr. DiMedici."

Danny closed his eyes and listened to her foot-steps fade. Everything hurt. He went to the phone, checked to make sure there was a dial tone, then turned off the lights and lay in bed. Checked the phone again.

He saw himself being carried far out to sea, swim-ming against the current, a tidal wave of blood rolling in from the horizon as he struggled toward shore. He hoped Lauren was alive and couldn't sleep tonight, hoped she'd need him. He lay in the dark and waited for the phone to ring.

CHAPTER 3

SHE HAD DONE all right for herself.

The house was set far back from the street, mostly hidden by groves of twisted jacaranda and eucalyptus trees, three stories of white brick, right on the beach. Moorish Modern, the layout in *Architectural Digest* had called it in its cover story.

There was a full-page photo of Lauren lounging in the living room, bathed in sunlight. Her bare feet rested on a polished coffee table that seemed to be cut from a single slab of rose quartz.

"Psychologist Lauren Kiel retreats to her beach-front Southern California hideaway, a hybrid of smooth Arabian classicism and contemporary elegance, where the eternal rhythms of time and tide renew and refresh her."

Danny had mailed a copy of the magazine to her office, marking the spot with an old photograph of the two of them at the central market in Merida, cheek to cheek, laughing, each of them cradling a stuffed iguana wearing a sombrero. An old Mexican had taken the photo for them, and refused any money. He said he and his wife, God rest her soul, had once been so happy, and seeing the two of them reminded him of those days.

Now he was parked at the end of her driveway, just before dawn, listening to the wind in the trees and hoping for a light to come on in her bedroom. He had given up trying to sleep at 4:30 A.M. and driven to the address in Lido Isle that Steiner talked about. The house was the kind of place they had talked about owning. After he had moved enough product. After Michael had laundered the money through offshore banks. She had gone ahead and done it on her own.

The magazine layout had shown skylit rooms with vaulted ceilings and bare walls. Lauren was quoted as saying that too many objects distracted from the sense of place, of serenity, which was the essence of home.

The master bedroom was on the top floor, the king-size bed draped with raspberry- and lemon-colored parachute silk. Three bottles of perfume and a tortoiseshell comb were arranged on the inlaid Empire dressing table he had bought her in Paris. On their first anniversary, he had filled the drawers with lingerie, reds and yellows, blacks and pinks, a cascade of colors spilling out onto the floor.

He kept a copy of the magazine for himself, spent hours with his fingers resting on the pages, imagining the two of them in that big bed, watching storm clouds boil across the horizon.

He shifted in his seat, stretching, banging his knees. The '68 Mustang fastback was built more for speed than comfort. Pretty soon the neighbors would be up brewing coffee and getting their morning paper and wondering what the ugly black car was doing in the driveway of that house with all the police activity. That's what he had been saying for half an hour, and he was still sitting.

Purple blossoms floated down from the jacaranda trees, lay thickly on the lawn and sprinkled across the hoodscoop. If he stayed there long enough, they'd cover him completely. Then he wouldn't have to worry about the neighbors, just hole up and wait for her to come home.

He took a deep breath, got out, and started up the winding driveway, shoulders hunched, walking fast.

A yellow ribbon circled the house, POLICE INVESTIGATION DO NOT CROSS repeated across its length in black letters. It was standard procedure, but it made a difference, it changed the terrain. The magazine was wrong. Lauren didn't live alone anymore; she had roommates: Steiner and Holt.

One hand slid along the brightly colored police line as he walked around back, feeling it twist through his grip. Cops marked their crime scenes like there was a party inside and they wanted to point the way with festive decorations.

The lots in Lido Isle were elaborately landscaped —he passed terraced flower beds and azalea bushes, intricate rock gardens and a wall of towering desert cacti.

The living room faced the beach, fifty feet of glass panels, two stories high. One of the smaller sliding-glass doors had been broken, sharp splinters sticking out of the frame. Cardboard had been haphazardly taped across the opening and yellow ribbon Xed across the cardboard, like that was supposed to keep out the angel of death. Little late in the game for that.

The sheer white curtains were pulled, but the wind coming off the ocean blew them back, affording a glimpse into the darkened interior. Somebody had spilled . . . He turned and watched the waves, his knees shaking. The curtains flapped behind him, snagging and ripping on the broken glass. It was an ugly sound. He had to resist the impulse to cover his ears.

Lauren was right. He *had* lost his edge. Once he had been stopped by a highway patrolman on the way back to Newport with a half-ton of sensimilla in the back of a refrigerated van. The patrolman told him his license-plate light was out. The two of them stood there discussing the lousy season the Rams were having while he tightened down the loose connection with a screwdriver he borrowed from the officer. Danny's hands were as steady as his smile. Now he was afraid to walk into a dark room.

His confidence had died in the farmhouse, along with everyone and everything else. He had dragged himself to the car, blood running down his side and into his boot. He had hoped Lauren would think a scar was romantic. Because he wasn't going to be so perfect anymore.

A small sailboat tacked back and forth across the water. The beach was deserted. A red balloon bounced over the dunes.

He got the divorce papers by certified mail three months after the farmhouse. The phone call came the next day. She wanted to confirm that he had received them. He slammed the phone down with a curse, called her back thirty seconds later, apologizing.

Danny told her he was going back to teaching.

She said she didn't want to be cruel. He told her, "Why stop now?" She said, "If you want to be a professor, you should find a nice professor's wife. Someone who'll be happy driving a three-year-old Volvo, who thinks snorting cocaine before a faculty party is the ultimate in wicked pleasures." She said could he try to remember the good times and not give in to bitterness or depression? "Not a chance," he said. "Not a fucking chance," replacing the receiver as carefully as if it were a letter bomb.

The sun had come up while he stood there staring at the waves. He still couldn't look at the house.

The last time they had seen each other was when he was moving his things out of their condo. He put his arms around her and smelled the sweetness of her hair, not wanting to let go. She said there would always be a part of her that loved him. "Which part?" he said. "Maybe we can make a deal." She laughed and kissed him and he actually thought for a moment it would all work out.

The only good thing about being raised Catholic was it gave you a belief in resurrection. The curtains behind him snapped in the wind. He ignored the sound. He was still waiting for the happy ending.

"Sir?"

Danny jumped at the low voice.

The little man in the faded bib overalls raised his hands as Danny stepped toward him. "Sir, please. It is Friday."

"What?"

"It is Friday, sir."

Danny followed him around to the front of the house and down the driveway, staring blankly at a shiny white pickup on the shoulder of the road. The truck was filled with lawn mowers and rakes, "MATSUDO LANDSCAPING" neatly painted on the side. "Your car, sir. It must move."

"Sorry." Danny hurried past, got into the Mustang, and backed out. As he drove away, he could see Matsudo in the rearview, standing in the street, watching him.

CHAPTER 4

THE TWINS, BOYD AND LLOYD, sat in a red Corvette parked along the beach, Boyd behind the wheel. A peeling bumper sticker on the back read: OFFICIAL PLAYBOY PHOTOGRAPHER, AUDITIONS WELCOME.

It was late morning and already the temperature was in the upper eighties. The motor was running, the windows up, and the air conditioner full on. Droplets of condensation rolled down the insides of the windshield. The grassy picnic area nearby was packed with college students playing Frisbee, family cookouts, and old couples on benches holding hands. The whole scene made Lloyd want to puke.

Lloyd pushed steadily at the cap of a half-pint bottle of unfiltered apple juice with his thumbs. A small Styrofoam cooler was half open between his legs. Empty bottles bobbed in the soup of melted ice, clinked against each other as the engine gently vibrated the car.

They had bought the juice at this health-food store that reeked of incense, Boyd demanding to know if it was organic while the longhair behind the counter kept repeating, "I just work here, man," in this faggy British accent, until Lloyd grabbed him by his ponytail and banged his face into the counter. "Take an interest, pencilneck," he said. "You don't know, find out." Lloyd didn't want to bother with the wimp, but otherwise Boyd might have done something *really* awful. They were already in enough trouble with Uncle Arthur over what they had let happen at the blonde's beach house. Like it was their fault.

The twins wore identical XXXL sleeveless T-shirts that said IRONWORKS GYM and cutoffs. The T-shirts were tight with muscle, the seams of the cutoffs split almost to the crotch to accommodate their thighs. Twenty-eight-inch thighs, twenty-one-inch arms, fifty-four-inch chests, and thirty-inch waists. They had pectorals like gladiators', wide and flat, the contours defined with tiny auxiliary muscles. Blood vessels thick as earthworms crawled along the humps and gulleys of their biceps. They were massive, but at five feet seven inches, the symmetry was off. Instead of looking developed they looked inflated. And the pressure had been kept on too long.

Boyd nodded at the park through his side window. "Check the whale in the apron standing there turning greaseburgers, little brats pounding on the picnic table for their potato salad and corn on the cob. Kids' hearts explode in the middle of the night, she'll be bawling how it isn't fair," Boyd snarled as the woman stacked hamburgers neatly onto a platter.

Lloyd couldn't get the blonde out of his mind. She and Dr. Tohlson had spent most of their time in her bedroom, but he had gotten a good look at her when she came downstairs. She left the drapes in the living room wide open. She had come downstairs in a wispy white robe that made her look like a bride, except she wasn't wearing anything underneath. He had gotten a boner looking at her, imagining how she'd taste, like pink lemonade, probably. He was getting another one just thinking about her. More trouble. Boyd said boners were a waste of good hormones. "Use 'em for your muscles, not your dick," Boyd said.

The cap popped off the apple juice and landed in the cooler. "Two points," mumbled Lloyd, still thinking of the blonde.

"You just can't get serious, can you?" said Boyd. "We got important business, but all you can think of is games."

"I'm not afraid of Uncle Arthur," said Lloyd, gulping down half the bottle.

"I'm not *talking* about Uncle Arthur," Boyd said. "I'm talking about the contest. Less than five weeks to go and you're still playing around. You're small. Your lats are useless."

"Not true." Lloyd's voice teetered and cracked. "I'm two thirty-seven, just a half pound less than you."

Boyd didn't even bother to look at him. "Your

lats are useless." He stared out the windshield.

A slender, deeply tanned teenage girl in a white string bikini walked along the sand next to the parking strip. A braided piece of rawhide around one ankle, soft brown hair bouncing against her shoulders.

"You faded on that pulldown superset, Junior. You died on me." Boyd held up both hands. "It was pull-downs-military presses-benches-pulldowns-flys-benches-and-pulldowns." He ticked off the exercises on his fingers. "So what happened to you?"

"Not my fault we're up all night," murmured Lloyd. "Can't train like that."

The girl in the string bikini passed in front of the Corvette. The suit must have been new—there were thin slivers of tanline along the edges of her breasts and butt. Her parents had probably thrown a fit when they saw it. She looked at the twins and smiled, lowering her eyes.

"Work on your hamstrings, airhead," Boyd spat after her. "You'll be up to your lazy ass in cellulite by the time you're twenty."

Lloyd drained the apple juice, watching the girl as she swayed down the sand. He didn't think her hams were so bad, but he felt sorry for her skin. His and Boyd's complexions were fair and smooth—in fact, they had hardly any body hair at all. When they oiled up before competition, they gleamed in the yellow and red stage lights like they were on fire. They still had a tan—it set off their blue eyes and stark blond crewcuts and made their posing routine look even more dramatic—but they were smart about it. Boyd had ordered these carotene-tanning pills from Canada that really worked, even if your cuticles turned orange. The pills gave them the healthy look that the judges liked, and the two of them didn't have to go out into the sun. Boyd said sunlight gave you cancer. Or wrinkles. The girl in the string bikini should know better.

He was glad Boyd was there to watch out for things like that, things that could ruin you, like sunlight or red meat or loud music. Boyd said sound waves could destroy these little-bitty hairs inside your ears, hairs so small you couldn't even see them. If that happened, you could lose your sense of balance and maybe fall off the stage someday, with everybody watching.

That skinny jig last week, strutting along with the screeching radio on his shoulder, he had deserved what he got . . . probably already destroyed his own hearing with drugs and didn't care who he hurt. It was self-defense—no two ways about it.

Sometimes Lloyd wished that he were the big brother, particularly when it came to deciding what movie to see or if there was only one piece of fresh peach pie left over. But it was settled—Boyd was two minutes older, and two minutes or twenty years, it was all the same. They might look like mirror images, but Lloyd was never going to catch up.

"Let's get big," said Lloyd.

"We're supposed to pick up the blonde's husband for Uncle Arthur," said Boyd. "You're gonna get us in trouble again."

"Please?" Lloyd opened the dash and took out a

handful of amber glass vials. "I feel small. Like people are going to be laughing because I look all shrunk."

Boyd thought about it.

"Please?"

Boyd pulled a small case from under his seat, removed the stainless steel hypodermic. Lloyd started to tingle just looking at it. His muscles felt hungry.

"What's on the menu?" said Boyd.

"Well," said Lloyd, squinting at the fine print on the vials, "there's this new human growth hormone Uncle Arthur said to try, HGH Meta-Adrenal Complex. It's supposed to boost energy and eat up subcutaneous fat, without the side effects of the other stuff—"

"That stuff wasn't so bad. Once you got used to it."

Lloyd shrugged. "Supposed to be better, I don't know." More vials. "And here's the old reliable, Pro-Anabol, for bulk without water retention. That should pyramid with the HGH real nice."

"Any more testosterone?" said Boyd.

"Bingo," said Lloyd, holding up three yellow vials.

"All *right*." Boyd returned the grin. He leaned against the door, pulled down his cutoffs and underwear. "Upper right quadrant, baby boy, and don't skin-pop me."

Lloyd watched the family in the park sitting down for lunch while he gently slid the needle in. They divided their buttocks into four parts, shooting up one quadrant at a time. It was supposed to minimize bruising. Lloyd had a hard time remembering from one day to another, but Boyd always knew, like he had written it down somewhere. Boyd was amazing.

The whale in the park was actually saying grace. Unreal. Boyd was complaining that the HGH stung. It must be good. Lloyd drew HGH and fluid back into the syringe, a tendril of blood rotating slowly through the viscous liquid, then slowly pressed the plunger until it was gone. You didn't need to back-pull an intramuscular shot, but Uncle Arthur said it was a good habit to get into. Besides, Lloyd liked the way it looked, like a little rose blooming in the syringe.

Now she was pouring drinks for the kiddies, looked like cherry Kool-Aid or Hawaiian Punch. Artificially flavored and sticky sweet, no doubt.

Lloyd took even more time with the Pro-Anabol, because it was thick and had a tendency to clump up. He rubbed Boyd's hip as he fed it into the muscle. To help it disperse. Boyd groaned and said it felt like his ass was on fire. A couple of kids dragging boogie boards glanced at the car as they walked by and started giggling.

The whale was pouring seconds. Artificial flavors caused hyperactivity, and sugar was the most addictive substance on the planet. Lloyd had read about it. In a sane world she'd be tried for murder. Or drug trafficking, anyway. Boyd's perfect white skin reddened where the hypodermic emptied into him. Lloyd pressed out the first vial of testosterone, reached for another.

"Do the extra one yourself," said Boyd.

"Thanks." Lloyd helped him pull his shorts back up. "Thanks a lot."

"Don't make a big deal out of it," said Boyd. "You need it." He loaded the hypodermic while Lloyd leaned against the passenger-side window, shorts bunched around his knees. "Lower left quadrant?" said Boyd.

Lloyd watched the waves rolling in. He smiled when he felt the bite of the needle.

CHAPTER 5

"I WAS HOPING you'd show, kiddo." Mavis beamed when Danny pushed through the doors of Motivation Associates. "It's a nuthouse here." She was a bosomy middle-aged woman with a frosted-pageboy hairdo and a bright yellow dress. Mavis had been Lauren's office manager since the beginning, when Motivation Associates was more a letterhead than a corporation. "The boss is missing, and no one'll tell me what the hell's going on."

"Don't ask me." Danny kissed her on the cheek and sat down on the edge of her desk. "I'm just the primary suspect."

She slapped his leg. "And I'm the queen of Sheba."

He was still a looker—God, what she wouldn't give for that smooth olive complexion and those dark eyes—but he looked tired, and there was a sadness to him that had never been there before. Men always got that look when they were dumped. Women could have a good cry with their girlfriends and get it out of their system, or at least hide it with makeup. Men always looked like wounded bucks. Surprised at the hurt of it. They got over that, of course. Most of them. Mavis had been divorced four times. They still sent Christmas cards, every one of them. Shoot, number three still sent a dozen roses every birthday. But he was a special case, strong as a stevedore yet tender as a boy. Danny reminded her of number three. Now more than ever.

Danny fiddled with the photographs on her desk, formal portraits of her with each of her six Persian cats. "Was Lauren seeing anyone special?" he said. "A boyfriend?"

"She didn't talk about things like that, hon, not to me, anyhow. I told her plenty of times she should work things out with you, get back together."

"What did she say?"

"It doesn't matter."

"I can take a punch."

"She said you were going in the wrong direction. I said, Boss, you got enough direction for the two of you. Told her there's not a dime's worth of difference between men, so you might as well stay with a good-looking one. Somebody who rubs your feet when you come home and doesn't scratch his dingle-dangle in front of company."

"That's me."

"You're close enough, but in the long run, I prefer cats—they're clean, don't borrow money from you, and don't burn holes in the sofa."

"Hard to love something shits in a sandbox, then

looks at you like it never saw the stuff before while you pick it up."

Mavis wiped tears as they laughed. "You got quite a mouth on you. That's probably why I told her to take you back. Not many men make you smile, I said. You find one who does, hang on with both knees."

"Quite an image there, Mavis."

The waiting room had a high ceiling and soft lighting bouncing off the beige leather sofa. A marble coffee table had copies of *Sailing, Fortune, Town & Country,* and *Aviation Week* fanned out. Three large framed color photos of Lauren on the walls: Lauren in a fuchsia ski jacket atop a powdery crest, goggles pushed back and face flushed; a night scene of Lauren and a group of people around a beach campfire; and Lauren onstage at an auditorium, the crowd of suits standing, applauding.

"I went by her house this morning," Danny said, staring at the photos. "She's come a long way fast."

"She works hard keeping it going," said Mavis. "Full throttle all the time. You'd be proud of her, hon. I'm not saying she's the easiest person to work for, but people like her live by different rules. You're like that, too."

"Sure. I'm just headed in a different direction."

"Stop feeling sorry for yourself."

Danny leaned over her desk. He smelled good. She liked a man who didn't think he had to smell like a jockstrap. The young ones were like that. It would have been terrible to have missed Glenn Miller and V-J Day and the suspenders her first boyfriend wore, but she was born twenty years too soon. No doubt about it.

"Could you let me see her personal calendar," said Danny, "and a list of her seminars for the last four or five months? I've got to find her."

"Police already took her calender. And her Rolodex. Said they needed it."

"Just let me see what they left, then."

"Well . . . I'm not supposed to let anybody into her office, but you're not anybody." Mavis fumbled in her desk for the key. "Voilà," she said, opening the door. She waved him over and they stood in the doorway. "Realtor called it a full hundred-eighty-degree ocean view, best in the building. And that's a rented Renoir," she continued, giving him the full tour. "Real one, too, and her Louis Fourteenth armoire and desk belong in Versailles. The boss says it makes the CEOs feel that they're getting their money's worth."

"She act worried at all the last few weeks?" Danny had walked over to the desk and was looking through the neat stacks of paper on top.

She felt bad for him. He was trying too hard to be nonchalant, but she could see the slight hesitation in his movements. He knew he didn't belong here.

He opened the top drawer and slowly pulled out the small framed photograph. He acted like if he breathed too hard it would crumble to dust.

"I'll tell you, kiddo, I had to fight to keep that one. The two cops wanted it bad."

Danny smiled at the snapshot. It was the one he had sent Lauren, the two of them clowning in

Merida, a stuffed iguana under each arm.

"The lady cop kept saying they needed it for their investigation," said Mavis. "I told her it was personal property and if she wanted to make a federal case of it, I'd call our attorney. The big cop said he understood. He's a sweetie, that one. Just a big old bear."

"Can I have it?" said Danny. "Just until I find her. Promise."

"You don't have to promise," Mavis shushed him. "It was her favorite picture, kept it right on her desk. Damned if I'm gonna let some redhead waltz away with it."

Danny followed her into the outer office.

Mavis pulled a sheaf of stapled papers out of her desk. "Here's the client list, if that'll do you any good. The big cop asked for the same thing when they came by yesterday. He also wanted to know about you."

"I bet." Danny riffed through the pages. "Computronics . . . AeroQuest . . . Techstar Research . . . probably not a window in any of these places."

"What's going on? I ask the cops a question, they don't answer, just ask me a couple more. She's a snippy thing. Had the nerve to ask me if I was covering up for you. I never liked redheads. You ask me, they have a complex."

"These are just for the last four months?"

"After she subbed for Toni Grant that week, the phone didn't stop ringing, then the *Times* profiled her in their business section and *People* magazine is interested—"

"Okay, okay." He folded the client list into his pocket.

"You know, this isn't the first time she's taken off without even a phone call," said Mavis. "The boss doesn't have to make explanations to me, or anyone else for that matter. She's gone for days sometimes. Just disappears. I call her appointments, tell them she had to fly to Washington for an emergency consult, very hush-hush. They fall all over themselves rescheduling. Next thing, the boss strolls in, acts like nothing happened."

"Let me know if she strolls in. You've got my number."

"This is different though, isn't it?" said Mavis. "The cops coming by and all—that never happened before. Her nibs even had the nerve to ask me the name of the boss's dentist. What kind of question is that? If she was in an accident they'd have to say something, wouldn't they?"

"Sure they would." Danny squeezed her hand. "It's going to be all right," he said, giving her a warm hug. "We'll get her back."

Mavis watched him leave. The boss was one sharp cookie. But if she let Danny slip away, she sure didn't know men.

CHAPTER 6

"EVERYTHING ALL RIGHT, Dr. Reese?" The security guard leaned his head in, not wishing to intrude any more into the brightly lit lab than he absolutely had to.

"Quite all right." Arthur Reese didn't turn his head from contemplation of the bell jars on his lab table.

The door clicked loudly shut in the stillness. It was after 10 P.M., but Reese frequently worked all night, particularly since Tohlson had been murdered. Fucking idiot. The whole project was in jeopardy.

He reached out and placed his hand on the nearest glass jar. A twenty-five week fetus was suspended in formaldehyde, pink lidless eyes staring back at him, tiny fingers spread wide. Reese had to resist the impulse to tap the jar, as though its contents would move or blink. There were a dozen bell jars lined up on the table, each one holding a fetus. Tiny astronauts with a trailing umbilicus.

More gristle than meat, Reese was a tough little bantam with a cropped bullet skull and a look of intense calculation. After spending much of his life among tribal people in inhospitable places, he took pleasure in the awareness that not only had he survived, he had dominated. Equally comfortable in a loincloth or the white lab coat he now wore, Reese was as burnt-black and unforgiving as a Ubangi shaman or a Yaqui medicine man—the very people who had contributed so much to his success.

The shamans had been invariably suspicious and often dangerous; it had taken months of cajoling and meek apprenticeship to gain even their first level of trust. Reese valued his pride, but he valued the shamans' botanical wisdom even more. He had formulated a topical antibiotic from swamp lillies and a cholesterol-lowering drug from a species of orchid found only at the base of Mt. Kilimanjaro.

The son of a Texas panhandle sharecropper, Reese had attended Harvard on scholarship, graduating first in his class. Then on to Stanford medical school and the University of Chicago for a Ph.D. in ethnobotany. His accomplishments covered half a page in *Who's Who in America*. Reese Pharmaceuticals was a privately held corporation with annual revenues of over $500 million. But it wasn't doing him any good at all.

The bitterness overwhelmed him. He scooted his swivel stool, pulled an agar plate out of the incubator, and transferred a tissue sample onto a slide with a glass pipette. Through the binocular lens of the electron microscope he could clearly see the DNA segments, those diaphanous ribbons of life, vigorously dividing at 100,000 magnification. The sample was proof positive of the success of the research he and Tohlson had been conducting. The tissue should have lost the ability to replicate days ago. Yet it continued spinning off perfect copies of itself. It was the most gorgeous thing Reese had ever seen, and for a moment made him forget the disastrous events of the last week.

Reese had been working on maximizing the human organism for twenty years, initially because it presented an unlimited profit potential, but more recently for personal reasons. Reese Pharmaceuticals was the industry leader in supplemental antioxidants and ergogenics of all kinds. Reese had even privately experimented on his two nephews—call it a quest for perfection. Their mother had died giving birth to them, and Reese had supervised their upbringing.

Boyd and Lloyd, the twins, might have the collective brainpower of a twenty-watt bulb, but they were superior physical specimens, the best that science could deliver. Reese's work with growth hormones and steroids had turned the twins into veritable protein factories, hybrid organic machines that produced muscle while they slept. He had just started them on a program of clenbuterol injections, a European drug originally used on farm animals. Clenbuterol made sheep and cows bigger, with less fat and more lean meat. Reese's improved version of the drug dramatically increased fast-twitch muscle fibers, which should give his nephews even greater quickness and explosive strength.

Reese caught a glimpse of his own reflection in the stainless-steel ventilator hood above the lab table and he turned away in disgust. He was fifty-two years old. His elbows were scaly and his gums were receding, millimeter by millimeter. In the last decade, his liver and kidneys had lost 11 percent of their efficiency, and his lung capacity was dropping, right along with his angle of erection.

Oh, he was still a powerful man, chesty and fit, his rounded biceps filling the sleeves of his shirt. He had worked out all his life, with the most sophisticated resistance equipment. He megadosed on vitamins and hormones and Retin-A, spent two weeks every year at a Swiss longevity clinic. It wasn't enough.

Reese pinched the skin at the back of his hand and released it, counting to himself. It took 4.5 seconds for the skin to flatten out. Ten years ago it had taken only three seconds. With every heartbeat his skin lost elasticity. In spite of all his efforts, Dr. Arthur Reese was getting old.

He had hunted big game all over the world, had tracked a bull elephant across miles of grassland by himself, knowing one of them would tire first. The elephant's head was on his office wall now, a gigantic testament to Reese's prowess. Tooth and claw ruled the killing ground, and those creatures with neither had best be swift. Or sly. Reese was getting old, but he had no intention of standing still for it.

The Hayflick Limit was the problem. Reese could improve the efficiency of the organism, boost its immune system, and fine-tune the metabolic rate. But all life-extension techniques were constrained by the Hayflick Limit, the number of times a cell could replicate itself accurately. Like a Xerox machine, copying from a copy of a copy, there was a point beyond which the reproductions lost definition, mutated into a cancer, organ failure, and death. The Hayflick Limit was a cellular kill-switch, making room for new life. Mother Nature liked them young. But then, so did Reese.

Reese wandered back to his lab table, lost in thought. The room seemed to hum with the intensity of his presence, a singularity that shoved aside everything else. There was only a place for one dominant male in any animal society, an alpha male whose will to power drove the species forward.

They had cracked the Hayflick Limit, he and Dr. Tohlson. Fetal nerve tissue, carefully extracted from fresh specimens—late second trimester was best—and spliced onto adult tissue, had set back the clock, pushed back the limit.

Reese picked up the bell jar and looked at the fetus inside. He felt like a gypsy staring at a crystal ball, reading the future in his reflection, the shape of things to come. The fetus slowly revolved as he turned the jar in his hands, serene in the formaldehyde, immune from the ravages of time. The fetal extracts had been his area of expertise. Developing an injectable modality to stimulate new growth in adults had been Tohlson's. They weren't ready for human experimentation yet, but they were close.

All Reese wanted was another twenty years.

Twenty years of vitality. Twenty years to feel the
ferocity of youth, the rage of life roaring through
him. He lightly ran his fingers over the seams of his
neck, touched the gray stubble on his cheeks. Reese
would keep the findings to himself, of course. His little secret. No monograph in the *New England Journal
of Medicine*, no write-up in the *New York Times*. They
could keep the Nobel. He'd keep his secret.

But Tohlson was dead. *Prematurely* dead. Boyd
and Lloyd had found him trussed up like a chicken
at Lauren Kiel's beach house. That was bad. The
fact that all of Tohlson's research notes were missing
was much worse.

Lauren Kiel had really surprised him. She was
beautiful, but too skinny and civilized for his tastes.
He liked them darker and dirtier and ready to tear
him in half if he relaxed his grip for an instant. She
was probably everything an ivory-tower type like
Tohlson had ever dreamed about: a cultured intel-
lectual with French underwear.

Her motivation seminar at Reese Pharmaceuticals had been the brainstorm of the marketing
department. They said she had done wonders at
Squibb and Genentech. Tohlson had attended every
session, and told him afterward that she was the
most intelligent and insightful woman he had ever
met. Reese had thought it was $25,000 worth of
bullshit, but he had signed the check. Well, she
had made fools of them all.

McVey had come to him one morning, his mouth
puckered in distaste, and said that Tohlson was
spending his nights with Lauren Kiel. Poor McVey.

As security chief for Reese Pharmaceuticals, it was his responsibility. He should have never have let it happen. To teach McVey a lesson, Reese ordered the twins to stake out her beach house. It was simple. All they had to do was stay on the beach and listen in, but they got bored—attention span of gnats, those two—and wandered off. Probably dragging the parabolic mike in the sand.

Reese unlocked the top drawer of his file cabinet and brought out the Polaroids McVey had taken at her house. The twins had called at 2 a.m., all panicky, trying to cover their asses, and Reese had sent McVey to make the best of it. McVey reported back at dawn. It was one of the very few times Reese had ever seen him excited.

Reese riffed through the stack of photographs. There was a shot of the living room, arcs of blood curving down the walls. Another of Tohlson dangling from the ceiling, naked as a jaybird, looking like a load of raw hamburger from the neck down. What the hell had he done to deserve that?

It was an artistic job, very impressive, worthy of a B'Dai warrior. Reese had spent a year with the People when he was thirty-four, wearing nothing but a jockstrap and red face paint, cataloguing herbal cures. One morning there had been yet another skirmish with a neighboring village over a disputed section of marshland—a rich source of feathers and bird eggs. One of the B'Dai, a new warrior, had dropped his short iron-tipped spear and fled. The others, shamed beyond words, hung their heads and gave up all claim to the marsh.

There was Tohlson from behind, a neat gridwork of punctures across his back, hands tied over his flabby buttocks.

The B'Dai found the coward hiding in his mother's hut and took him away, while the mother wailed and rubbed ashes on her belly. All day the warriors labored, cutting a narrow maze into a thorn thicket with their hand axes. Late in the afternoon, they led the coward into the center of the maze and shoved thorns into his eyes. He didn't make a sound.

The coffee table was awash in blood, Tohlson's feet visible overhead, the broken sliding-glass door in the background. McVey had removed the body and had the twins smash the door. He said it would confuse the issue. As if it wasn't already confused enough.

The whole village had climbed the trees overlooking the maze and taunted the coward, who just stood there in the soft light of the setting sun. Just before darkness, the warriors set the edges of the thicket on fire. The coward flinched at the crackling sound, took a step forward, hands outstretched. The villagers shouted contradictory directions to him and bounced pieces of fruit off his head. As the flames got closer, his efforts became desperate. He lunged first in one direction and then another, tearing himself to shreds, his screams rising up like smoke.

Reese checked his watch. The twins were long overdue. He had sent them out this morning with express orders to pick up the husband. He wanted Lauren Kiel, and the husband was a good place to start. Just ring his doorbell, he had told the twins. If he's not there, sit in your car. Wait for him to come home. They probably drove past his apartment and decided to go work out.

The last photo was a closeup of Tohlson's face. McVey must have stood on a chair to get that one. Tohlson's mouth was stuffed with something silky and his eyes were bulging in agony, caught forever in death. On his cheek, a bright red lip print. A perfect kiss. That was a beautiful touch. You had to hand it to her.

CHAPTER 7

YOU COULD HEAR the Locker Room three blocks away, a heavy bass note that rolled through the night.

Danny drove the Mustang up to valet parking, next to the two-hundred-horsepower imports parked out front in the winners' circle: a Lotus, two Porsches, a black Euroteched Mercedes 500SL, and a red Ferrari Testarossa with a PROSPERITY IS YOUR DIVINE RIGHT bumper sticker.

A trio of sleek Hispanic valets, cinched into canary-yellow tuxedo jackets, watched him while they swayed to the rhythm that pounded through the walls of the club. One of them finally sauntered over, slid a cardboard stub under the windshield wiper, and handed a duplicate to Danny.

"I won't be long," said Danny as the valet revved off into the back lot, grinding every gear. In the shine of the coral Targa he checked his angry reflection: soft gray cotton pleated pants, baggy gray shirt with tiny black flecks, buttoned to the top. No tie.

He pushed open the front door to the Locker Room, found himself eye to eye with posters of Lyle Alzado and Howie Long snarling out from their shoulder pads. Black-and-silver pompoms and Raiders pennants lined one wall; a cracked football helmet presided over the reservations desk. Another wall was dominated by a life-size photo of Kareem arched in an elegant skyhook, the ball frozen inches from his long, tapered fingers. Another of Magic grinning as Kurt Rambis hurled his elbows into the face of a bleeding Larry Bird.

The hostess walked over and stood too close. She was new, which wasn't a surprise. When the Locker Room was part of his regular circuit, he had seen them go through three hostesses in one month, but that was partially because of Grand Prix weekend, when every moron in a decal-studded race suit thought he had grab-ass privileges. This one had spiky blue hair, white lipstick, and a short satiny dress that pushed her breasts up and out. It was amazing what they were doing with plastics nowadays; gravity didn't stand a chance.

She squeezed his upper arm with her fingertips, led him back to the upper-level bar. This close, he could hear the tinkling sounds of her movements as she walked. Her earrings were a cascade of tiny gold baseball bats; the matching charm bracelet was heavy with little gold megaphones, footballs, and basketballs. She reminded him of those Tibetan

prayer wheels that spun in the wind, sending a constant stream of salutations to the gods.

The crewcut bartender wore a bored expression
and a football jersey with the nametag JOHN on it.
He took Danny's ten-dollar minimum and jabbed a
thumb at the sign behind the bar—"Locker Room
special: end-zone peach margaritas and slam-dunk
kamikazes."

Danny had John open a couple of dark Becks.

The dance floor below was packed, reflections
of the crowd bouncing off the mirrored walls.
Overhead, on projection-TV screens, mud-smeared
giants from past Super Bowls crunched soundlessly
above the heads of the dancers like a storm raging
over a school of herring.

Couples bit their lips as they bumped and shuffled, clapped their hands, and hunched each other's
knees. Frazzled and sweaty cocktail waitresses in
cheerleader outfits edged through the crowd, holding up trays of fluorescent drinks. A tall, fat man in
a black corduroy suit was at the edge of the floor—
eyes closed, pocked face turned toward the mirror
ball overhead, he jerked spasmodically, punching
the air with his thick arms. Everyone gave him
room.

Danny put the first empty on a passing tray and
started on the second beer. He spotted Barton at the
center of the crowd, dancing with a scrawny woman in lace leggings and merry-widow corset. Unless
things had changed dramatically in the last year,
Barton's partner was somewhere close by, holding a
couple of ounces of heavily stepped on coke, broken

down into half-gram packets. And there was Jo-Jo, the China White king, leaning against a pillar near the men's room, wearing a suede jacket, Wayfarer sunglasses, and his go-for-it smile. Eugene nursed a kamikaze in a corner, chain-smoking clove cigarettes and coughing. Every few minutes, someone with an interest in downers stopped by to shake his hand with a twenty-dollar bill. Business as usual.

Danny finished the second beer. The DJ tonight was a slinky black man with a bleached-white afro and four gold hoop earrings through one ear. He popped and dipped in his clear plastic booth, working the twin turntables and blowing kisses to the crowd.

Bingo. There he was, next to the EMERGENCY EXIT sign, a stocky, brown-skinned man in tight leather pants and Harley-Davidson jacket, with a beeper on his belt. His thinning slicked-back hair was pulled into a stubby ponytail—ponytail? He was barechested under the jacket, the gold chains and crucifixes around his neck swinging from side to side as he danced. The blond co-ed he was with shimmered in front of him, wriggling to Public Enemy's rap exhortations. She bent toward his leather pants, lip-synching the words to him with a glossy red pout, eyes luminous as magnesium flares.

Danny worked his way over and made eye contact. The man stopped, grinned, and embraced him, enveloping them in a fog of Paco Rabanne.

"Dan-ny," he shouted in his ear. "Qué pasa, man?"

"We need to talk, Cubanito."

"Long time, man." Cubanito bounced to the music. "Missed you, no shit."

"It's important," said Danny, the two of them frozen in the strobe light.

Cubanito looked back at the co-ed. She stood on the floor, glaring at the both of them. "Vámonos," said Cubanito. He pushed open the emergency-exit door. Alarms went off.

Danny waved to the co-ed. She flipped him the finger.

Cubanito waited just outside the door. A moon-faced bouncer in referee stripes stuck his head out, saw Cubanito, and went back in. They walked toward where the attendants were sitting, squatting on their haunches under the sputtering arc lights. One of them spotted Cubanito and raced off.

"Ain't seen you, man," said Cubanito. "Nobody has." His motorcycle jacket had little gold dollar signs for zipper pulls. Cubanito had once told Danny, completely serious, that God must really love the rich, otherwise he wouldn't have made so many poor people for them to eat.

The attendant pulled up in the red Ferrari from the front. He got out, making little bowing movements to Cubanito, wiped the door handle as he held it open. Cubanito bent down and looked along the length of the car for dings or scratches.

Danny eased into the narrow passenger seat, smelled fresh sweat and Paco Rabanne and butter-soft leather. Whatever had died to cover those seats had not died in vain. "Where's the DeLorean?"

"Don't remind me." Cubanito banged his knees

as he got in. "I unload it on some dusted-out illegal think he's superpimp."

"Your dust."

"Look at me, man." Cubanito edged the low-slung Testarossa over the speed bump. "I don't move that shit no more. No Sherm, no crank, no snap-crackle-pop. Save the lowlife product for the lowlifes. Me, I repositioned myself." He clicked the shift into second and peeled away with a screech. "Just prime flake for prime people, man. Dust got no class."

Danny felt a vibration move past the soles of his feet, through his legs, and up his spine as Cubanito moved from second to third gear. They were doing 80 MPH before they hit the traffic signal. He cinched his seatbelt.

"You looking sharp," said Cubanito, glancing over with a predatory leer. "Guinea charm, man, good as the real thing. 'Making a good appearance is making an investment in yourself,'" he recited. "You know who said that? Ed Sanders, that's who." He slipped a cassette into the Blaupunkt and the sound of a waterfall churned out of the door speakers. "Man change my fucking life."

A clear drop of mucus hung from Cubanito's nose. He sniffed it back. "Way you dropped out of sight," he said, "I figure maybe federal indictments or a grand jury make you keep your head down . . . " Cubanito's face was a smooth brown mask. "Or you could be busted, start narcing out your friends." He saw Danny's expression. "Hey, anything's possible, man. You show up all a sudden, talking favors, make me wonder, that's all."

Cubanito cut off a station wagon on the freeway entrance ramp—"Punto!"—shifted into fourth and raced down the asphalt, the acceleration pressing them back into their seats. "So, okay, what can I do for you?"

"Start by cracking the window," said Danny. Fresh air and the throaty engine rumble filled the car. "I'm looking for Lauren."

"What are you going to do to her?"

"Talk to her."

"Talk, huh? Okay," said Cubanito. "I see her every few weeks, but not back there. Rainbow or Portofino Club, usually. She got tastes, man, you know her." He twisted a flake inhaler with his thumb, popped the top, and stuck it in one nostril, snorted, shifted to the other. "Ummm." He tapped the peeling gold crown of the dashboard Madonna for good luck, held out the inhaler to Danny. "C'mon, man, don't be shy."

Danny shook his head. "I'm in training."

"See, now you're acting like a narc again. They got every excuse you wanna hear why they can't do some shit with you. All they wanna do is *buy* some shit, you understand?"

Danny understood. He put the inhaler to his right nostril. It was still warm. He sniffed. Before he could put it into the other, the rear end of his skull started expanding. He hit the other one anyway.

Danny hated cocaine. Hated the sudden rush, the bitter taste at the back of his throat, the nasty letdown afterward. He avoided anything that

made you feel like a rat on a treadmill. Long before
Cubanito got repositioned, Danny dealt exclusively
in high-grade pot, sensimilla and Hawaiian buds,
Thai sticks and Afghani red. He sold quantity to
eager middlemen with a yuppie clientele: real-estate
brokers and record execs who needed something
to take the edge off their frantic workday, something friendlier than Valium. It was a good life for
five years—clothes and cars and travel and never
checking the price tag. The pot trade attracted
less craziness, the psychos and cowboys gravitating
toward coke, speed, and bathtub pharmaceuticals.
Danny always said that pot didn't have the same
profit potential as coke, but at least you didn't have
to kill anyone. He had been wrong.

They drove easily down the 405 freeway, heading
south, barely conscious of the movement, sliding
back and forth through the five lanes of traffic like
the Ferrari was greased with hot light. The road
hum broken only by Cubanito's perfect tenor singing scraps from "Guys and Dolls." " 'Got a horse
right here, name's Paul Revere' "—Cubanito's finger
stabbed at the cars alongside for counterpoint—
" 'and the man say he'll win if the weather's clear.' "

"When did you see her last?" Danny said, the feeling starting to come back to his brainstem.

" 'And if the man say the horse can-do, can-do,' "
sang Cubanito, the red glow of the instrument panel
reflecting off his face, " 'can-do, can-do.' " He was
shiny with excitement, a pyro watching a forest fire
roar down a mountain. "Yeah, she some beautiful
woman, your wife, man. Woman like that leave me,

I have to kill her or cut off my prick, 'cause I ain't *never* gonna get it so good again."

"Thanks, Miss Lonelyhearts," said Danny. "Let's try it again. When was the last time you saw her?"

"Maybe . . . two months." Cubanito pulled up alongside a black Corvette, glanced over at the driver, pushed in the clutch, and tromped on the accelerator. The tachometer screamed into redline. "Players." No response from the Corvette. They pulled away. "I'm shiekin' these two actresses got purple hairs like parrots, and I tell you, man"—he smacked his lips—"such sweet, long-legged birdies . . . "

"She with anybody?"

"Some whitebread." Cubanito giggled, a girlish, incongruous sound coming from him. "Dance like he afraid he move his ass, it break off and fall on the floor."

"Did whitebread have a name?"

Cubanito shrugged. "The parrots and I duck into the head, and when we come out they're gone."

"Ever see them together before?" Danny squinted. There were too many lights, headlights and taillights, LEDs and yellow arc lights, neon glare from off the freeway and searchlights from the malls bouncing off the clouds. There was always a going-out-of-business sale somewhere.

"Maybe . . . three times." Cubanito snorted twice and wiped his nose with his sleeve. Snot glistened on the leather jacket, looked like slug trails. He offered the inhaler. "C'mon, man, get right." Danny shook his head. Two girls in a white VW bug stared at them as they passed.

"You don't know his name? She didn't introduce him?" Danny thought he was yelling, but he couldn't tell. Whatever—it made his head feel better.

"EEEasy," said Cubanito. "Slow down, man. Yes, I sees her, but I don't talk to her. She don't *like* me. Remember?"

"She said you looked like you were in training for a pinky ring."

"What's that mean? That's an insult, right? Well, *fuck* her, man, excuse my langwich, but *fuck* her. I look like I'm standing still? Look what I'm driving." He caressed the soft leather. Dreamy with pleasure. "I walk into the dealership with a shopping bag full of hundreds. Manager runs over like I'm some beaner got lost, and I empty the bag onto his floor, say, 'Gimme the red one, asshole.' Guy even fill up the tank for free," he said.

"I was going to ask you about that." Danny let his head loll against the headrest, a smile playing around the edges of his mouth. "What are you doing driving a narc car?"

"Are you fucking with me, man?"

"This is the same kind of car that asshole on *Miami Vice* drove, right?"

"Yeah, Sonny Crockett."

"That guy's a narc." Danny kept his eyes closed so that he wouldn't laugh. "You're driving a narc car, Cubanito."

"Yeah, but that's just like his job, man," Cubanito insisted, waving the inhaler. "In his heart, Sonny's dealing."

"I don't know, seems like a bust to me."

"You're fucking with me, man, but that's okay. Another year, I'm out of the business anyway, diversify myself stone legal—you'll see. Maybe buy a McDonald's or a Seven-Eleven, hire some wetbacks to keep the costs down. I'm learning all the time, man, like from *Inc.* and *Fortune* and *Money* magazines. Beautiful names, man. God bless America, you know what I'm saying? I even bought these flash cards with words on one side and what they mean on another. That's how come I'm talking so much better, 'cause I study in the shitter. Someday, I want to be a lawyer . . . or maybe just go on quiz shows, you know, like *Jeopardy*, man."

Cubanito was on a prime-flake speed rap, too far gone to stop. He was going to race down every neurological alleyway, every thought, every sensation emptying out of his mouth, and there was nothing Danny could do but wait for it to be over.

"Stone legal, man, the only way to go. I tell you, these new guys . . . Colombians were bad, but these fucking Jamaicans are crazy. They kill for nothing, man. Your grandmother step on their shadow, they gonna *joint* her. They gonna chop off her arms and legs and leave her bleed to death in a Dumpster. No shit."

It wasn't the killing that repulsed Cubanito, it was the sloppiness, the random aspect of it, that he couldn't tolerate.

Once, before he started specializing, before the Ferrari, when Cubanito sold anything anyone wanted to buy, he had moved a bad batch of synthetic heroin. He didn't know it was bad until his junkies began turning up dead, spikes still sticking out of their arms and ankles.

Danny had run into him on the Newport pier, Cubanito listening to the waves and quietly saying he was a businessman and no fucking chemistry major was going to cost him customers. It was a bright, sunny day, kids on boogie boards yelping with glee in the cold water, and Danny hadn't even tried to talk him out of it. Maybe he didn't think Cubanito would really do anything, or maybe death was an abstraction at that point. He just said, "Later," and went to meet Lauren.

"Are we driving anyplace in particular?" Danny's headache was getting worse.

"We not so different, you and me," said Cubanito. "You look for your wife, I look for somebody, too. Not for love, though. It's money for me. You worry about your cash flow, the pussy take care of itself." He looked over at Danny, then back at the road, having received a confirmation that was apparent only to himself. "Money's better, Danny," he said gently. "Men like us, it's too late for love."

Danny looked out the windows at the darkened homes by the side of the freeway. The inland areas were hotter and smoggier than the beaches, but the houses were a lot cheaper, cheap enough that even mechanics and cops and schoolteachers could afford to raise kids. Inland was families and Little League and going to Sizzler on special occasions. The biggest worry anyone had was getting to work on time.

Cubanito nodded at the stereo. "How you feel, man? Confident? Your prick hard?" He pulled out the cassette and held it up. "Say thanks to Ed Sanders."

"Cubanito, as a friend, I'm suggesting you lay off the coke."

"Hey, man, I'm offering you the whole twelve-tape set, 'Dare to Dream: Ten Keys to Financial Security, by Ed Sanders.' "

"Cubanito—"

"Is scientific, man, like college, only makes you money. You think is just waterfalls on the tape, but Ed Sanders himself is on there, *behind* the waterfall, talking to your subunconscious mind, secret like, whisper into your brain—

" 'Hey, vato, you can do it, man, you're one smart motherfucker and the whole world want you to be rich.' It works, Danny, for true, man. This Ed Sanders is a fucking millionaire."

"Look, would you recognize this guy who was with my wife if you saw him again?"

"Three hundred ninety-nine dollars for the set," said Cubanito, "if you buy from Ed Sanders." They blew past a black Porsche. "I sell you for a hundred dollars, total. I can do it 'cause I never pay the three ninety-nine myself, so I pass the savings on to you. Copy mine from some chubby dumbass secretary, gave her a gram and eight inches." He grinned. "Cutting your overhead is the second key."

Danny turned the tape deck off. "I know it's going to be awfully quiet in your head without Ed talking to you, but see if you can turn the car around and take me back to the Locker Room."

"My feelings hurt, man. You don't wanna be rich?

Okay. You just want your wife? Okay. I help you find her, but first . . . "

"I'll buy the goddamn tapes!"

"Forget it, man. I was try to help you, but even Ed Sanders can't help you 'cause you got a negative attitude." Cubanito took an off-ramp, drove past several traffic lights in tense silence before he slowed and pulled the Ferrari against the curb. "There's a man here I have to talk to." He nodded to André's, across the street. He was breathing through his mouth as he watched the restaurant.

Cubanito looked just like he had on the Newport pier, tight and hard, remorseless as a shark. It made the hair on Danny's arms stand up.

Cubanito snorted, shook the inhaler, and snorted again. "Ahhhhh." He dabbed at the inside of his nose with a moistened finger, then held it out. Danny waved it away. Cubanito's eyes were glistening with anticipation. Danny could see himself in them.

He had left Cubanito on the pier and gone to a new restaurant in LA with Lauren, one that served only champagne and caviar. They had ordered golden-black Iranian beluga, seventy-five dollars an ounce, served in the mouth of a ice-sculpture sturgeon. Lauren had plucked out the eye of the fish—it was a bead of caviar the size of a tiny pearl—and bit it so it squirted across the table. Danny had laughed and kissed her hotly. The next morning he read about the chemistry major in the newspaper. When Lauren asked him what was wrong, he wouldn't answer.

"You been away for a long time, man," Cubanito

whispered. "Everything's different now. More heat, more money . . . I want to see if you're still the same."

"Keep going, don't stop now."

"There is a man sits at a table outside." Cubanito pointed. "Comes here every night. He's rich, this one, but greedy. He sells gold coins to people too smart for banks, trades me stacks of gold panda bears for bags of my best cocaine. He says he is my friend, then tries to go around me. 'I'm just eliminating the middleman,' he tells me when I find out, not even scared. He's a rich man but foolish, because my people will not deal with him. Never. Only with Los Nombres."

Cubanito pulled down his lower lip, his hands shaking with rage. "You see? You see it?" He let go his lip. "Thirty-eight eighty-three. They do that at Castro's prison on the Isle of Pines, tattoo a number inside your lip, mark you like a dog. My people will not talk to men without numbers. This man has a silver limo out back and a tub-of-shit Samoan donkey in the limo, and he say to me, ' That's business.' Should I allow this?" He slammed a fist into the dash, the Madonna shaking from the force of the blow. "You want my help? I break my stones helping the old Danny, this new Danny needs to show me his street manners first. Take care of the donkey, and I find your long white bitch for you."

"I look like King Kong?"

"You're not so big," Cubanito admitted. "But you're tricky, man. That's better. Like the time with the trucker."

"I broke three bones in my hand on that guy."

"Hey, don't worry, man. I got faith in you."

It was a fair trade. Cubanito passed out thank-you dimes of coke to every manager, bartender, bouncer, and valet in three counties—he dealt in favors and information as much as anything else. If Cubanito said he'd find Lauren, he would.

"I don't want to read about anything that happens tonight in the papers," Danny said.

"Does it matter?"

"It matters."

"Tonight we keep our souls clean." Cubanito shrugged. He snorted more flake, tapped the Madonna, and grinned. "Tomorrow's another fucking day."

Danny had promised himself that he'd stay away from dealing and dealers. Away from situations where people could get killed for being uncool and killed ugly for failure to deliver. He'd promised. But then he'd also thought that he'd get over Lauren. Assured himself that if her love could fade, so could his. It had been a long time since he had been right about anything.

CHAPTER 8

DANNY WALKED ALONG the row of potted palms and decorative brickwork fronting the street. There were no neon, loud music, or charm bracelets here. André's was too small to need valet parkers and too exclusive to need a winners' circle. If you could afford the prix fixe menu, you were a winner. He passed the outside patio, heard muffled conversation through the thick hedge, the tinkle of stemware and giddy laughter. The bubbly sounds of the good life, the sweet life, floated into the night until they burst against the stars.

Jaguars and Bentleys, Mercedes sedans and Rolls Corniches lined the lot—there were no stiff-suspensioned sports cars at André's. In a world of potholes and detours, these people demanded insulation from light, motion, noise, and worry.

Danny was wearing a white apron, one hand holding a serving tray aloft. On the tray a cut-glass water pitcher filled with cooking oil. He had slipped a pimply busboy twenty dollars at the kitchen door, the kid blinking, not understanding the request, but fluent in the lingo of cash.

The silver Rolls was parked in the shadows, pointed away from him. Danny moved briskly toward it, tray perfectly horizontal, strictly professional. The dark figure in the driver's seat turned his head, following Danny's progress in the rearview mirror.

As Danny approached the Rolls, he stumbled, the pitcher sliding off and shattering on the pavement next to the front door. Danny lurched and sprawled across the hood. The metal was barely warm against his cheek. He felt the Rolls shudder as the driver shifted and opened the door.

A bad sign, definitely a bad sign.

The Samoan was half out of the seat, built like an upright piano, monstrous neck bulging from a black suit, cursing in a language full of vowels. As his feet swung to the pavement, he slipped in the puddle of oil. Danny pushed off from the hood and kicked the door shut. There was a crunching sound and a howl from the Samoan as he fell backward. Leviathan getting the harpoon amidst icy spray and the slap of wooden oars.

Grunting with the effort, the Samoan pulled himself out of the car, slipped, caught himself on the roof, and slipped again.

Danny slammed the heavy door on him again. The Samoan's cries, more anger than pain, should have warned Danny off, but he was flushed with the momentary clarity that action gave him and contemplation rarely did.

The Samoan scuttled out, grabbed Danny by the sleeve before he lost his balance and fell, a scrap of Danny's shirt in his fist. Danny backed away, panting. He should have brought a tire iron or a pipe wrench. Maybe an antitank gun.

The Samoan tried to stand, but his legs splayed out, skating wildly on the oil. He reached for Danny even as he fell, grunting with frustration, his broken fingers twisted into talons.

Danny danced in and away, careful to keep away from the spreading puddle on the pavement. He feinted and kicked the Samoan in the face.

The Samoan got to his knees, startled. Sheets of blood poured out of his nose and dripped off his chin. He cupped his hands in front of him, stared sadly at the blood running through his fingers.

Danny took a running start and kicked him again, drove the Samoan's head against the doorjamb. It sounded like a baseball bat hitting a bag of soup bones.

Danny suddenly went all rubbery, sat down and waited for the sirens, the screech of brakes, the SWAT team. He didn't care anymore. He could hear Detective Holt's ever-so-solicitous inquiry: "Do you have problems with your temper, Mr. DiMedici?" I have problems with everything, lady.

The conversational hum continued without pause from the patio, a cork popped. He rose slowly. His foot throbbed, one shirtsleeve was in tatters, and a good crime lab could probably run a set of prints off his ankle where the Samoan had grabbed him—fee-fi-fo-fum. The guy had an unlimited pain threshold.

Danny limped over to where the Samoan had collapsed against the rear wheel, stood over him cautiously, ready to bolt. He'd seen too many horror movies where the creature was never quite finished. Danny slipped in the oil and fell to one knee, yelped . . . No, the Samoan was out, head flopped to the side, mouth hanging open. Danny slowly dragged the big man free of the oil and broken glass. By the time he was done, he was dizzy and soaked with sweat.

Blood drained from the Samoan's flattened nose and streamed across his cheeks. Danny picked shards of glass out of the man's face, listening to his breathing. It was thick and ropy but steady. A glistening red bubble formed on the Samoan's lips. Danny popped it with a forefinger. He removed his apron, folded it into a pillow, and propped up the Samoan's head with it so that he wouldn't strangle on his own fluids. He laid the Samoan's hand across his chest. So many bones were broken that it looked like he was wearing a catcher's mitt.

The Samoan coughed and a tooth fell out of his mouth and rolled onto the pavement. Danny hesitated before picking it up. He examined it in the dim overhead light. The tooth was smooth and yellow, jagged at the root, where it had splintered off from the jaw. It didn't look that big. He ran his thumb over the worn surfaces, seeing coconut palms and typhoons, manta rays and red hibiscus, Lauren crouched on the crest of a wave, surfboarding on a sea of blood. Once upon a time . . .

Danny had to reach out to steady himself. He might have killed the Samoan. Danny had spent years studying the Mayans and Aztecs. They had gods for everything—corn gods and rain gods, gods that drowned children and gods that made mescal. Cubanito believed God was a Republican, and Lauren didn't believe in anything. Danny didn't know about heaven or hell, but he believed that a killing got noticed, it drew attention to you, and that was the last thing he wanted.

There was no going back to his little room in the Shore and pretending to be invisible. Holt thought he was guilty, Steiner thought he was innocent, but neither of them had a clue. They thought of death as merely cause and effect, a crime followed by punishment. But a killing stuck to you. And what was worse, it attracted still more death. All the midnight swims hadn't been enough to prevent whatever had happened at Lauren's beach house. He wasn't going to stay home anymore, waiting for a phone call.

Whistling came from the far end of the parking lot. " 'Can do . . . can do, if the man says the horse can do . . .' " Danny looked up to see Cubanito applauding, head thrown back in delight.

CHAPTER 9

THERE WERE A DOZEN small tables on the patio of André's, each one flanked by white wicker chairs. Candles on the table and Mozart on the sound system.

Danny sat down, still flushed from his attack on the Samoan.

A waiter with a moussed-up pompadour and no sideburns glided over. "Good evening," he said. "My name is Rick. May I bring you something to drink?"

"Rick, bring me a double Irish and four aspirin."

When Rick returned, Danny was rubbing at the blood spots on his knees with a wet napkin.

"Oh," said Rick, setting down the Irish and the aspirin, "that looks awful, simply awful." He squatted down and took the napkin, dipped it into the water glass, and worked at the stains. "Rub *with* the grain of the fabric. Such beautiful material, too. Italian, isn't it? I've done the same thing myself."

Danny merely grinned.

"Here, you try it," said Rick. He hurried toward another table, turned, and wagged a finger at Danny. "Now, as soon as you get home, you soak that with Perrier. Stain'll lift right out."

Cubanito's low whistle preceded him as he walked out from the main restaurant. He trailed a hand across Danny's shoulder as he passed, then moved to a nearby table, where a man and a woman were sitting.

The man was wearing a blue blazer with gold buttons and an elaborate gold-threaded crest on the breast pocket, white duck trousers, and deck shoes with the laces undone. He was in his mid-forties, tall and lanky, with sun-bleached hair, neatly parted to the side. Smooth, pinched face, thin lips, arrogant mouth. He looked like he enjoyed saying no, preferably from behind a blindingly polished desk the size of an aircraft carrier.

The woman had on a simple black dress and a single strand of pearls. Her dark hair was swept high on her head. Fifteen years and fifteen pounds ago, she had been a runway model. She still had the cheekbones, but her neck was losing the battle.

"Hola," chirped Cubanito. He did a slow samba footstep before sitting down between them.

The woman glanced at Cubanito, winced at the sight of his leathers as though she had bitten into a bad oyster. She looked at the man. "Edward?"

Edward had taken a beeper out of his pocket and pressed the call button. "Mr. Sanchez, good to see you, super. I'd offer you a glass of Cristal, but . . . " He glanced at his watch and smiled. "You only have about seven seconds before Matuiai arrives."

Cubanito picked up the woman's champagne glass. "Mr. Sanchez? Whas a matter, Eddie, we not buddies no more?" He took a sip, swirled it around his mouth, gargled, and spit it back. "Is a leetle sour, chica. You should get your money back."

Edward had his thumb flattened against the beeper while he looked around.

Cubanito picked up Edward's wrist. Checked the gold Rolex. "How much time I got now, Eduardo?" He released the arm, let it drop to the table. "Time enough, eh? I think maybe your donkey fall asleep."

Cubanito reached over and stroked the back of the woman's hand, felt her flinch and start to get up. Cubanito placed the index finger of his right hand against the base of her throat and pushed her back into her seat. People at the other tables looked over, then went back to their conversations.

"Remove your hand from my wife," hissed Edward.

"Such a pretty wife, too," said Cubanito. "Such a . . . co-quette," he pronounced, petting her arms. "That's French, you know?"

The woman sat stiffly, staring at Edward with contempt.

Edward had pulled out a checkbook and was furiously writing.

"We've had a misunderstanding, Cubanito. It happens all the time in business, and I'd like the opportunity to make it up to you, to give you a little token of my—"

Cubanito tugged at a loose strand of the woman's hair. "I likes a woman with such a nice, long neck."

The woman glared at Edward. She must have terrified her maids.

"Edward. Are you just going to sit there while this . . . person molests me?"

"No one is being molested, dear, just a little misunderstanding."

"That's right, dear, you know it when I molest you," said Cubanito. He gave a low chuckle. The woman felt it roll down between her breasts like a bead of sweat.

Rick walked over. "Is everything okay here? Can I bring anyone anything?" They ignored him.

"Just a little misunderstanding, huh, Eddie?" said Cubanito as he continued to stroke the back of the woman's neck. "Fucking misunderstanding like that put you right out of the game."

"What can I do to remedy the situation?" asked Edward. "I want to make sure that something like this doesn't happen again."

Cubanito was staring at the woman's face with a look of surprise.

"Señora," he said, patting her hand. "Por favor." He crooked his pinky toward her face and she pulled away. "No, no, no," he soothed, pulling her close. "Por favor, señora."

The nail of his left little finger was over an inch long, an eighteen-karat gold claw epoxied into place at the best salon in Newport. He held her to him with his right arm and gently reached into her nostril with the gold nail. "Por favor, por favor," he said. Slowly, lifted a tiny rust-colored scab from the inside of her nose. He held it in front of her for a moment so she could see, then flicked it away.

She stared straight ahead while Cubanito kissed her hand. She was focused on something far in the distance, something beyond reach.

Cubanito dabbed at the tear running down her cheek with a knuckle. She wasn't flinching from his touch anymore.

"A woman who loves the white lady needs a man with the cojones of a bull." Cubanito glanced at Edward and shook his head. "But, señora, you must take care. After you taste the lady, you must rinse your nose with water, otherwise . . . " He held up his little finger and smiled.

Edward had sunk back into his chair. He seemed lost in his clothes.

Cubanito reached into his jacket pocket. Looked over at Edward. "Con su permiso?" he mocked. Edward didn't make a sound. Cubanito dipped his index finger into a tiny jar. "Vitamin-A cream," he said to the woman as he delicately stroked the inside of first one nostril, then the other. "Squeeze from the liver of fish. Verdad. It heals you fast, chica, my word on it."

Cubanito pressed a small triangle of white paper into her hand. "For you, señora"—a smile of warning for Edward—"and for you alone. A gift from Cubanito." He kissed the inside of her arm. "With all due respect and affection." He stood up and bowed to her. She stared straight ahead, the white triangle trembling slightly in her hand. "Eduardo," said Cubanito, his voice soft and husky. "Give me your fine Rolex watch."

"I beg your pardon?"

"Your fine watch, por favor . . . "

"It cost me over fifteen thousand dollars!"

That same warm chuckle. "That's why I want it, Eduardo."

Edward slowly unhooked the watch and handed it over. "Are we square?" he asked as Cubanito walked away. "Are we square?" he called. People at the other tables looked over at him and started laughing.

Danny finished his Irish and left a big tip. Rick could buy himself enough Perrier to bubble clean a dozen Italian suits.

CHAPTER 10

"DR. REESE, YOUR NEPHEWS are here." The voice of the security officer posted at the main entrance was crisp yet deferential. He sounded like he was standing at attention.

"Send 'em up," Arthur Reese growled, snapping off the intercom in his private office. It was almost two-thirty in the morning, his favorite time of the day. Most people's biological rhythms were slowed; they had difficulty focusing. Reese preferred to phone his staff during the middle of the night, berating them, demanding explanations.

He propped his white shoes up on the desk and sighted between them. A few minutes later, the door opened and Boyd and Lloyd squirmed in his expectant gaze like a couple of fat partridges caught in the open, waiting to be blown to pieces.

They sat down carefully in the chairs in front of the desk and looked at the floor.

"I don't see him," Reese said casually, stroking

his bony chin with the back of his hand. The white lab outfit he wore was fresh and clean—he changed four or five times a day—but his tobacco-stained fingers reeked of formaldehyde. "You must have left the husband in the reception area."

"W-we knocked, but he wasn't there," said Boyd.

"So you gave up?" said Reese.

"We waited and waited and didn't know what else to do. So we came back," said Boyd. Lloyd nodded his head in tandem.

Reese steepled his fingers and sighed. The twins were his greatest achievement and his most bitter failure. They were raw power, totally obedient, but their performance was erratic. Throw a stick into a boiling volcano and they'd fetch it. As long as they remembered what it looked like. Neither of them had ever had a cavity, a pimple, or a headache. Their skin was smooth and taut, their urine clear enough to drink. The only thing missing was a sense of purpose. Curiosity. Pride. Everything that he valued. Reese had wanted them to be more than human, to be the next great leap forward in evolution. What a waste of DNA. They didn't even dream.

"We thought you might want us to do something else, Uncle Arthur," said Boyd. "Work out, maybe, or take some shots. Ever since Dr. Tohlson got killed, we've been under a lot of stress. It's just eating up our muscle tissue. We felt like we had a responsibility to you, because of the experiments. That's why we came back. So we could stay big for you."

Boyd was twice as smart as his brother, just enough brains to get them both in trouble.

Reese swiveled his chair slowly around the room, taking in the rows of stuffed-animal heads that ringed the office: gazelles, wildebeest, mountain sheep, pronghorn antelope, a battleship-gray African rhinocerous, a Cape buffalo, its face placid in death. A black-boar head hung over the door behind the twins, watching them, its curved tusks gleaming.

"Well, boys, the ungulates understand," said Reese, pulling at his wrinkled neck, "but that's the way they are . . . trusting. But, Mr. Boar"— he winked at the evil piggy—"ol' Mr. Boar says he'd have waited for the husband to come home. He'd have waited forever if I told him to."

The twins shifted in their seats.

Reese lit a cigarette and did another circuit of the room. There were a Bengal tiger head in full snarl, cheetahs and jaguars, matched wolverine bookends. An upright polar bear filled one whole corner, poised on his pedestal, watching and waiting.

The twins kept their eyes downcast. They called the office the staring room. To Reese, the office was a monument to the superiority of homo sapiens, the killer ape.

"Boys"—Reese brushed ashes off the front of his white coat, leaving black smudges—"the carnivores are not very sympathetic. They think you'd starve to death in their world. If you lasted that long."

"I'm sorry, Uncle Arthur," blubbered Lloyd.

"Don't whimper, damnit!" Reese flipped his lit cigarette at Lloyd, bounced it off his cheek. Lloyd bit his lip and rubbed the red spot.

"What am I going to do with you two?" Reese said. "First you screw up the surveillance at the beach house, now you give up on the husband. You couldn't even find the brother—"

"That one wasn't our fault," said Boyd. "No siree."

"I don't wanna go back to the loading dock, Uncle Arthur," said Lloyd.

"Spiderman didn't even have an address for her darn brother," said Boyd, leaning forward in his chair. "We drove all up and down PCH looking for the turnoff. Spiderman's the one you should be mad at."

"Did I hear my name mentioned?" said a silky voice. McVey had come in silently through a side door to the office. He stood with his head cocked to one side, a tall, very slender man in a vested blue suit. In the room full of staring animal heads he looked like a giant heron that had flown in by mistake.

"Yeah, you heard your name, Spiderman," said Boyd.

"I'm sorry, Dr. Reese. I wasn't aware you had . . . company."

"Quite all right, Frank." Reese lit another cigarette. "I must apologize for my nephews' rudeness."

"No need for that, sir." McVey had wispy hair and a delicate, feminine face. He smiled at the twins. "Boys will be boys."

"Why you being so nice to him for, Uncle Arthur?"

said Boyd. "This is all *his* fault. He's head of security, and there wasn't no security."

Reese picked a bit of tobacco from between his teeth, flicked it toward McVey. "Got a point there, Frank. Kid doesn't get many things right, but he's got something this time."

McVey brushed his hair back from his high forehead. "Security is a relative concept, Dr. Reese, and I don't feel this unfortunate . . . incident should be used to condemn a program that has proved remarkably efficient."

"Incident. That what you'd call it?" Reese rocked back and forth in his leather swivel-chair. "How much do you weigh, Frank?"

"Would that be stripped, sir?" McVey stood next to the lion head, idly running his fingers through the thick mane.

"Right down to your skivvies," said Reese, his jaw jutting with pleasure.

"A hundred forty-seven pounds, skivvies included."

"And you're what? . . . Six-foot-four?" said Reese.

"Six-foot-four-and-a-half inches, sir. As you well know."

"Pure ectomorph," said Reese. "Your basic toothpick. My nephews are pure mesomorphs and weigh over two hundred thirty pounds each. Less than five percent body fat, and a VO_2 max of sixty-five. Their potential strength limit is off the scale, and they never get tired. But you could whip their ass, couldn't you, Frank?"

"Bull!" said Boyd.

"Yeah, bull!" said Lloyd.

"I really don't like getting into those questions, sir," said McVey.

"But if you wanted to, you could," continued Reese. "Use some jujitsu or that CIA mumbo jumbo on the boys. If I was to ask you to, you could do it. Isn't that right?"

McVey patted down his wavy, sand-colored hair. The more he attempted to restrain it, the more it billowed out of place. "It wasn't exactly the CIA, Dr. Reese," he preened. "And as you indicated, the weight differential is sizable, so whipping their ass might present a problem—"

"No shit," said Boyd.

"Watch your language," ordered Reese.

McVey turned to Boyd. "However, I could rather easily kill the both of them before they had a chance to trip over their own feet."

"Try it." Boyd stood up. "Try it, Spiderman."

McVey casually picked a piece of lint off his jacket and watched it float to the floor.

Reese laughed and slapped his desk. "Dominance and subordination, that's what being a primate is all about, eh, Frank? Knowing which ass to fuck and which one to kiss."

McVey shifted and cleared his throat. "Lauren Kiel evidently has the only record of Dr. Tohlson's research," he changed the subject. "I completed voice-stress tests on Dr. Tohlson's staff. None of them were privy to his recent experiments with D-adrenal complex."

"As expected," bristled Reese. "That four-eyed son

of a bitch made a fool of both of us. His computer files are incomplete. The early experiments are detailed, but the later entries are gibberish. Lab notebooks were a fraud, too. I'm very disappointed in Tohlson. In fact, it seems like everywhere I look"—his gaze withered the twins but left McVey unflinching—"I'm surrounded by incompetence and duplicity."

Reese let the personnel department hire the drones and drudges, the lab techs and the programmers, but he personally recruited all his senior staff. He preferred extremely able individuals who, for one reason or another, were utterly dependent on him. Borderline personalities who didn't fit into the neat bureaucracies, men who made enemies and broke rules. Sexual deviants and substance abusers. People with *problems*. He viewed himself as a ringmaster who could make even the most erratic and volatile individuals bend to his will and perform to their utmost. He was their court of last resort. And they knew it.

Tohlson had been a brilliant researcher, innovative and rigorous, but his personality quirks had caused him to be fired from a succession of top-level jobs. Reese had plucked him from a state university, given him a fully staffed lab and an open-ended budget. If the competition couldn't woo him with money or threaten him with blackmail, Tohlson would remain loyal. That was the theory. Reese hadn't counted on the stupid bastard's falling in love. Live and learn.

McVey had his difficulties, too. Reese had heard

about McVey through contacts in government, and while it had taken a long time to find him, McVey had leaped at the proposal. It wasn't so much the protection and anonymity that Reese offered. It was the chance to use his special talents again. There was so little opportunity for a man like McVey to be really appreciated.

"Have the police found the body yet?" said Reese.

"They'll get a phone call in an hour," said McVey.

"I still don't know why you didn't get rid of it," said Reese, "or just leave it in the beach house."

"Doctor"—McVey held his annoyance in check— "a body is an opportunity. By controlling its discovery, we gain a measure of control over the police investigation. This way, we use their efforts to further our own. It's called piggybacking. I might point out that the police located *both* the brother and the husband. We need them in the loop."

McVey had an arrangement with the master programmer of the firm that installed police computer systems. McVey got the secret access code to every PD in Southern California. The programmer got to keep his little secret. Every time the two detectives entered their daily reports into the system, McVey delivered a printout to Reese.

Reese blew smoke rings at McVey.

McVey leaned forward, his long fingers resting on the edge of Reese's desk. "There's no reason we can't proceed with our original strategy, Doctor. We can use Ms. Kiel to mount a disinformation campaign. Let her sell the competition a set of flawed research. Send them down a blind alley. By the time they run their own experiments, they'll never catch up. She'll cooperate, I promise you that."

The silence in the room was so acute that the only sound was the hum of the air conditioner.

McVey removed his hands from the desk. "I turned in a missing-persons report on Dr. Tohlson yesterday," he said stiffly. "Once they find the body, the police will stop by for some routine questions. I've completed my search of Dr. Tohlson's house. There's nothing there that can hurt us . . . or help us, either. I removed the tap already and have begun following up on his phone log."

"I want the brother brought in," said Reese. "Him and the husband. She didn't do this on her own."

"According to Detective Holt's report," said McVey, "the brother is a hermit and a marijuana user. Probably delayed-stress syndrome. The husband was a mid-level drug dealer. Evidently retired." He gave a barely perceptible shrug. "I don't think either of them have the expertise or corporate connections we need to worry about. If you wish, I'll have my people take care of it."

"I don't want anyone else involved," said Reese. "Just the four of us in on this one, Frank, one big happy family. Boys, stop by the performance lab and get a muscle biopsy. Then get some sleep. You're looking puny. Frank, you stay close by." He dismissed them with a wave of his hand.

As the door closed behind them, Reese rocked back and forth, puffing away. He liked to turn the heat up on McVey, loved to watch him twitch like a locust on a stone griddle.

There were actually very few pharmaceutical manufacturers who could use Tohlson's notes, companies that had both the resources to work on cellular life-extension projects and were privately owned. Most of the public firms had steered away from fetal-tissue research after the government had expressed moral reservations and their annual meetings were picketed by right-to-lifers.

Reese considered it a fortunate circumstance when the competition was hamstrung by ethical considerations. In fact, he had McVey funnel money to a fundamentalist Christian broadcaster who urged his listeners to boycott those corporations "using the slaughtered innocents for vile profit."

Besides, his own method of extracting the fetal cells was critical to the project and, like Tohlson, he also kept dummy lab notes and incomplete computer records. He cupped his hands behind his head, appreciating the irony of the situation.

CHAPTER 11

GRAY LIGHT WORKING toward morning, Danny on dawn patrol. He squinted, face pressed against the windshield, wiping at the condensation of his own breath. The orange streetlights looked like distress flares falling through murky water. A rippling of the darkness that didn't illuminate as much as give the air a phosphorescent glow.

Danny's foot still throbbed from where he had kicked the Samoan. Definitely getting too old for this.

Once upon a time he had enjoyed his capacity for violence, the exhilaration of being free from doubt, beyond good and evil. Now he just felt sore, and wondered if the Samoan had a wife who'd cry when she saw his broken face. A woman who'd cradle his head in her arms and sing him to sleep. If someone like the Samoan could be taken down, then they were all of them walking bags of blood waiting to burst—and it gave him no pleasure, no pleasure at all.

The traffic was sparse on Pacific Coast Highway. He passed rusted-out vans loaded with surfboards and shiny tanker trucks. A VW bug plastered with THINK PEACE bumper stickers came across the center line, right at him, the driver scraggly and wild-eyed in Danny's headlights. He veered onto the shoulder and kept driving.

This was one of the barren stretches of PCH, a mix of commercial and industrial outposts in between the small beach towns—wet-suit sales, doughnut shops, used-car lots, heavy-equipment depots, and all-night gas stations advertising COLD BEER and CHEAP CIGS!

After Cubanito dropped him off at the Locker Room, Danny had decided to go see Michael. Michael and Lauren weren't all that close, but he was her brother. Even more important, he was Danny's friend.

A skateboarder shot down an overpass in a crouching knot of elbows, kept pace with him for a block, and just as suddenly dropped off into a side street. Danny hunched over the wheel of the Mustang, looking for his turnoff.

Hawaiian Shaved Ice. Leather Bikinis. Fresh Seafood. Surfside Apartments, an ancient, flaking stucco building filled with riggers who worked the offshore oil platforms. Twenty days on and ten off. No alcohol or gambling allowed.

In the beginning, Danny had delivered two jars of black beauties, strictly pharmaceutical, to a guy in room 31, carried them over his shoulder in an army duffel bag and dropped them on the squeaky bed.

The guy had been even more nervous than Danny, pulled a gun and kept saying, "What am I, stupid or something?" Danny had looked from the gun to the orange shag carpet, not wanting to die in such an ugly room. He had never handled speed again.

He almost missed the cutoff, remembering. Block after block of chain-link fence on the ocean side, marked by NO TRESPASSING, CALIFORNIA OIL COMPANY signs, then skidding into the sudden gap in the fence and onto the service road, a narrow ribbon of gravel winding through the oil fields.

The car lurched over the ruts in the old road, low beams bouncing off the dirty yellow fog. Dust floated in through the open window as Danny tried to find the way, sticking his head out to see ahead. The road kept dropping off suddenly, sending his head against the roof. A local talk-show radio host was arguing with a caller about the proper method of dealing with rapists. Danny cursed as he checked his nose where it had smacked against the doorpost. He had managed to survive the Samoan, now the trick was surviving Michael's private driveway.

The grasshopper pumps creaked as they bob-bob-bobbed up high-sulphur crude; ghosts of trilobites and dinosaurs, pterodactyls and proto-mammals, low rungs on the evolutionary ladder, now fuel for the freeways. Some of the pumps were marked with spray paint: *Dead Boys, Psychotech, WASP.* Everywhere the litter of grease-caked fifty-five-gallon drums and broken beer bottles. No deposit, no return.

He jerked the wheel onto the right-hand fork of

the road, veered into the weeds to avoid a series of deep potholes. "Shit!" as his forehead whipped into the steering wheel. He took a left, another left, and drove on. Sound of breakers. He was getting closer.

The caller told the talk-show host she wanted rapists executed. After a last supper of their own genitals. The host cut to an Alka-Seltzer commercial.

More turns and drop-offs. The graffiti stopped this far in. Out here it was just overgrown and unattended, waist-high weeds around the pumps and wooden fencing fallen on its side.

Michael's house was suddenly right *there* in the mist, a small cinder-block bunker set out alone on a bluff overlooking the ocean. The house was surrounded by pumps, hard pack, and scrub grass. There was a satellite dish on the flat gravel roof and a four-wheel-drive truck with a broken right headlight parked alongside.

The previous caretaker, a retired rigger, had sodded in a lawn, put in a birdbath and a white picket fence. His wife had planted marigolds and petunias, hung a hummingbird feeder from the porch. After they left for a trailer park outside of Palm Springs, Michael moved in. He drained the birdbath, took down the hummingbird feeder and the fence, tore out the sprinkler system. He said he got free rent and no neighbors for checking the pressure gauges and reporting trespassers, and that was it.

Danny turned off the engine and stepped out into the fine gray mist that blew in from the sea. It may have started out smelling of seaweed and jellyfish, but by the time it got to Michael's, it tasted like gasoline at the back of your throat.

Michael stood in the front yard wearing baggy madras Bermudas and a white letter sweater, a Pebble Beach Country Club golf cap rakishly tilted back on his head. His ancient jungle boots were spit-shined and laced halfway up. Even with his question-mark posture, he was huge: six feet six, with a wide, flat chest and spindly legs. He kept one hand in the sweater pocket; the other held Lurp on a taut leash. The black Labrador retriever squatted and strained, still tugging at the chain even as he crapped on the brown lawn.

The two of them looked like the kind of terra-cotta lawn sculptures sold at the roadside in Mexico for the vans full of tourists who drove down for cheap lobster and huaraches.

Michael with the shaggy mustache and long, curly hair, a fat joint clutched in the corner of his mouth. And Lurp was all wrong, too. He didn't look cute or sad; he just looked cranky and consti- pated.

They were never going to sell. The sculptor was going to have to stick with the old reliables: black lawn jockeys and pink flamingos, brown-skinned Madonnas and haughty matadors.

Michael watched Danny with Lauren's blue eyes. Blue ice. Symphonia Antarctica. A sad song for a continent under wraps.

It was after 5 A.M. Danny's gray silk shirt was streaked with sweat and dirt from André's parking lot, and his face banged up from the bumpy ride through the oil field. He needed a shower and a good night's sleep. He needed a friend.

"You look like shit," said Michael.

"Yeah, and good morning America to you, too." Danny dabbed under his nose with a fingertip, wiped the blood on his pants. He had a knot on his forehead where he had hit the steering wheel. "Why not just put in a mine field, set up some claymores?"

"More fun this way."

Danny rubbed the top of Lurp's head, watching Michael. The dog yelped, as though in pain. "You been holed up too long, Mildred," said Danny. "Some visitors would do you good. Keep you up to date on the current fashions."

"Wouldn't surprise me a bit," said Michael, hitching up his Bermudas.

"You missed a spot," said Danny. He nodded at a clump of wilting dandelions. "Those flowers are spoiling the ground-zero effect you've worked so hard to achieve around here."

Michael jerked a .45 automatic out of his letter sweater and emptied the clip into the dandelions. "Better?" He smiled, blue eyes flashing.

Danny stood with his mouth open as the echoes rolled around him.

Lurp howled and continued to rip at the sand with his back feet.

Michael jerked the leash, and the three of them walked onto the porch. "Missed you, bro," he said, laying a hand on Danny's shoulder, light as a falling leaf.

Danny embraced him. He felt Michael flinch then hug him back.

"Love your cologne," said Michael.

"Cubanito." Danny shrugged. "I think he gargles with the stuff."

Michael hooked Lurp onto a long chain on the porch. "Been too long, bro," he said, opening the door. "*Entirely* too long."

CHAPTER 12

DANNY SHIVERED AS HE WALKED into Michael's house. Thick curtains and an 8,000 BTU air conditioner kept the inside at a constant sixty-five degrees year-round, a single season rolling down the calendar. The huge unit filled the front window—it squeezed all the moisture out of the room and dripped it into Lurp's water bowl on the porch. Michael called it part of his closed-system eco-strategy.

"Nanook"—Danny raised one hand in salute—"I bring you greetings from the Great White Father in Washington."

Michael returned the salute, the joint moving from one side of his mouth to the other, all on its own. He laid the .45 on the electrical-spool coffee table, took off his letter sweater and handed it over. He had on a freshly pressed but faded Izod polo shirt, the little alligator frayed headless. On the sweater were a pair of crossed golf clubs and three gold chevrons. A *State Champions* badge over the heart.

"Sorry I didn't call first," Danny said, the shoulders of the sweater drooping on him. "I thought you'd be up, and didn't want to use the phone."

"You don't need an invitation, bro," said Michael. "Sooner or later, always figured you'd turn up." He pinched the joint out between his thumb and his forefinger, swallowed the roach. "I just hoped it'd be sooner."

Two sides of the living room were stacked with book-cases running from floor to ceiling, the books filed according to subject. Air filters hummed in every corner, sucking up smoke and dust. Three televisions, a video recorder, two computer terminals, and a fax machine faced the sofa. The walls were filled with awards and photographs, neatly arranged, precisely balanced. Danny had never been in Michael's bedroom, but he was sure you could bounce a quarter off the sheets.

Four junior-achievement blue ribbons were displayed over the sofa in a perfect square. At the center of the square was a gold plaque identifying Michael Kiel as the *California Jaycees, Man of the Year, 1976*. Two Silver Stars and three Purple Hearts were pinned on a velvet strip above the computer, right next to Lauren's diplomas and two sets of wedding pictures: Lauren and Raj, and Lauren and Danny.

"Beer?" Michael ambled into the kitchen.

"Coffee."

"Turning into a lightweight, bro."

Danny checked the photos while Michael made kitchen noises. A much younger Michael in camouflage pants, beefy and bare-chested, sitting in the lap of an enormous stone Buddha. Another of a sad little Vietnamese girl wearing a UCLA sweatshirt that hung to her knees. A large glossy of red bougainvilleas blooming through the shattered cockpit of a downed Huey—red flowers, black gunship, a revolutionary springtime.

Pictures of Lauren. Lauren with her first bicycle, her feet barely reaching the pedals, angry at being photographed in the act. Lauren in curlers, sticking out her tongue at the camera. Lauren lying on the beach, tanned and elegant in a lavender bikini, white-blond hair and smooth cleavage. There was sand sticking to the inside of her thighs.

It made Danny's chest hurt to look at her. He sat down on the couch. He tried to let himself be lulled by the steady sounds of the air conditioner and the air filters, the whispered counterpoint of the laser printers as they made hard copies from the computer. Stock quotations scrolled across one of the computer screens in soft yellow light; the other one showed a succession of multicolored bar graphs. One TV was tuned to a financial-news network, another to a Road Runner cartoon, and the third showed a Japanese commercial for Scotch whiskey, all with the sound off.

"This is real cozy," called Danny. "I feel like I'm inside a digital watch."

"Thanks." Michael came back with a bottle of beer and a steaming mug of coffee for Danny. "Chicago

Board of Trade just opened." He nodded at the financial-news network. "Coffee futures are down eleven cents. You want action, you came to the right place."

"You heard about Lauren?" said Danny.

"Sure. Your two cops—"

"*My* two cops?"

"They ain't mine, bro. They humped up to the front porch yesterday, had me call a tow truck before we even got to the questions. Seems like they broke an axle fifty yards past the turnoff." Michael laughed so hard he started coughing. "They lost it in a monster pothole. Old cop said it took them over two hours to hike in and find the place, thought he was going to have a coronary—"

"Don't believe it."

Michael raked a hand through his tangled hair. "Seemed like a nice old guy. The whole time they're here, he just sits on the couch looking at my medals and the pictures, back and forth, back and forth. Swear he had tears in his eyes. She's something though, isn't she? A number one, all the way."

"What did you tell them?"

"Everything I know. Nothing." Michael finished the beer and belched. "She asks me if I know that possession of marijuana is a misdemeanor in the State of California. She actually said *State of California*. Cracked me up." He shook his head and hit the remote, replaced the Road Runner with a game show. Bill Cullen was smiling and motioning to a rebus with most of the pieces blocked out. " 'Miles to go before I sleep,' " Michael answered the puzzle.

The pale white skin on one side of Michael's neck was mottled with leathery scar tissue that disappeared down his back. He went outside only early or late, said direct sunlight made him feel like he was on fire all over again. He lit a fresh joint from the neat row laid out on the coffee table, inhaled, and passed it to Danny.

"We've got to do something." Danny held the joint for a few moments, just to be polite, then gave it back.

Michael dragged deep. On the game show a bouffant redhead winced as she stared at the rebus puzzle board. " 'Miles to go before I sleep,' *dipshit*," said Michael.

"She's in trouble," said Danny.

"She's fucking illiterate, is what she is."

"Not her," said Danny. "*Lauren*. Lauren's in trouble."

Michael switched to *I Love Lucy*, Ricky jabbering silently at Lucy, somehow more comforting in black and white. "Lauren's always in trouble." He glanced from screen to screen. "Get used to it."

The Michael sitting on the couch wasn't the same one in the Vietnam photos. All the meat on him had disappeared, ounce by ounce, pound by pound. His arms were white strings hanging from the sleeves of his polo shirt, his chest flattened to the breastbone. Only his big hands had stayed the same size. They were strong and supple, seeming to move of their own volition. Danny had seen him roll a joint with one hand while punching in computer commands with the other.

"You want to do something," said Michael, "do something with that, will you?"

Danny finally took a drag. He had already fallen from grace, might as well make it a double back flip. Another drag. He closed his eyes. An image of deep green forests and ancient limestone heads formed at the back of his lids. The heads were mossy with history, their thick-lipped Mayan features knowing and arrogant through a curtain of leafy vines. Red-haired monkeys watched from the trees overhead as he and Lauren kissed in the clearing below. All the time in the world.

They sat in silence, passing the joint. When it was done, Michael lit another.

"I went by Lauren's place," Danny said at last. "Couldn't even go in. Scared off by those yellow ribbons the cops put up. What a weird color to mark off a crime scene. Makes it look like a wedding."

"Who can understand cops? I give your two detectives a lift back to PCH, and the lady cop tells me I can be ticketed if I don't get the broken headlight fixed." They howled as Michael imitated the expression on her face. "I told her not to sweat it," said Michael, " 'cause I never leave the perimeter. The old guy just pats my shoulder and says, 'Semper fi, son.' "

Electronically, Michael could leapfrog all over the globe, shifting money across national boundaries with a phone call, getting the latest information with a speed-of-light bank shot off the nearest Telstar. Physically, Michael stayed put. Anything he wanted, anything he needed, got delivered to the front gate. The last time Michael had left his oilfield outpost was to appear in court with Danny when the divorce was final. Lauren had a seminar scheduled, and he said he figured Danny could use a little moral support.

"They think I killed Lauren," Danny said. "You believe that?"

"I figured," said Michael. "Lady cop keeps asking me if you were jealous, if you held a grudge, if you were violent . . . Why she got such a hard-on for you, anyway?"

"Sunspot activity. I don't know."

"She seemed okay to me, real methodical. Little formal, maybe. Wouldn't sit down the whole time. But I guess she has to be, otherwise people take advantage."

"Yeah, next thing you know they'd be borrowing her handcuffs or asking for half a cup of hollow-points."

"She's just doing her job," said Michael.

"I love this." Danny shook his head. "You're sitting around with the cops smoking a joint in the Captain Video room, probably got your .45 lying on the coffee table, and *I'm* the one they're hassling."

"I think it's your attitude, bro. You probably get searched at airports, too." Michael pulled his gold cap low over his eyes, puffing away watching the TVs.

"All right!" Michael threw his hands upright. "Cocoa's gone to thirty-eight cents a pound, and our hero, the man of the year emeritus, went long, very long." His face was drenched in ecstasy.

"You're really not going to help, are you?" said Danny.

"You got to deal with life as a series of commodities and transactions," said Michael. "No offense, Danny, but you're gonna die broke. Forty-one cents a pound! Extra point! Goddamn, I love this game. You want to make a lot of money? A lot? Just tell me what the weather's going to be in two weeks. Could you do it? If your life depended on it, could you do it?"

"Could you?"

"Damn straight." Michael nodded. "Two months ago, a Cambridge entomologist on R 'n' R in Central Africa reports to the Royal Zoological Society that the local beetles and centipedes are digging deeper nests, tunneling down an extra three or four inches . . . "

"The Mayan calendar was carried through thirty thousand years in the future," said Danny. "Every day had a different god and a different set of prayers. It didn't help. The jungle still won."

"No Mayans here, bro. So if you see rhinoceros beetles digging in, kiss the cocoa harvest goodbye and head for the ark, because it is going to be one rainy mother-fucker. Supply and demand is just reading between the lines."

"She could be dead, Michael. She could be stuffed in a trash bag somewhere."

"Lauren? Not likely. You want to go hit some golf balls? I got buckets of 'em. Do you good."

"Don't you care?" said Danny.

"Listen, bro, people who care about Lauren end

up paying for it. I'd rather work on my short irons."

"Don't blame her for your problems, okay?" said Danny. "You want to live in solitary for the duration, fine, but don't blame her."

"What's wrong with this place?" said Michael. "You want to see *The Maltese Falcon* or *The Wild Bunch* or *Debbie Duz Dishes*? I got them all. Three thousand dollars a month for international videotext—gets you a printout of any book or magazine you want. Is it snowing in Kamchatka? Surf up in Bali? Ask me, go on, ask me! I got access to more data banks than Exxon does. What do you want to know? Come on, what do you want to know?"

"I want to know where she is," said Danny. "I want to know that she's all right. I want to know what's going on. Can you tell me that, Michael?"

"You're wasted, man." Michael laughed. "Smoke some more pot."

Danny pushed away the joint. "My whole life has turned to shit in the last thirty-six hours, and it wasn't so good to begin with. I wake up every morning for the last two years and have to remind myself we're not together anymore. You don't know what that feels like, Michael. You don't know what it's like to be in love with her."

Michael said he needed another beer and stalked into the kitchen. Danny could hear him in there, muttering, angry at Danny, angry at himself. They both knew it would pass.

Danny was wasted, all right. He felt dizzy and couldn't focus, but what he had said was the truth. Michael didn't know her. No one did.

Lauren was a professional. She never raised her voice or lost an argument. If she had the capacity to feel, she never gave in to it. But when it was just the two of them, she was different. They'd lie awake in bed for hours. Lauren needed to be at the brink, but she needed to feel safe. And when he was no longer able to give her that sense of security, when he pulled back, she had cut him out of her life. Just like that.

They had met when Danny was leading a university group to Copán. It was his favorite Mayan site, a ceremonial city in the middle of nowhere, a skeleton city for priests only. Murky green sunlight filtered through the canopy of trees while parrots screeched overhead. Their last day together, they had found three chips of carved jade; they stayed up till dawn smoking hash on top of one of the pyramids. Once they thought they heard a jaguar scream and he held her close, felt her heartbeat. She was still married to Raj then, so that's all they did. That was enough. He had never hated a sunrise so much.

Michael came back with a beer, swept up ashes from the coffee table with the side of his hand, and neatly tucked them into the side pocket of his Bermudas.

"You'd have liked the Mayans, Michael." Danny had a silly grin. Between the pot and the lack of sleep, he couldn't differentiate between what he was thinking and what he was saying. The utter lack of outside noise, outside light, heightened the intimacy between the two of them. "I mean, here's a whole civilization of anal retentives who spent all day fine-tuning their calendar. Perfectly organized, everybody knowing what they were supposed to be doing every minute of the day. No wasted movement."

Michael lit another joint.

Six years later, Danny ran into Lauren on the other side of the country, in the apartment of a guy he was setting up a major deal with. He was done with teaching by then, and she was done with Raj. Ton of bricks, right through his heart.

He and Lauren just walked out together, left her boyfriend and the deal and everything else. There was never any question about it. Nobody gets more than two chances and grateful for that. Two hours later, they were driving along the beach road with the top down. She had her shoes off, one foot out the window, wiggling her toes in the wind, and he floored it, tickling her with the acceleration. He looked over at her, laughing and free, and said, Marry me or I'll drive over a cliff, because we'll never be this happy again. She kissed him and said, Wanna bet?

"You're missing a major opportunity in strategic metals." Michael pointed at the TV with the can of beer. "Miners go on strike in Zambia, cobalt's going through the roof."

Danny blinked himself awake. Lauren's kiss still warm and sweet on his lips.

"You okay?" said Michael.

"Let me tell you a story," said Danny. "Once upon a time there was a rich kid named Bronco Billy, the boy wonder of Wall Street. One day Bronco Billy burst into flames on the trading floor. He slumped against a marble pillar, still shouting and waving his arms. No one was sure if it was a successful takeover or a major miscalculation, but they all gave him plenty of room." Danny yawned. "All except for a fat broker in a seersucker suit who leaned close, nodded, and raced off, his clothes already beginning to smolder."

"Sounds like a margin call to me," said Michael, distracted, glancing at the screen as he wrote rapidly on a legal pad, then put down the pen. "Okay," he said, pointing. "Let me see it."

Danny waved him back. "I'm fine."

"That's why I want to see it."

Danny slowly unbuttoned his shirt, exposing the thick five-inch-long scar curved across the right side of his abdomen.

Michael traced the path of the scar with a fingertip, lightly testing the area with his thumbs. "That hurt?" Houdini had had such perfect coordination that he was supposedly able to pick up needles off the floor with his eyelashes while hanging by his heels. Michael had the same delicate touch.

Danny didn't remember much about the operation except the graceful way Michael had held the instruments. He was already going into shock by the time he got there, the front seat of the car soaked with blood. Michael, skin-and-bones Michael, had eased him out like he was weightless, given him a shot of morphine, and laid him on the kitchen table. Danny remembered asking if he could have one of his Purple Hearts and Michael saying, "Anything you want, bro, just please don't die."

Danny slipped in and out of consciousness, watching Michael's serious face and his hands swooping back and forth. Michael kept saying not to worry, that he had been the medic for his five-man recon team, and Danny was lucky he hadn't caught an AK-47 round. Danny said he didn't feel so lucky, then passed out. Michael nursed him for a week. By the time Lauren came back from her conference in Europe, Danny was able to go for short walks and tell her it had been nothing.

"You ever pass blood?" Michael asked, "or get sharp pains behind the scar?"

"Sometimes." Danny yawned, settling back into the couch. "If I sit funny or get up too fast. Like somebody poked me with an icepick."

"The bullet glanced off your pelvis," Michael muttered. "Probably left some bone splinters I didn't catch. Damnit, I told you this isn't an ER. I don't have that kind of equipment."

"Hospitals have to report gunshot wounds to the police, Madge. You know that."

Michael buttoned up Danny's shirt, smoothed it flat. "I should have caught it"—he shook his head—"but I was afraid if I didn't stitch you up fast, you'd develop septicemia."

"I'm not going to report you to the AMA." Danny could barely keep his eyes open.

"A wound like that creates a pocket for infection." Michael's voice faded into the hum from the air conditioner, the whisper of the laser printer. "I think I got all the bullet fragments, but you should have some X rays." Michael had gotten up from the couch. He stood in front of his wall of photographs, staring at the picture of himself with his arms around two muscular black marines, the three of them brave and smiling for the camera.

"Honky-Tonk, here, tripped a booby trap on night patrol around Chu Bai. But he's like you—he's lucky, gets a clean exit hole. Top radios in: 'We've met the enemy and we're sitting tight.' Fuck this John Wayne stuff. I shoot Honky-Tonk up with streptomycin and we sit around waiting for a dawn dustoff. Honky-Tonk's doing fine, talking about his mama's okra and laughing 'cause he's got his ticket back to the world, and how much fucking longer till dustoff, man? Four A.M. I lift his field dressing and the stink rises up like steam in the moonlight and he sees my face and starts to cry."

Michael took a drag, slowly exhaled through his nose. The circles under his eyes were so dark you'd have thought he was in camouflage. He turned to Danny, but Danny was already snoring. "Yup, turning into a lightweight." Michael tucked the letter sweater around him. "I tell you, bro," he said softly. "Howard Hughes was right. It's a dirty fucking world out there. Give it half a chance, it'll kill you dead."

CHAPTER 13

THE CRIME-SCENE WAGON raced down the narrow road from the opposite direction, Yakabofski flashing the light bar at Holt as they passed. She whacked the steering wheel and cursed her bad luck.

It was barely dawn by the time she arrived at the scene, a vacant field near a new housing development on the outskirts of Newport Beach. Yakabofski and the other CSI boys from county had staked off the area for a grid search when there was more daylight, but Steiner was already walking around with a huge mug of coffee and a doughnut. He suddenly dropped to his hands and knees and picked at something in the wet grass, his nose almost touching the ground.

A couple of whites were parked at the edge of the field, the uniforms just standing around yawning. It was too early in the morning to worry about looky-loos, but they still should have made an effort. She glared at them as she crossed the overgrown lot, ignoring their friendly greetings.

She high-stepped over burst bags of garbage and soggy cardboard boxes, wet weeds slapping at her jeans. A rusted washing machine, motor gutted for scrap, leaned against a NO DUMPING sign. She felt her jaw clench looking at the sign—contempt for the law, high and low.

Holt had dressed in a hurry and broken the zipper on the brown corduroy slacks she usually wore for rough ones. And the middle-of-the-night calls were always rough ones. Having to wear the jeans made her feel unprofessional. Then she'd had a blowout and spent twenty minutes wrestling the spare into place, bent over on the shoulder of the freeway while truckers roared past, hooting their airhorns.

She took the coffee Steiner offered. It was still warm, strong and black with a touch of cinnamon. He put a fresh pot into a thermos every night, just in case. Karl also kept a backup in an ankle holster and a change of clothes in his trunk. Better safe than sorry, he had repeated every day for the first month they worked together.

Steiner eyed her grease-stained hands and grinned. "What'd you do, Jane, stop and change your oil?"

"I'm in no mood, Karl."

"Neighborhood kids called it in couple of hours ago," he said as they walked toward where the trees began, his suit jacket flapping in the wind. "One of them fell over it. A real doozy, too." They stood over the black plastic trash bag, passing the

coffee back and forth, feeling the morning damp-
ness. "Hell of a thing for little kids to come across.
I told Yakabofski, Forget finding anything usable
after they been around."

Holt moved downwind, squatted, and ran the tip
of her pen along the cut seam. She peeled back the
powder-smudged bag as gently as if it were a birthday present and she wanted to save the wrapping
paper.

"Techs from CSI already dusted it." Steiner took
a bite from the doughnut as he crouched next to
her. "Nothing there, I guarantee. This one's got a
real professional tone to it."

"Wipe your mouth, Karl."

He rubbed at his lips with the back of his hand,
licked the grape-smeared knuckles.

The man's face was exposed first, a waxy death
mask contorted in agony. The mouth was agape,
the head flopped to the side so that one brown eye
stared at her, bulging out of its socket. There were
purplish bruises around the neck.

As Holt worked her way down with the pen, the
smell rolled out, waves of it, burning her eyes.
She turned away and took a shallow breath. One
Memorial Day weekend, her family had gone up to
the summer home. She had opened the meat locker
before anyone realized that the power had been out
for two weeks. That was the summer she became a
vegetarian.

"Only good thing about getting old, Jane"—
Steiner reached over and jerked the bag open, the
stink blooming forth—"the nose starts to go."

She kept a handkerchief soaked with Tuxedo in the brown cords, but she'd forgotten to switch it to the jeans. Another perfect morning. She calmly pulled on a pair of surgical gloves, trying not to let Steiner see her revulsion, and went back at it, leaning full over the body, taking inventory. Her eyes watered, but her movements were unhurried.

The body was nude, faintly yellowish and puffy with the first stages of decomposition. Dozens of small puncture wounds neatly crisscrossed the torso and down the thighs, dried streamers of blood running down from each hole. There was a crusty pink stocking tied tightly around the left wrist and another around the right ankle. Yakabofski had bagged the hands to maintain any evidence under the fingernails.

"Late thirties, early forties, my guess," said Steiner, waving the jelly doughnut. "Couple days in the sun inside the bag, gets hard to tell."

She lifted the right hand with her pen. Red ligature marks cut deeply into the wrist. The fingers were visible through the clear Baggies, stiffened into claws. From the knees down, the skin was wine-colored. It looked like he was wearing purple cowboy boots.

Steiner nodded to the legs. "Tells the tale, huh?"

The man must have been hanging for five or six hours before he was taken down, but it was the boots that were interesting. The line of demarcation in simple suicides by hanging was from the waist down, a dark mottling where the blood had pooled. Hip-waders, the morgue attendants called them, because even laid out on a slab, the half-and-half look remained. This one was probably three or four quarts low, and she knew exactly where he had lost it.

He had been castrated, fine copper wire wrapped tightly around the base of his penis and testicles and his sex sliced off. The coil of wire was still attached to a stump of abdominal flesh. It looked like a shiny vagina between his legs.

"You find his genitals?" she said evenly.

Steiner shook his head. "I'll make sure the lab checks the garbage disposal at the beach house, just in case." A column of ants flowed across the black trash bag toward the body. Steiner's hand lazily reached down, pinched one, then another, while Holt removed the bag on his right hand.

"Clear polish on the nails. No calluses on his hands or roughening of the skin," she said. "White-collar job or a soft life."

"CSI noticed the manicure when they scraped for tissue." Steiner looked up at her, an ant still wriggling between his thumb and forefinger. "I told them—nice thing about working Newport, you meet a better class of stiff." He crushed the ant and tossed it aside.

She sighted along the line of punctures across his chest. "They have any idea what might have done these?"

"Yeah," spat Steiner. "The asshole with Yakabof-ski said he thought it must have been a sharp, pointed instrument."

"Par for the course." She nodded. "Why go out

on a limb when you can run back to a nice air-conditioned autopsy room and run ten thousand dollars' worth of tests." She looked closer at the face, pointed at a slight indentation on each side of the bridge of the nose. "Glasses."

Steiner leaned over the body, peering at the faint marks. "I missed that." He grimaced. "Clean got away from me." He refilled the mug from his thermos and they passed it back and forth, not saying much, just looking at the body.

Every job had moments when you'd want to rush things, Steiner had told her, moments when you'd be tempted to hurry on through and get to the good parts. He said that it was exactly at those times that you had to force yourself to go slow. Smoke a cigarette, drink a cup of java, listen to the background sounds. Steiner said it was the uncomfortable parts of a job that were the most important. That's where a good cop could make a difference.

Holt had learned more from Steiner in the first week they were partnered than in her six months at the academy. One more semester at USC and she'd have her master's in public administration, one step closer to her goal of being the first woman police chief of a major metropolitan area.

When she made it, she'd owe a large debt to Steiner. But she'd never be able to put him on her staff. He was old school, too idiosyncratic, too willing to go outside channels. He didn't complain about Miranda and he wasn't on the take, but his warrant requests were overstated and he was too friendly with his snitches. He wouldn't make it in her administration. It was one of the few things Holt regretted.

After a while they turned the body over, the two of them grunting with the effort and the rubbery feel of the flesh. The puncture lines continued around the torso. Steiner tapped a large wrinkled mole between the shoulder blades. "These things can turn to cancer just like that"—he snapped his fingers—"I seen it happen."

She felt the base of the skull while Steiner spread the buttocks and examined the anus for semen. Then they turned it over again and watched some more. Steiner checked the arms and between the toes for needle marks. The sun was higher now; flies buzzed the body. She absently waved them away and scrutinized the scalp, separating the damp strands of hair.

"You ever wonder why a corpse's eyes always seem to follow you wherever you go?" said Steiner.

A tiny clump of hair came out in Holt's hands. She continued working through the scalp. Sometimes the CSI vacuum missed something. But all she was seeing was dandruff and the beginnings of male-pattern baldness.

"Makes me think that they're keeping track of what we do," said Steiner.

"This one just looks dead to me," said Holt.

"You got no romance in you, Jane."

"Not anymore, Karl."

Steiner pulled another doughnut out of his suit-jacket pocket and offered her a bite. She shook her head. "Hardly squashed at all," he said. "I think it's a cream-filled."

"I'd rather go pick up the swimmer."

He snatched a fat green fly out of the air, shook it in his fist, and hurled it to the ground. There were traffic sounds in the distance now, commuters in a hurry to get to the office.

"I said I think it's time to pull in the swimmer, Karl."

"Little premature for that, don't you think?" Steiner watched the fly twitch.

Holt's mouth tightened. "We have a man here with a broken neck, full of holes, and drained of blood. You have any doubts that he's the one that died all over the wife's nice carpet?"

"Oh, I don't disagree with you at all." Steiner held a rock over the fly. "This is the guy from the beach house, the wife's boyfriend. Mr. B-positive himself." Direct hit. "That don't mean the swimmer did it."

"You know, Karl, the cop who taught me how to read a crime scene told me to always look for the personal touch. You find a body with a handful of dollar bills stuffed down his throat or a burnt candle pushed up his rectum, look for somebody that wants to leave a message. That's what you said. Now, I look at this body and I see somebody trying to make a point. Somebody violent and jealous. Somebody so arrogant that he just dumps the body by the road like a load of garbage. Now, what do you see that I don't?"

Karl stood up slowly, his knees popping with the effort. He offered her a hand, but she got up on her own, pulled off the surgical gloves, and dropped them on the body. Steiner draped the black trash bag back into place, and they walked back to their cars in silence.

"The swimmer's not right for this one, Jane," Steiner said when they reached his new department-issue Plymouth. "Books and clothes scattered everywhere, doesn't even wear a wristwatch. He's a fella that keeps a routine just to stop himself from flying off into a million pieces."

Steiner reached into the front seat, took out a bottle of Mennen Skin Bracer, and rinsed his hands. "No, Jane. Whoever did the job on Mr. B-positive was neat and tidy and knew what they were doing every step of the way." He shook his hands dry in the morning light. "Whoever did it kept him conscious the whole time, so he could think about what was coming next." Steiner sniffed his fingers, then ran them through his hair. "I think the boyfriend was strung from the overhead fixture in the living room. Given just enough slack to breathe while somebody worked on him, slow and easy. I think whoever did it played him like a piano. That sound like the swimmer? You said it yourself. He's a jitterbug. He'd do it fast and simple." He got into his car, buckled the seat belt, and adjusted the rearview. "You wanta go get some breakfast?"

"And what was the wife doing all this time?"

Steiner shrugged. "That's what makes our job so interesting, Jane."

One of the uniforms came by and started to speak. "Not now," said Holt, without looking at him. "Call the lab and stay here until they pick him up." The officer stalked back to the squad car, cursing under his breath.

Holt stuck her head through the open window, close to Steiner's upturned face. "Let me get this straight. The swimmer's impulsive and doesn't hang up his clothes. So he didn't do it. Maybe the wife did it. Except we don't have any motive for her. We also don't know how she managed to hang him from the ceiling. And she's missing anyway, so we can't ask her. Is that it?"

"Jane, all I'm saying is, right now, the swimmer's not a perfect fit. I don't know what turns up tomorrow, but he's not going anywhere and neither are we." Steiner turned the ignition. "C'mon, I'll buy you breakfast."

"You're flooding it."

"I was starting cars before you were born," he said, grinding away.

"Well the new ones have fuel injection, so don't pump it. Just hold down the accelerator."

"You were saying?" Steiner shouted as the car revved into life.

"I'm not eating a breakfast that comes in a paper bag," said Holt. "I want to eat off a plate and use metal utensils. I want to go someplace that has hot water in the bathroom and a mirror over the sink."

"Only the best for my partner." Steiner put the car into gear. "Let's go, Jane. We get there before seven, they put extra Velveeta on the hash browns!"

CHAPTER 14

"HEY!" EILENE CALLED to him as he passed her window, beckoned from the couch. "I want to talk to you."

Danny went back down the stairs and stopped in the open doorway. He had slept a couple of hours on Michael's couch, woke up groggy and hung over, the room reeking of pot and Michael glued to the computer screen, muttering, "Fuck, fuck, fuck."

Eilene wagged a bottle of fluorescent-green melon liqueur at him. It was late morning, but she was still in panties and her boyfriend's baggy EVEREADY T-shirt. "I know what you've been up to."

"Yeah, then tell me." All Danny wanted was to shave and lie down in his own bed for a month or two.

"You're not fooling anybody," Eilene singsonged, sloshing liqueur on the sofa. "Oopsie." She blotted the upholstery with the bottom of her T-shirt, flashed white Calvin Klein jockey shorts with the

123

cutaway thighs. She caught Danny looking and gave him a bleary wink. Her eyes were red and puffy, but they didn't miss a thing.

"Nice talking with you." Danny turned away.

"They were here, you know."

He came back in.

"Oh, now we're interested. How nice. Busy guy like you, barely has time to nod taking down the garbage." Eilene patted the cushion next to her.

Danny brushed aside corn chips and sat down. The room felt sour and unhappy. All the framed Vogue covers on the walls, the ballet posters, and deco furniture weren't going to change that.

"Why is it that for a year I never see you in anything but shorts or sweats and today you show up in last season's Armani?" Eilene appraised him coolly, her eyes momentarily in focus.

Danny could see her striding through Nordstroms, the consummate fashion arbiter, adjusting a salesgirl's belt in passing.

"It's a good look for you," Eilene said. "But get it pressed and lose the shoes. If you'd like some advice on accessories—"

"Was it an old guy and a tall woman?"

"That was *last* night . . . or the night before—I forget. The tall girl's quite chic, but she dresses to emphasize her height, which I just do not understand." She hiccuped into her cupped palm. "Excuse me. I'm five feet eight inches, which is your perfect height, fashion-wise."

"Fashion-wise?"

"Right." She offered him the bottle. He shook his

head. "Did you know we used to watch you? Blaine and I. You'd come back late at night and we'd be fooling around on the couch or on the floor, and you'd just stand there on the steps, dripping wet. Sometimes, if we pretended not to notice, you'd peek in."

"No comment."

"What does that mean?" A dazed smile spread across her face. " 'No comment,' like some CEO on *60 Minutes* caught with his hand in the cookie jar." She straightened Danny's wrinkled collar, absently gauged the quality of the fabric. "We always wondered why you'd go swimming in the dark. You have such a nice body. Sometimes Blaine would make me do things on the couch . . . " She put a fingertip in her mouth and gnawed the tip. "You know, things. We'd pretend our eyes were closed, but we could see you."

"Who came by looking for me?" Danny said. His cheeks were burning.

"Oh, you're no fun! Okay, they came by around nine and went up to your place. They must have pounded on the door for five minutes. Happy?"

"What did they look like?" asked Danny.

"They're never going to buy off the rack, I'll tell you that. Probably a fifty-four jacket at least."

"They were big?"

"Not tall-big, barndoor-big," said Eilene. "Yuck. Men like that always look like they're about ready to split a seam. Did I mention that they were twins? Well, they were. Identical twins. I told them you weren't home."

"What did they want?"

"Said they were Jehovah's Witnesses. I am sure. 'Jehovah's Witnesses don't wear Hawaiian shirts,' I said. 'They wear black suits from K Mart.' Then one of them—"

"They were wearing Hawaiian shirts?" said Danny.

"Didn't I say that?" said Eilene. "Anyway, one of them gets this mean face like I slapped him or something, and he sticks his finger at me and says, 'Clean up your act!' And the other one goes, 'Ditto!' Then they left. Weird. You owe somebody money?"

Danny shook his head.

"Well . . . you must have done something," said Eilene. "Are you listening to me? How about if I go take a shower and you go get some more booze. There's money in my purse."

"I'm really tired." Danny pulled his arm from her grasp.

"I'm not stupid," Eilene said. "I know what you're thinking." She kept biting her lower lip, trying to stop it from trembling. She wasn't successful, but just making the effort made Danny like her.

"You should get some sleep," he said.

"You don't know what it's like to have somebody you love walk out," Eilene said, "not even tell you why. Just wake up one morning alone, stare at their pillow, and start to cry."

Danny didn't say a word. Eilene leaned against him, sobbing into his shoulder. Danny patted her back, watching the window.

"I used up my sick days and my vacation," she

said, "and work keeps calling, asking when I'm coming in—and I can't, I just can't. You don't know—"

"Keep your door locked and your drapes pulled for a few days," said Danny.

"Like you really care." Eilene's mascara was running down her cheeks in black streaks.

Danny went into the kitchen, found a dish towel, and wet it with cool water. While he wiped her face, she sobbed something about the cute ones and the nice ones and the ones who treated you like shit. She snuggled against him as he walked her into her bedroom, her fingers tickling his chest. He pushed the wrinkled clothes off the bed.

Eilene pulled off her T-shirt and stretched. "You won't have to do a thing," she said. "I'll do it all." She had soft white skin and freckles everywhere.

"Get some rest," said Danny, easing her under the covers. "When you wake up, clean your apartment. Wash the dishes." He smoothed her hair. "Don't expect to feel good anytime soon, because you won't. And thinking you're supposed to will only make it worse."

"I'd do anything in the world if Blaine would just come back," Eilene said. "Anything."

Danny nodded.

"I don't care what he's done." Eilene's eyes were half shut. "When you love them, you don't care. That's funny, isn't it."

"Shhhhhhh," said Danny. "Go to sleep."

Eilene yawned. "You sound like my guardian angel. Sexy one, too. My luck." Her eyes were closed now. "Stay till I fall asleep. Please?"

Danny turned off the lights and pulled the drapes in the living room almost shut. First the two cops, now a set of twins. He watched the stairs as her breathing steadily deepened, watched them until she began to snore.

CHAPTER 15

THE HOT SPRAY MADE Danny jump. Then he closed his eyes and turned the shower up, letting it soothe out the kinks, wash away the fatigue. He couldn't stop wondering about the two guys in the Hawaiian shirts. They weren't cops. Cops didn't come in matched sets. His foot still hurt from where he had kicked the Samoan. Newton's third law of thermodynamics: For each and every action there is an equal and opposite reaction. Or was it the second law? He remembered all the wrong things these days.

The farmhouse. Danny remembered waking up in the white-pine cabin, ears ringing, still groggy, wisps of smoke hanging in the air like mist. Wilson stood over him, pale and flabby, his shirt a cascade of pineapples and hula dancers. The hula girls shimmered as Wilson jabbed the sawed-off shotgun at

Danny's head. He looked like the ugliest tourist in the world.

"Rise 'n' shine, slick," said Wilson, kicking Danny in the side.

Jerry and Janice huddled in one corner, Janice talking to the baby in her belly, soothing it. T-Bone covered them with a Mac-10. He held the little machine gun easily in one of his huge hands; Danny's .38 was sticking out of the waistband of his jeans. T-Bone had a shaved head and a Fu Manchu mustache. All his flesh had disappeared after years of mainlining speed. The only thing left was knobby bones and meanness.

Jerry asked Wilson if they were busted.

Wilson was confused for a moment, then snickered. "Sure, farmer. This bald-headed sumbitch is Kojak and I'm McGarret, Hawaii Five-Oh!"

"Yeah," said T-Bone. "You're under arrest, fuckface."

There was a knock on the door. A shy kid in fatigues peeked in and told Wilson no one else was on the property. He called Wilson sir.

The kid was named Stevie. He was a PFC at Camp Pendleton and had supplied the concussion grenades that had smashed through the farmhouse window at dawn. They needn't have bothered. Danny had rolled off the couch when the dogs started to bark, reaching for his revolver and yelling for Jerry. Then the room had exploded with light.

Wilson walked into the kitchen and dug out a handful of the coffee cake that Janice had fixed the night before. Danny told them to take the whole load, no one was going to give them any trouble.

"That's real neighborly, slick," said Wilson, crumbs clinging to his jowls, "but we wouldn't want to just eat and run. Besides, I want to see the operation. I'm a curious kind of guy."

Wilson was just playing with them. Danny knew that. But there was nothing to lose.

Danny crossed the farmyard, Wilson three steps behind, the shotgun cradled in the crook of his arm. There was a freshly painted white fence around the house, and the flowers that Janice had planted were blooming through the fence pickets. Red and yellow and orange flowers—it looked like the house was on fire. Jerry's garden was overflowing with melons, purple cabbages, lettuce, kale, cukes, and tomato plants, neatly staked, still green. The morning was warm. Birds flapped overhead.

"Jesus." Wilson shook his head in disgust as he kicked through a dew-sparkled spiderweb. "How the fuck can people live like this?"

Danny showed Wilson the greenhouses bursting with high-grade sensimilla and explained how they had installed methane-powered generators so the electric company wouldn't notice any increased usage from the grow lamps. He pointed out the mobile lighting system that tracked across the plants, mirroring the movement of the sun. Jerry couldn't name the state capital, but he could do things with pot that Luther Burbank would envy.

Wilson gazed open-mouthed at the setup, inhaled the ripe sweet greenhouse smell. "No wonder no one wants my ragweed."

"They're yours," said Danny, his eyes moving slowly through the rows of plants, looking for something sharp or heavy.

"Oh they're mine, all right." Wilson smiled. "Can't argue with you there." He pinched off a bud and smelled it. "Amazing. We could have worked together. My distribution, your goods—you'd be sitting pretty."

"I'd be sitting right where I am now," said Danny. "Sooner or later."

"Maybe so, maybe so." Wilson's soft cheeks bobbed with a secret joke. "But later's always greater. That's what I say."

Danny edged toward the pruning scissors that hung on a hook.

Wilson poked the shotgun at Danny. "What's your hurry? We got time." Danny stopped. "This place used to be a chicken ranch, right? I heard you chop a chicken's head off, it runs around for five minutes looking for it. That true?" Danny just watched him. "Well," said Wilson, "guess it don't matter. One nice thing about being way out in the boonies, you got privacy. You could do anything out here—no one'd be the wiser."

"There's neighbors just over the hill," Danny lied. "Why not just take what you want?"

"You remember the first time we met, slick? There was a party at the mansion. You showed up with that pal of yours, Ricky Ricardo."

"You had a silver punchbowl filled with crystal methedrine and a couple of tanks of nitrous," said

Danny. "About two A.M., T-Bone went into convulsions."

"Yeah, it was a good party," said Wilson. "I gave you a present, and you sent the bitch back. Here I am making my introductions and you throw her back in my face."

"I'm married."

"Hey, slick, you could have gotten a blow job, be polite. You didn't have to embarrass me."

"If you have a problem with me, let's go someplace and take care of it," said Danny. "Janice and Jerry aren't worth your trouble."

"Heck"—Wilson rolled with laughter—"it's no trouble." The hula girls were shaking all over his shirt.

When Danny and Wilson walked back into the farmhouse, Jerry and Janice leaned against the wall with their hands and feet spread. T-Bone sprawled on the couch, smoking, his machine gun making lazy circles in the air. Stevie sat in the rocking chair, his head in his hands.

Wilson took Danny's .38 from T-Bone, unloaded the shotgun, and tossed it to Stevie.

Jerry jabbered away. He told Wilson that they wouldn't tell anyone. He told Wilson about karma. Janice took his hand, tears streaking her face. "Don't, honey," she said. "They don't care what we do or say. They just want an excuse."

Stevie stood up. "Wait just one minute, Mr. Wilson. You told me we were just going to rip 'em off—"

Wilson sidled over to Stevie. "Think fast," he said

as he pressed the barrel of the .38 under Stevie's jaw and pulled the trigger. The shot was muted by the soft skin, but the top of Stevie's head hit the ceiling at the same time the shotgun hit the floor.

Jerry cried out, and Janice held him. Danny didn't move but shifted his weight to the balls of his feet.

Wilson turned to Danny. "Gee, slick, I didn't know it was loaded." T-Bone laughed and ground his cigarette out into the couch.

Wilson ordered Janice into the kitchen and told her to rustle up some breakfast. He wanted biscuits and gravy, coffee cake and eggs, sausage and bacon. He wanted a real country breakfast.

Janice carefully poured a couple of mugs of coffee, filling them to the brim. She laid them on the counter separating the kitchen from the living room and began cracking brown eggs into a bowl. She moved as if she knew just where she was going.

"Make sure you don't cut yourself on those sharp knives, moms," Wilson said to Janice. "I faint at the sight of blood." T-Bone laughed louder and louder.

Janice slid a plate onto the counter next to the coffee cups.

"Looks good." Wilson reached for it. "I must of worked up an appetite—"

Janice slammed a carving fork down onto his outstretched hand, pinning it to the wooden countertop.

Wilson shrieked and shot at her, missed, trying to pull his hand free.

"Babe!" Jerry ran toward Janice. T-Bone cut him down with a burst from the Mac-10. It sounded like a chainsaw. The Mac-10 jammed. T-Bone cursed, pulled back the bolt, and shook it. Danny punched him in the face and knocked him to the floor. T-Bone hung on to the gun, working the slide, still trying to clear it.

Jerry crawled to Wilson and grabbed at his knees while Wilson howled with pain, trying to pull his hand free without putting the gun down. He kicked at Jerry, but Jerry wouldn't let go.

Danny smashed T-Bone in the face with a heavy ceramic ashtray as the Mac-10 fired. It felt like a wasp sting, a sharp jab in the side, then burning.

Janice threw the pot of hot coffee onto Wilson. Danny saw the brown liquid arching through the air as Wilson raised the .38 and shot her twice in the chest. She and Wilson screamed at the same time, the coffee scalding him as she died. Still pinned to the counter, his face blistering, Wilson leaned down and snapped off two more rounds into Jerry's neck. Jerry finally let go, rolling onto his back, the life fountaining out of him.

Danny tried to pry the Mac-10 out of T-Bone's grip, but T-Bone clawed at him, fighting on out of instinct, a brainstem rage as implacable as a great white shark. The gun went off. T-Bone's eyelids slowly closed and he fell back onto the couch.

When Danny turned around, Wilson was smiling, the .38 pointed directly at him. The burning in Danny's side had spread so his whole body felt on fire.

Wilson had pulled his left hand free, but it was in shreds. Blood dripped from the hand onto his deck shoes. "I'm gonna miss ol' T-Bone," he said. "Probably take me a whole ten minutes to find another one like him." He pulled the trigger. His smile went blank as the hammer landed on an empty cylinder. Again and again and again.

Danny raised the Mac-10.

"Hold on there, slick." Wilson dropped the pistol and held his hands up. "Don't be shooting some unarmed man." His Hawaiian shirt was shimmying. Shake-shake-shake. "Don't you do it. You'll never forgive yourself. Trust me."

Danny emptied the Mac-10 into Wilson's chest. The hula girls kicked and swayed, wiggled their hips as the shirt turned red. Their grass skirts flew everywhere. They saved the last dance for me, Danny thought. He had always had a way with women.

The room had gotten very quiet.

Danny checked on Jerry, but his head was tilted at an impossible angle on the braided rug, blood spreading out from his body like one of the auras he and Janice talked about. They could have told you everything you'd want to know about crystals and pyramids and being in tune with the natural cycle. Jerry hadn't liked Danny even bringing a gun into the house. He'd said he didn't believe in violence. It didn't solve anything.

Janice stared at Danny from the floor. Mouth open, eyes like mud. He kissed her forehead, remembered her honest laugh. She and Jerry were going to raise chickens and goats and babies and live where the air was clean and the people were friendly.

Danny sagged against the tile wall as the water sprayed over him. Lost in the billows of steam. He was never going to find his way out.

CHAPTER 16

IT WASN'T THAT DANNY belonged back at Lauren's house. He just didn't have any choice.

The conversation with Eilene had knocked him off balance, her loneliness triggering his own, filling him with a longing so acute his teeth ached. No one died of a broken heart. God didn't want to put people out of their misery. Solitary confinement, that was the sentence.

So here he was, back at Lido Isle. Only this time Danny had left his car at a nearby shopping center, changed into shorts and a tank top, and run the three miles to Lauren's beach house. He raced past the gated driveways and landscaped groves, waving to the matrons in their Mercedes station wagons. Just another investment banker living the Pritikin life-style.

Someone had been to the living room since Danny's visit the day before. The broken glass door was now covered by a single sheet of cardboard taped into position. The cardboard presented no obstacle to anyone intent on entering. It depended on intangibles to keep people out: the force of law, the weight of authority—both of which were represented by a Newport Beach Police Department notice defining the house as an "official crime scene."

It was the same tactic used by everyone from the pharaohs to the Maoris. To protect the sacred, put a curse on it. Make it taboo. The nearest house was hidden by a high fence. The beach was almost deserted. Just a couple of jocks running along the tide line and a girl lying on a Mickey Mouse towel. Danny didn't believe in curses. Or the force of law, either. But he didn't like the door being sealed.

Danny took a final look around, then pulled off the cardboard. He listened in the open doorway. There was only the wind in the trees behind him, and the seagulls overhead. Silence from the house. He pushed aside the curtains and stepped into the living room. The drapes fell back into place behind him.

The outside light coming through the curtains didn't penetrate far. The room was dim and swampy. And hot—Danny could feel sweat rolling down his bare legs. He thought of newts and salamanders and blind white things that wriggled when you turned a log over.

He exhaled slowly as his eyes adjusted. Then the stink hit him and he was gagging, eyes tearing. The room was collapsing around him, smothering and wet, sliding down his throat so he couldn't scream. He banged against the glass, trying to find his way out through the billowing drapes. He tore down the curtains, found the door, and stumbled outside onto the white sand.

Danny stayed there, on his hands and knees, gasping in the cool breeze, trying to get the smell out of his lungs. Every time he coughed, he could taste the rotting sweetness of the room. He spit and wiped his tongue with his shirt. On the beach, the two jocks were running back in the opposite direction and the Mickey Mouse towel was empty.

The sun was shining, the air was clean, and he was going to have to go back inside. Eilene was right. When you loved someone, you'd do anything. Anything.

CHAPTER 17

"HEY, JUST LIKE SIEGFRIED and Roy, huh?" Detective Steiner's voice was muffled, his broad, beefy face planted between the gleaming jaws of the stuffed lion on the wall of Dr. Reese's office.

"Karl, will you knock it off."

"C'mon, Jane," Steiner said, carefully removing his head. "How often do you get to play lion tamer?"

She peered at the degrees and plaques that were arranged under the elephant head like a necklace, not to mention awards from the Explorers Club and the National Geographic Society.

"I tell you, this is a real man's office," said Steiner, voice rising with delight. "None of those friendly little couches or boat paintings on the wall." He threw punches at a snarling wolverine head. "Makes me feel like a rookie again."

Holt surveyed the room full of heads and grimaced. "It's a waste, Karl, and your boyish enthusiasm for the great white hunter is antediluvian."

"Antediluvian?" Reese smiled from the side doorway. He sauntered to his desk, hands in the pockets of his white lab coat. "Actually, that's exactly the right word, Detective. An appreciation for the trophies of the hunt is an ancient emotion, perhaps one of our earliest—"

"Dr. Reese, could we skip the anthropology lesson?" said Holt.

"Gee, Doc, you move so quiet, I didn't even know you were there," said Steiner. "What's that, some kind of a jungle walk, like you use to sneak up on some poor dumb animal with his tongue hanging out at the water hole?"

"Something like that," said Reese. "Please"—he indicated the chairs—"make yourselves comfortable."

Holt stepped around the zebra-skin rug and stood in front of the desk.

Steiner leaned against the wall, his head at the same level as the two antelope heads he stood between. As he watched Reese, he lightly tugged at the tuft of brown hair that hung from the lower lip of the one on his right.

Holt laid out a half-dozen mug shots on the desk. One of them was an old picture of Danny with longish hair. "Did you ever see any of these men with Dr. Tohlson?"

Reese picked each photo up by the edges, looked at it carefully, and laid it in a neat pile. "I'm afraid not. Dr. Tohlson was a very private man."

"Not private enough," said Steiner, his cockeyed

grin rising suddenly into braying laughter.

Reese looked startled.

"Sorry, Doc." Steiner wiped at his eyes. "We been pulling double shifts since day one on this case, and I'm getting punchy."

"No offense taken. You do any hunting yourself, Detective?"

"A little, when I was younger . . . got a nine-point buck once. Never anything like you're up to." Steiner stooped down and began slowly moving his hands across the zebra skin. "By the way, Doc, we really appreciate you sending your security man down to the morgue to ID Tohlson's body. Short notice. And I wouldn't wish that job on anyone."

"I'm sure Mr. McVey's seen worse."

Steiner looked up. "No kidding? I haven't." He grimaced at the memory and ran his hand through the cropped nap of the skin. "This is real, isn't it? You should feel it, Jane, soft as a kitten."

"Quite real, Detective." Reese laughed. He swung his legs up on the desk, planted a shoe on the stack of photos. "Oops."

"We'll want the names of all of Dr. Tohlson's colleagues and subordinates"—Holt glared—"anyone else Lauren Kiel might have taken an interest in."

"Our work is sensitive, Detective." Reese patted his jacket pocket. "I trust you'll be discreet."

"I'm not interested in your work, Doctor. I'm interested in mine," said Holt.

Holt and Reese watched each other across the desk. He pulled a cigarette pack out of his pocket, saw it was empty, and crushed it.

"This the bullet hole, Doc?" said Steiner, examining a perforation in the zebra hide.

"That's right."

"One shot?" said Steiner.

"All you need, Detective. Any more than that, you're just running the meat."

Steiner got slowly to his feet, groaning with the effort. "One shot," he murmured, shaking his head.

Holt ignored him. "Doctor, we also requested Tohlson's personnel file."

Reese punched the intercom. "Louise, bring in Dr. Tohlson's file, please."

"Mr. McVey put a hold on the file, sir."

"Just get it, Louise." He looked at Holt. "My security chief thinks we should have waited for a court order. Some of the information in the file is proprietary. I'd like your assurance that it will be kept confidential."

Steiner flopped into the armchair with a sigh. "This Tohlson guy, was he into satanism or anything like that—you know, whips and chains?"

"We don't inquire about the religious affiliations, ethnic backgrounds, or sexual preferences of our employees." Reese winked at him. "That would be a violation of their civil rights."

"Christ on a crutch, don't I know about that." Steiner held up his hands in apology to Holt. "Sorry."

Reese's secretary walked in with a folder in her hand. Reese pointed to Steiner.

"Don't mind telling you, Doc, this case is getting to me," said Steiner, leafing through the folder. He wiped sweat from his upper lip, his hands trembling slightly.

"Karl?" said Holt.

"Detective?" Reese bounded from behind the desk, took Steiner's carotid pulse with his index and middle fingers. "What medications are you on?" His voice was soothing and professional.

"You name it, Doc, it's in my medicine cabinet. I got this high blood pressure makes my head feel like a thermometer on an August day." Steiner's face was the color of raw steak.

"Louise! Bring me some sublingual Angidyne samples, a hundred milligrams." Dr. Reese loosened Steiner's tie. "Slow, steady breaths, Detective."

"I'm okay, Doc," panted Steiner. "It's just that if a murder case isn't closed out in two weeks, odds are it won't *ever* be solved." Holt squatted next to him, pale and anxious, holding his hand. "Detective Holt told me that." He squeezed her hand. "I believe it, too."

Reese's secretary ran in with the Angidyne. Reese tore one of the foil wrappers open and handed two pink tablets to Steiner. "Place these under your tongue, Detective. That's right."

Holt and Reese watched Steiner. Louise stayed in the doorway, not sure what Dr. Reese wanted her to do.

Steiner sighed. "That's better. Thanks, Doc."

Reese patted him on the shoulder and walked back to his desk. "I think you should schedule an appointment with your personal physician."

"Soon as I get a chance." Steiner fanned himself with Tohlson's personnel file. "Promise. I don't mind telling you, Doc, ID-ing Tohlson's body is the first real break we've had in this case." He blotted his forehead with his sleeve, his color beginning to return to normal. "A stiff makes all the difference in the world. No offense. I understand that you and Dr. Tohlson were close."

"I like to feel that I'm close to all my employees," said Reese. The phone on his desk rang. He picked it up, listened, and held it out to Steiner. "It's for you."

CHAPTER 18

DANNY WAS BACK in the living room. Back in the heat. He stood there, caught in the shaft of light where he had pulled down the section of curtain. He breathed through his mouth as he looked around. It didn't help much, but at least the hairs in his nose didn't burn.

He started across the room and his steps *crunched*. He didn't want to look down. He got dizzy when he did. A thin crust of blackened blood covered the light blue Bukhara carpet. Green mold sprouted across the blood. In a few more days, the fungus would make as intricate a pattern as the Oriental's. The long-dead desert women who had woven the rug might have found that amusing. Allah is great, is He not?

Danny's knees were shaking. He tried to walk softly, but each step cracked the glaze of blood, fractured the surface. He was half afraid he'd slip through and keep falling down down down.

There was a cream-colored sofa facing the sliding glass, one of those modern designs that you couldn't get comfortable in. An overturned end table. Brass-and-onyx floor lamp. They didn't count.

Danny's attention was on the coffee table at the center of the room. The center of the rug. The coffee table was cut from a single slab of rose quartz, polished to a translucent glow, shot through with veins of silvery mica. The table was the ultimate crystal radio set, able to beam in the death broadcasts from hell, to fine-tune the worst nightmare and bring it on home. And it had.

Blood had puddled on the pale pink quartz and run down the sides onto the rug. The coffee table radiated pain; it set the whole room buzzing. Static. Or flies. Danny would have covered his ears if he thought it would do any good.

Above the table was a heavy iron candelabra, candles guttered down to stumps.

The white walls were splattered with blood. The man who had died here had been hung from the candelabra. Cut and bled. Then spun like a top, spun so fast his life flew out and splashed the walls. It looked like hieroglyphs on the plaster.

He had a gift for nonsyllabic languages. Picture languages. Egyptian. Sanskrit. Babylonian. Mayan glyphs in particular. All he needed was the basic grammar and the meaning just leaped out at him. Whispered in his ear. A curator from the Smithsonian had offered him a position, said it took more than scholarship to make a true reader. It took a gift, he said, an ability to slip back in time.

Danny stared at the blood on the walls, trying to see the message left behind by the man who had died here. The walls weren't giving anything away.

He had hoped that somehow being here would make a difference, would make things clear. Instead, it had just confirmed his suspicions.

Lauren must have killed the man who died here. The man had died the spinning death, a Mayan sacrifice. Who else could it be? The Mayans were all dead. There were just Lauren and Danny. Like Michael had said, it wasn't Lauren who had to worry. It was the people around her. The people who *loved* her. They had to worry.

Danny had come back to the house to find out about Lauren. He had found out about himself instead. It didn't matter what she had done. He still loved her. She hadn't committed a murder. She had committed a ritual.

Danny moved silently through the house. Lauren's study was functional and elegant: rows of books in antique bookcases and comfortable leather wingchairs. A spotless kitchen, the milk still fresh in the refrigerator. Formal dining room, stiff and cold. Lauren would have eaten upstairs, in bed, as always.

The second-floor bedrooms were devoid of human presence. Each had a double bed, dressers, and sitting chairs; all had Portault linens. But no one had ever slept in those rooms.

Every room had been carefully dusted for fingerprints. The furniture, the door handles, the telephones. If anything, the white dust only increased his sense that he was entering a place that had been undisturbed for centuries.

Danny lingered on the steps to her third-floor bedroom. He knew the floor plan by heart, had memorized it from the *Architectural Digest* article. The whole top floor was the master bedroom suite, with huge windows looking out on the water.

He was at the top of the stairs now. The dressers had been emptied, her clothes dumped onto the floor. That wasn't in the article.

Danny stood in front of the full-length window, hands in his pockets to stop them from trembling. A storm was moving in, dark clouds piling up on the horizon. The beach was empty. Everyone had run for cover. Even before they knew if it would blow over. No one had faith. No one wanted to take a chance of getting caught out in the open.

He was prepared to stand there all day watching the water, thinking about anything in the world except what she had done in this room without him.

He walked around the room, touching the furniture, straightening pictures. The inlaid Florentine writing desk, the iron-handled antique Japanese merchant's chest. Everything in the room was familiar; they had bought most of it together.

Over Lauren's bed was the painting of Kali, a tantric watercolor, very rare, very old. It pictured the four-armed Indian goddess standing over the entwined bodies of two lovers. The goddess was bare-breasted and youthful, a garland of skulls around her neck. Kali's two lower arms held lotus blossoms, the symbol of eternal life. One of her upper arms waved a scimitar. From the other hand dangled the severed head of the man at her feet. Kali smiled a distant, dreamy smile of total bliss.

The glass was broken out of the frame and Kali's black hair daubed with yellow paint. Danny had done it. He had turned the goddess into a blonde the day he got the divorce papers, shattering the glass with a punch. He looked at the scars on his knuckles. The painting made the bedroom seem as bad as the room downstairs.

When Lauren asked him how he wanted to divide their things, Danny told her to keep it all. He didn't need anything else to remind him of her. She made him take the matching Bukhara. She said the carpets had been in Raj's family for three hundred years and it was time to break up the set. Then she laughed and said she was going to keep the Kali just the way it was. She liked what he had done to it. Danny sat down on the bed and pulled at the sheets. After a few minutes, he went into her bathroom and splashed cold water on his face. He'd clean the handles later. When he dried his face, he smelled her on the towel. He buried his face in it.

The medicine cabinet was open, the vials unscrewed. Someone had emptied three months of birth-control pills, punched them out of their plastic containers, broken the containers, and thrown the whole mess onto the floor in the corner. The glass jar of little soaps on the sink was undisturbed. Red and yellow soaps, blue and green, soaps shaped like flower buds and hearts and quarter-moons.

The morning after they had first slept together, he had washed his face with one of these funny little soaps. The little red heart had made a thin, fragrant lather. He had almost cut his throat shaving.

There was only one toothbrush. It was the most beautiful sight in the house.

Her vanity was topped with a crystal perfume bottle at center stage. She had the perfume blended especially for her by some French guy in LA, cost her over five hundred dollars an ounce. It was so subtle that it seemed more like an extension of her own clean smell. The whole room was permeated with it.

He went through her CDs. There were a few new ones, but she still had all their old classics. He put on the Neville Brothers' "Tell It Like It Is," programmed the player to repeat it six times, and lay down in the center of her bed. He just wanted to lie here and feel close to her. And if he felt like it, after he heard it six times, maybe he'd have it play another six times. Maybe he'd play it all day and all night, too.

" 'If you waaaaant, someone to play with,' " crooned Aaron Neville in his rich tenor, " 'go and get yourself a toy' "—his plaintive voice filled the room with longing—" 'because my time is too expensive, and I'm not your little boy.' "

Danny closed his eyes and mouthed the words along with Neville. He felt like he was falling slowly through the bed, wrapped in her sweet smell.

They had slow danced to this song on their honeymoon, danced naked in their room, bodies pressed so close neither of them could tell where one left off and the other began. He had leaned his face into her hair, felt her rub her thighs against him. She wrapped her laughter around them.

The song began again. He sang out loud now, his voice cracking as he started to cry.

The wind shook the windows of the beach house. Perfect. Lauren had insisted they go someplace rainy for their honeymoon, because she had gotten married to Raj in the blinding sunlight of India and it hadn't worked out. Maybe her next marriage, she'd want to get married in a blizzard.

Danny had taken her to the Washington State coast, found a bed-and-breakfast on the edge of the rain forest, and rented the whole thing for a week. He had passed out hundred-dollar bills to the staff and told them to take some time off. He and Lauren had danced through the empty house while the trees bent outside and the rain beat against the glass.

Danny's eyes flew open as he felt the cold barrel of a gun press against his forehead.

"You're under arrest," hissed Detective Holt, her eyes bright. "You have the right to remain silent."

Steiner stood off to one side, shaking his head.

"Anything you say can and will be used against you," said Holt. "If you cannot afford a lawyer—"

Danny slowly closed his eyes. " 'Life's too short to have sorrow,' " crooned Neville. " 'You may be here today, and gone tomorrow. So you might as well get what you want, so go on and live, baby, go on and live . . .' "

Danny and Lauren were dancing as Holt droned

on in the distance. The rain pounded against the windows of their honeymoon hotel. He could smell Lauren's hair, feel her nipples burning into his chest. If he could keep his eyes closed, the storm would wash Holt clear away.

CHAPTER 19

"DO YOU UNDERSTAND?" said Detective Holt. "Do you understand what I've just read to you?"

Danny looked up. Heavy-lidded, his gaze focused on some distant point far beyond her. Holt wondered if he was on drugs. He wiped at his eyes, the steel in him snapping back into place. "Yeah, I heard, Detective." The same smart-ass approach he had taken back in his apartment.

Holt stepped back but kept her weapon on him. He aroused an anger in her that she couldn't explain, an anger that threatened her professional judgment. It was more than his attitude or his actions. She wanted to teach him a lesson.

"It's okay, Jane," said Steiner. "Mr. DiMedici isn't going anywhere. Are you, Danny?"

"No place at all." Danny smiled. "You don't look so good, Karl."

Steiner sat down heavily in the vanity chair, both he and the chair groaning. "Little tired." He wiped his forehead. "Too many stairs lately. Thanks for asking."

"You've violated a crime scene, Mr. DiMedici," Holt said. "Tampered with evidence." Glass tinkled, and she looked over at Steiner. He was sniffing the crystal perfume bottles atop the vanity. "Karl? Do you mind?" He shrugged.

"It's good to know she's like this with everyone, Karl," said Danny. "I thought it was just me."

"She cuts no slack, son, no slack at all." Steiner dabbed the perfume stopper against his wrist and sniffed. "Nice."

Holt bit her lips shut. Maybe that's what it was about Danny that made her so angry. He and Steiner had fallen into a natural banter, an easy camaraderie, as if they were sharing a private joke at her expense. It made her feel that Danny was deliberately undercutting her authority, challenging her competence. Couldn't Karl see it?

"Please turn around and place your hands behind your back." Holt jerked her handcuffs out of her purse. "Now, Mr. DiMedici."

Danny stared past her. "Karl?"

The crystal stopper dropped to the floor, and Holt turned. "Karl!"

Steiner twisted in the chair, sweat pouring down his face, staining the collar of his shirt. He massaged his left arm, his eyes glazed with pain.

Holt's handcuffs clattered in her shaking hands. Steiner slid out of the chair, his mouth moving wordlessly to her, but she could not move, could only watch him fall.

Her father had died the same way last year, died in front of her, clutching his chest. That time, she had rushed to where he lay on the living room carpet, knelt over him, feeling her breath rattle into his sour lungs. She kept it up while her mother's screams traveled through the house, continuing her efforts long after she knew it was useless. She tasted death on her lips for weeks afterward.

Steiner looked at her with surprise. He was still staring at her when Danny rolled him onto his back and started CPR. Danny's movements were measured and precise. He pinched off Steiner's nostrils while he gave him mouth-to-mouth, Steiner's huge chest rising with the force of Danny's exhalations. "That's it, Karl," he said between breaths, his confidence rippling through the room like a warm wave. "You can do it."

Holt jerked. She took a faltering step toward Danny, then turned and scrambled for the telephone. The average 911 response time for this exclusive section of Newport Beach was under four minutes, best in the city. He was going to be all right; he was going to be fine. She gave the emergency operator the address twice, then hung up and sat beside Karl.

"I'm sorry, Karl. I . . . " Holt grabbed his cold hand and squeezed it. Danny's arm brushed her leg while he worked, but he didn't acknowledge her; he just kept encouraging Karl in between breaths. She found herself joining in, the two of them repeating, "That's it, Karl, you can do it," until she heard the paramedic's siren in the distance.

CHAPTER 20

"THIS IS GREAT, MAN." Cubanito smiled, eyes fixed on the traffic light outside the Newport Beach police station. As he raced the engine of the Testarossa, the fuzzy dice hanging from the rearview mirror bounced. Two cops crossing the street to begin their three-o'clock shift gave him a dirty look, but he ignored them, tromping on the accelerator. "I been hoping for something like this."

"You were hoping I'd get arrested?" said Danny. "What?"

"I said," Danny shouted, "you wanted me arrested?"

"No, man," he said, eyes still on the signal. "I mean *us*. You and me." The light changed and he floored it. Black smoke pouring from the tires as they hurtled across the intersection, past the two cops who stood on the steps of the station house, hands on their guns. "Is like, now we partners."

"Look, I appreciate you bailing me out," said Danny, "but—"

"Fucking team, man. Starsky and fucking Hutch."

Danny was still wearing the shorts and CATALINA MARATHON tank top he had been arrested in. "You know where the Vons market is on Lido Isle? I have to pick up my car."

Cubanito glanced over. "You should dress better when you get busted, man. You got a reputation to think of." Cubanito held out the flake inhaler. "Toot?"

"You walked into the police station *holding*?"

"I got rights," Cubanito said with an outraged expression. "This is America, man, no illegal search and seizure here." He waved the inhaler like a flag.

"Just keep that away from me, okay? I'm in enough trouble."

"You look wasted, man." Cubanito shook his head. He tapped the dashboard Madonna and hit himself in each nostril. "Losing your touch." His thinning hair was slicked back, and he had thrown a handful of Paco Rabanne under each armpit. He was ready for anything. "If I did my old lady and her boyfriend, I sure wouldn't go back there. And if I went back there, I sure wouldn't get popped by no cops."

Danny stared straight ahead. "I didn't do my old lady. And I didn't do my old lady's boyfriend."

"Desk sergeant said you did. Jaime Rodriguez. He's okay. Jaime said the old cop got a heart attack on account of you."

"Well, Jaime's wrong."

"Jaime said it was a lucky thing I come down so fast, 'cause the lady cop was working on the judge to revoke bail. My Jew lawyer is the best, man. He shows up, they gonna cut fucking *Manson* loose."

"Charlie and I both thank you," said Danny.

"If I tell you somebody can help you find your wife, maybe you thank me again, huh?"

Danny turned and looked at Cubanito.

"I close down a couple of spots after I drop you off," said Cubanito. "I don't need much sleep," he sniffed.

"Just give me a name," said Danny.

"Amber, man. The bitch's name is Amber. She lives in Sunset Beach, right on the water. Four houses down from Fatburger."

"This Amber knows where Lauren is?"

"I seen them at Bobby McGee's dancing together—" Cubanito shrugged—"wearing sunglasses like they're outside. Once I seen the two of them with whitebread." He sniffed again. "When you find your woman, man, ask her why I'm not good enough to talk to but she can drive her Mercedes with a whore who swims in hot oil. Ask her that."

"I don't get it."

"This whore Amber, she wrestles in oil at Benson's, with other girls and with men who pay. I seen her. She wins, too. You go see her, man, you better bring money."

"You're sure?" said Danny. It didn't make sense. Lauren liked to go slumming, but she never brought it home with her.

"Bartender at Benson's gave me her address," said

Cubanito. "I tell him I want to fuck her. He say, 'It's against policy.' So I give him Eddie's watch, and he write out directions on a napkin."

"You gave him the Rolex?"

"That fucker Eddie . . . " Cubanito looked more hurt than angry. "That watch was fake, man. Who can you trust anymore?"

"Probably not the guy who's just watched you nose-rape his wife."

"I tell the bartender it's not real," Cubanito said. "He say it don't matter if the bitches don't know."

"Sounds like a philosopher," said Danny.

"I been thinking," said Cubanito. "Maybe when I retire, I buy a few of those hot-dog stands. Set them outside the courthouse, 'cause everybody's nervous and hungry when they goes to court. Maybe have these chicks sell 'em, with shorts and a funny little hat."

They slowly passed two high school girls in a VW convertible. The driver beeped and waved. Danny could see the girl in the passenger seat blush. They looked like sisters. Their mother told them not to talk to strangers and they thought she was old and out of it.

"Cash business, man," said Cubanito. "Taxes are communist. Cash. Maybe Kentucky Chicken or a Seven-Eleven. I read in this *Forbes* magazine you can make big money selling cinnamon rolls to secretaries for lunch, 'cause they're sick of chocolate chip cookies."

"Where does that leave Famous Amos?"

"Fuck Famous Amos, man. Fuck that dude."

"You're going to be a real hit at the Toastmasters," said Danny.

"Yeah, I hear you. Only thing is, I fucking *love* dealing. It's inside work, plenty of pussy, and you don't have to get up early in the morning."

"Yeah, sport of kings."

"That's jai alai, man."

The two of them laughing and slapping palms, the tension between them suddenly broken. Cubanito weaved through traffic singing and snorting away. For a few moments, Danny forgot where he had been or where he was going. He just enjoyed the sense of movement and the sound of Cubanito's voice.

"You really not dealing anymore?" Cubanito said a few blocks later. "Verdad?"

"Over and out," said Danny.

"Not dealing *nothing*?"

"Slow down. Sometimes there's a radar unit parked up ahead."

"That's a waste, man. You got talent, a God-given talent."

"God's going to have to give it to someone else," said Danny.

Cubanito shook his head sadly. "Don't you miss it, man? Sometimes? Just a little."

"Never."

"Don't let it be money stop you," said Cubanito. "If you're tapped out, you come in with me. We move a couple of loads and you have enough to buy your way out of anything. My Jew lawyer's your Jew lawyer. You know what I mean?"

"Thanks anyway."

"Dealing spoils you for anything else," said Cubanito. "I'm still gonna get out. Few more months, a year at most."

"Sure."

"Last month I drive to Las Vegas, make a delivery," said Cubanito. "Two in the morning, all by myself out in the desert and the sky is so big and deep I get dizzy looking at it." His eyes glistened with tears. "I'm lost in the desert sky, man, toking flake, racing the night, and I finally have to roll down the windows and feel the wind blow through me, 'cause it's all so fucking beautiful. I tell you, Danny, I *gotta* quit dealing 'cause nothing this good can last."

Danny had to look away. "The good times never do," he said softly.

They stopped at the light in front of the Alumni Club, a white brick fortress surrounded by acres of groomed Bermuda grass. Four Mexicans moved slowly across the lawn on their hands and knees, faces bent low as they carefully picked out weeds and tiny pebbles kicked up by the traffic. Cubanito's mouth tightened as he watched them work.

One of the Mexicans looked up and saw them. He was still on his hands and knees. A trickle of sweat ran down his face from under the broad-brimmed straw hat he wore.

A horn beeped behind them.

"Light's green," said Danny.

Cubanito and the Mexican watched each other. More beeps behind them.

Cubanito slowly pulled away from the intersection. He watched the Mexican in his rearview mirror, watched him get smaller and smaller until he faded into the landscape.

CHAPTER 21

DANNY KNOCKED AGAIN, louder this time. Still no answer from the orange door with the fingerprints smudged around the knob. He was at the fourth house from the Fatburger, just like Cubanito had said, standing there the landing in jeans and a faded Levi's jacket.

Amber's walkway was littered with soggy advertising circulars, broken glass, and an empty pizza box. She probably used a bent coat hanger for her car antenna. Danny punched the peephole and walked back to where he was parked.

On a weekday afternoon the parking lot running the length of Sunset Beach was quiet, almost empty. At night it was a combat zone. Rabbit convertibles filled with blond cheerleaders from Newport Beach High cruised alongside low-riding '57 Chevys from the barrios of Santa Ana. Suzuki Samurais cranked out heavy-metal music, while the JesusMobile, a white minibus fitted with loudspeakers, counterattacked with warnings of damnation. The kids hung out the windows of the cars, waved to each other, chugged cans of malt liquor, and threw the empties in their wake. Sometimes a girl would stand up through a sunroof and take off her blouse to cheers from the cars around her. Danny had stepped over three used condoms and a crumpled religious tract on the way to his car. So far, it looked like sex was doing better than salvation.

Danny sat in his car, radio on, twirling the dial as he watched the house. The radio evangelist was begging listeners not to spend their "seed money" but to send it to him, so that God could make it grow. When the man started talking in tongues, Danny imitated him, his eyes following every car that drove past.

Danny started the car, then turned it off. There was no place to go. The list of Lauren's clients he had gotten from Mavis was useless. Useless to him, anyway. He had called a dozen corporations, pretending to be part of the police investigation, asking questions. He said he was trying to locate one of their executives who might have had a continuing relationship with Lauren Kiel. Someone awkward and slender and wearing glasses. The personnel director at a software-design firm said that description fit half their employees. Everyone he talked to wanted to cooperate. No one knew anything.

He was never going to make it as a double agent or a private eye. More career options down the tubes. One of these days he was going to have to make a decision about that. Make a living. Make a start.

The money he had stashed during the good times was nearly gone, spent on travel, months of travel, aimless and empty. Central America, Egypt, Italy, Nepal, Angkor Wat, Bali. Ruins for the ruined.

Danny got out of the car, slipped four more quarters into the meter, and cut through the Fatburger parking lot to the beach. Greasy wax-paper wrappers and Styrofoam cups tumbled around his feet. He turned up the collar of his jacket as the wind whipped the sand.

The beach side of the houses had small patios and decks loaded with lawn chairs and tiny hibachis. A couple of scraggly surfers, feet propped up on their boards, watched him as he passed. Their eyes were hidden behind sunglasses as they sipped their beers, waiting for the evening swell.

A drooping volleyball net was stuck in the sand behind the fourth house. Its deck was enclosed by a four-foot concrete-block fence. She was sitting on a white beach towel, legs bent in front of her as she leaned forward.

"Amber?"

She didn't even look up. "Who wants to know?" She had a rough, husky voice.

"I'm a friend of Lauren Kiel's."

Amber glanced up at him. "Oh yeah, I seen your picture. The husband." She tossed her head, sent the thick black braid from one deeply tanned shoulder to the other. She was wearing a gold lamé bikini bottom and no top.

Danny landed lightly on the deck. "I knocked on your front door," he said.

"Good for you." Amber was sinewy as a gymnast, with small breasts and thick brown nipples. "Do me a favor, okay, don't stare at my tits."

"I'm not," said Danny.

"Right," said Amber, and bent back over. She spread warm pink wax along her right leg with a wooden tongue depressor, dipping it out of a Crockpot. The tip of her tongue poked out of the corner of her mouth as she worked.

Danny's eyes followed the tongue depressor's progress from her ankle to her thigh. The wax had the consistency of honey.

She slowly rotated her leg to cover spots she had missed, stretching it straight out at him without any apparent effort. He squatted on his haunches, her foot an inch from his amused face. She pulled aside the gold bottom and waxed the hollow at the side of her pubic bone.

"This would *not* be happening if we were in Kansas," said Danny. "I don't care what they say about one nation indivisible.'"

"Hand me one of those strips," she said. "This stuff's setting up."

Danny fumbled around on the tray full of cosmetics, knocking over a couple of bottles of polish before he passed over one of the rolls of gauze. "I want to talk to you about Lauren," he said.

Amber unrolled the cloth with a snap of her wrist. "You're not like I pictured you," she said, pressing the gauze into the wax.

"What were you expecting?" said Danny.

"I don't know. Somebody bigger . . . taller, I don't know."

"I used to be taller before the divorce."

"Is that a joke?" Amber scratched her breasts. "I don't like funny men. I always think they're laughing at me." She moved her leg closer to his face, brushed his lips with her toes. "C'mon, make yourself useful."

Danny put his hands on her knee.

"Not there," said Amber. "Start at the top." She reached under the edge of her bikini bottom, peeled the wax down a few inches. "One long, steady motion. Like skinning a chicken breast. Think you can handle that?"

Danny wondered what she'd do if he sank his teeth into the fine high arch of her foot, just clamped down and wouldn't let go. Probably break his jaw. He'd wake up in the hospital and find out she was a black belt in Korean karate or a *sabot* instructor to the French foreign legion.

"Go on," said Amber. "You won't hurt me."

He jerked the strip of wax and gauze down her leg.

"Owww!"

Danny was smiling now.

"Shit"—she ran her hands down the inside of her thigh—"once you get the go-ahead, there's no stopping you."

Danny stared at the flap of wax that curled in his grip. Hundreds of tiny hairs speckled the surface.

"Don't stop now." Amber held out her leg.

Beads of sweat dotted Danny's forehead as he waxed her. He pulled aside her bikini bottom, scooped two fingers of warm wax out of the Crockpot. She rolled her eyes and moaned theatrically as he dabbed wax at the edge of her crotch. A tuft of dark pubic hair brushed against his knuckles.

"You sure you haven't done this before?" Amber said.

"I'd remember." Danny grabbed the gauze at the top of her thigh and ripped it down her leg in one fluid motion. It sounded like silk panties being torn in half.

She rolled over onto her belly, looked back at him over her shoulder. "Now, do the back of my legs. I get stubbly, it'll show under the stage lights."

The back of her bikini bottom was just a lamé thong that ran between the cheeks of her ass. The sun felt hot on Danny's back. He took off his jacket.

A seagull floated overhead as he worked. It dipped suddenly and veered off with a shriek. Down the beach, a group of scrawny Vietnamese kids was having a kite war. A red hornet, a green dragon, and a black bat parried and thrust in the air, trying to cut each other's strings with their rag-and-razorwire tails.

Amber let her head drop back. "You got a nice touch. For a man. Lauren said you were good."

Danny pulled the last of the wax off. Lightly ran his hand over the backs of her legs. They were soft and perfectly smooth. He kissed the warm skin where her thighs met her buttocks, more as a signature than a caress.

Amber sighed with pleasure. "You want to start something?" she said, looking at him.

He shook his head. "I'm looking for Lauren."

"Why?" Amber turned over. "Just because she dumped you?" She squirted baby oil into her hand and rubbed it into her breasts. "Lauren dumped me, too, but I'm not chasing after her." She looked up at him. "I mean, why bother?"

"Because I love her."

"Love? Shit, if that was reason enough, I'd be looking for her, too." She reached for the drink next to her, looked into the glass while she swirled the ice. "Love," she snorted.

"What did you mean?" said Danny.

"What do you think I meant?" Amber said. She saw the look on his face. "You think I'm not good enough for her? Buster, you don't know your little girl."

"That's not it," said Danny.

"Hey." Amber jabbed her drink at him. It splashed across the deck, a dark stain on the bleached wood. "I'm making five hundred dollars a week doing bikini contests. You hear me? I'm up for a Coppertone commercial."

Danny just stared at her.

Amber shrugged and picked up a thin gold chain from the deck. She clasped it around her right ankle. Sunlight sparkled off the chain as she ran her hands down her outstretched leg. "Feels good. I'm going to have you do me on a regular basis."

"Were you doing Lauren on a regular basis?" Danny said softly.

"You got a problem with it?"

"Depends," said Danny. "I was just getting used to the guy with the glasses. I thought *that's* who she was seeing."

"She is seeing him. But he's just business. We're all just business to Lauren. How'd you hear about him, anyway? He's, like, the *big secret*."

"Friend of mine saw them at Players."

"That was before she knew he was such a hotshot," said Amber. "Before she told me she was a solo. Should have known. Guy's even whiter than she is. He looks at me like I'm not good enough to jack him off . . . "

Amber fished an ice cube out of her drink. She absently circled her nipples with it, stiffening them, lost in the memory.

"What's the name of the guy with the glasses?" Danny interrupted her.

"What does the name Amber sound like?" she said. "Somebody blond and sexy, right? I changed my name, just for the contests. It was Lauren's idea. She called it associational transference. I wrote it down. It means that chicks with names like Kathi and Kristi and Candi go over big with the judges, even though the crowd likes me better. 'Cause their names make the judges think of Beach Boys songs and wine-cooler commercials."

"Do you know where she met this guy?" Danny persisted.

"This associational transference stuff works, too," said Amber. "I mean, I made out okay before, but ever since I got a blonde name, I make the finals.

It was Lauren's idea, but I came up with Amber. You know, like Amber Lynn, the porno star."

"How much is this going to cost me?" said Danny.

"There's a lot more to winning contests than having a great ass and shaking it for the frat boys in the front row. You got to be scientific." Amber pulled down one of her lower eyelids. "See? Violet. Just like Liz Taylor. Colored contact lenses. Judges notice things like that. Especially in a yellow spotlight. A blonde name and a yellow spot, I got 'em by the balls." Her hand made milking motions. "Then there's my tits."

"What about them?" said Danny.

"Don't play dumb." Amber placed her hands under her breasts and jiggled them. "They're too small."

"For whom?"

"Whom?" She raised an eyebrow. "You're sweet. But judges like big ones, what can I tell you. Unless I get a boob job, I'm never going to do better than runner-up. Only thing is . . . "

"You need money for the operation," said Danny.

"Lauren said you were real brainy."

"That's me. How much does this operation cost?"

"Five thousand bucks. I want to go to the guy that did Michael Jackson's chin."

"Half now and half when I find Lauren." Danny pulled an envelope secured with a rubber band out of his pocket and tapped one of her breasts with it. "You can do one tit at a time."

CHAPTER 22

DANNY THOUGHT OF A cool blue lake, backstroking across the surface while eagles drifted overhead. Sweat trickled down his face in the glare of the late afternoon sun. Far ahead, a horn beeped, followed by another and another.

The light turned green, but the intersection remained blocked by cars that tried to sneak through. Danny snapped on the radio, punched all the buttons, and turned it off in disgust.

Amber hadn't been much help. Danny wanted specific names and companies, details she shrugged off. She had met Four-eyes only once, she said, "accidentally" running into him and Lauren at DeVilles. He was just like Lauren had described him—soft and pale and nervous. Supposed to be some big shot scientist, but Amber wasn't impressed. He didn't even know the difference between a Porsche Targa and a Porsche Cabriolet.

She had tried to get him to dance, but he had shaken his head and kept his eyes on Lauren even when Amber was talking. The guy was really lame. Not that most of the ones Lauren brought around weren't; they were either sweaty egberts like Four-eyes or these flashy, loud jerks who slid their hands over her tits while bragging about the big deal they were working on.

Danny let a diesel Mercedes pull a couple of car lengths ahead. Breathing room. A rusted-out Fiat in the left-hand lane darted in front of him, so Danny had to hit the brakes. The Fiat had a crumpled door, broken windshield, and a peeling EASY DOES IT bumper sticker. Danny laughed in spite of himself. He wasn't sure if the bumper sticker was supposed to be a reminder to the Fiat's driver or a warning to the other cars—but whatever its purpose, it wasn't working.

"You stupid or what?" Amber had screeched at Danny, explaining for the third time what she and Lauren used to do. "Sometimes me, sometimes her, sometimes both of us." She bent over, painting her toes with iridescent orchid. "A couple of them just wanted to watch while Lauren and I went at it. I'll tell you, pup, guys in suits are the sickest people in the world."

Danny sat there on the deck, watching shiny Amber's mouth move, trying to imagine her with Lauren. "She paid you to fuck these guys?"

She looked at him. Unblinking. "Let me tell you," she said slowly. "It's not the kind of thing you do for free."

"Right."

"Lauren had everything on videotape," Amber said. "The first few times, I just figured she got off on that stuff. We'd lie in bed after the guy left, do a few lines, and replay it for grins. After a while, though, I start thinking . . . "

"Who was the big shot scientist working for?" Danny held out Lauren's corporate client list to her. "Look at these names. Any of them sound familiar?"

"For a couple thousand more, I could get implants in my cheeks, make me look like a fashion model." Amber sucked in her cheeks and made fish kisses at him.

Flashing lights atop the ambulance on the side of the road brought Danny back to rush hour. A burly man in overalls pulled at the silver bicycle wrapped around the front wheel of his pickup, cursing, oblivious to the paramedics working on the kid in multicolored Descente tights sprawled nearby. The bicyclist's right foot flopped back and forth as they applied pressure compresses. The line of traffic inched past, drivers craning their heads out the windows for a better look.

Amber said that Four-eyes called himself a doctor, but she didn't think so, because when she made a joke about seeing him for her next Pap test, he didn't understand what she was talking about. Lauren said that Four-eyes had the best dope in the world. And that didn't make any sense either, 'cause he sure didn't look like any dealer Amber had ever seen. Then Lauren had dumped her. Just like that.

So maybe Four-eyes was a dealer after all. He had to be something special for Lauren to do that.

Danny didn't offer to explain things to Amber. He just held out Lauren's client list and asked her to try again. She squinted over the list like it was an entrance examination in a foreign language, finally narrowing it down to two companies, a pharmaceutical manufacturer and a hospital-supply conglomerate. She figured that was close enough.

Danny drove past the accident scene, the ambulance lights splashing across his windshield so he blinked, staring straight ahead. He could hear the bicyclist crying. The traffic ahead thinned out and Danny hit the accelerator. He passed the Mercedes, doing fifty-five in third gear, leaving it all behind. Amber was right. Her answer was close enough. Close enough for Danny to know that Michael had lied to him.

CHAPTER 23

MICHAEL SAW SAND being kicked up in the distance. It had to be Danny. Who else would be driving that fast? Oh well, too late for regrets. He checked his grip, then hit a perfect eight-iron, a gentle chip shot that bounced off the flattened rock about ninety yards out.

The dust-covered Mustang skidded up to the house. Lurp lifted his head up from the porch as Danny blew past him, flung open the door, and disappeared inside. Lurp was a great watch dog. You could do whatever you wanted and he'd just watch.

Michael bounced one more shot off the flat rock, tapped another ball into place from the overturned bucket. He was wearing tartan knickers, bright red golf shoes, white letter sweater, and the Pebble Beach Country Club cap. Hell of an outfit to face incoming fire. And there was definitely incoming. He had done three tours, most of it in-country. He knew when the shit was about to come down.

Danny came out of the house, saw Michael on the bluff, and stalked over. Michael kept his eye on the orange-striped range ball.

"Where is she?" Danny gritted the words out.

"Just a second," said Michael, taking a two-thirds backswing.

"Now, you fuck!"

"Little slip of the PGA rules there, Danno," said Michael, head down, left knee cocked. "No profanity when a player's lining up his shot. Gentleman's game, you know."

Danny snatched the eight-iron and threw it over the cliff.

Michael watched it pinwheel down into the surf. "Clear violation, Danno. Two-stroke penalty on that one."

"She was here, wasn't she?"

"Why are you shouting?" said Michael, careful not to look at Danny. "I'm the guy who should be upset, that's my Ben Hogan you tossed in the drink. Now I'm not playing with a full set. I can make do with a pitching wedge—"

Danny grabbed him by the throat. Michael's letter sweater billowed in the wind. "Okay, okay." Michael pushed at Danny. "C'mon, bro, one of us could get hurt."

Danny's eyes were cold and dark. Michael could drown in those eyes and no one would ever find the body. "Guess which one of us could get hurt?" Danny said, tightening his grip.

Michael felt his neck snap as Danny shook him.

Michael was bigger, but Danny had the intensity, Danny had the high ground. Same old story. If Michael didn't get himself a cause, a crusade, he was going to lose forever. He wondered what one cost.

Danny's mouth looked like he was shouting, but Michael could hardly hear him, he was too busy watching the black spots that glided past his eyes. Danny shook him once more and dropped him. Michael curled up on the ground, sucking air, his face so red that the old scar tissue stood out like a topographic map.

"I thought we were friends," Danny said.

Michael sat up slowly. "We are." He coughed. "That's why I tried to keep you out of this. But you just can't let go." He could still feel the imprint of Danny's fingers on his neck.

"I talked to Amber," said Danny.

"Amber, huh." Michael's voice was still raspy. He wiped his nose. "That must have been an experiment in terror. From what I hear, anyway."

Michael watched the evening swell break against the string of offshore oil rigs. In response to the concerns of the environmentalists, the oil companies had decorated their drilling platforms, painting them soft pastel blues and yellows, installing fake palm trees. They looked like floating condominiums.

To the north, Michael could see the dome housing the *Spruce Goose*, the gigantic all-wood airplane built by Howard Hughes. The dome was right next to the *Queen Mary*, anchored in Long Beach. The *Spruce*

Goose had been turned into a tourist attraction, the *Queen Mary*, into a mall. The first time Danny visited him, he said he wished life were more like a Japanese monster movie. Then he and Michael could sit on the bluffs, drink a few beers, and watch the *Spruce Goose* break out of its dome and attack the *Queen Mary*. BATTLE OF THE BEHEMOTHS! Maybe Godzilla would show up at the last minute to save the city.

It had made Michael realize how much he liked Danny. Danny was always good for a laugh, and he never asked for anything. Danny had brought him Lurp. Just pulled this puppy with floppy ears out of his jacket and said, "With your personality, you could use a friend that doesn't talk back."

Danny stood over him. "I'm not leaving until I get some answers."

Michael pulled a joint from his knickers, fired it up. It took both hands to hold the Zippo steady. He coughed and offered the joint to Danny. "Miller time."

Danny backhanded it away. "I don't want any pot. I just want some answers."

Michael took a long hit, keeping his eyes offshore. "Strangling me isn't going to help."

Danny watched him smoke, trying to decide something. "You could have told me," he said, sitting down beside Michael.

Michael puffed away. A group of seagulls circled the nearest oil platform. They did it every evening, waiting for the cooks to dump the garbage. "What's got you so worked up?"

"I went back to Lauren's," said Danny. The sunset bathed his face in warm light. He looked young and innocent. He looked hurt.

Michael squinted in the haze of smoke around him. Lauren had been hysterical the night she called him. He thought she was just fucked up. Neither she nor Michael had any sense of limits. They just kept getting higher and higher until they crashed. He had ended up in this oil field. Lauren had gone on to bigger things. Much bigger. He wiped at his eyes. She had been laughing that night, shrill one moment, baby talking the next.

"I think I suspected Lauren from the beginning. . . " Danny's voice was so soft Michael could barely hear him. "It's just too hard to imagine her as a victim. But I didn't think you were part of it. Not until I talked with Amber. You left your fingerprints everywhere but at her house."

Michael picked dirt off the spikes of his golf shoes.

"I was falling apart this morning," said Danny, "and you just sat there listening to me." His eyes were on fire in the twilight. "You could have let me in on it."

Michael took a long drag on the joint and held it. "Okay, bro," he said, exhaling through his nose. "Here it is: Lauren's executive-management seminars you know about. Very professional. *Very* expensive. But you know Lauren, too. Straight money isn't as big as crooked money. And even if it were, it's not nearly as much fun. These clients of Lauren's—corporate big shots—watch her in action and it's all over. These kind of guys don't send flowers or candy, they try to impress her with their latest project—new products, mergers, LBOs —the hush-hush stuff that's going to land them on the cover of *Fortune* in six months. Executive pillow talk she calls it. They tell her, Lauren tells me. The first tip she got, we made two hundred thousand dollars on. Then we got serious."

"What was Amber?" said Danny. "Just a pinch hitter?"

Michael shrugged. "She made Lauren laugh."

"This guy who died at her beach house must have had no sense of humor at all," said Danny. "Who was he, anyway?"

Michael hesitated, then gave in. "Tohlson, Dr. Tohlson. He was a researcher for a local firm, Reese Pharmaceuticals."

"He making synthetics for you and Lauren?" said Danny.

Michael shook his head. "Just information. Dope's too high risk, you should know that. White-collar crime is a much better bet—enforcement's underfunded and the statutes are out-of-date. Dope is a federal strike force and action news."

"Yeah, it's a random world," said Danny. "Wars and pestilence and those ever-changing consumer tastes. Little inside information must make it all bearable."

"No such thing as certainty," said Michael. "All I'm doing is improving my odds. Even with all the data I can access, there's still plenty of surprises. I got killed last month on titanium."

Danny tossed pebbles over the edge. "What the

heck, it's not real money. Just blips on the computer screen, right?"

"Best kind of money is the kind you don't have to touch." Michael grinned. "Just key it anywhere you want, at the speed of light. Liechtenstein, the Bahamas, maybe the Cayman Islands. If you're really smart, you set up a holding company in one tax haven and just transfer the money to another holding company someplace else. Safe and sane."

Danny got up and went to the golf bag. The butt of Michael's .45 stuck out of one of the pockets. He pulled out the driver. "Don't worry," he said as Michael scrambled to his feet. "I know what I'm doing." He gripped the club like a baseball bat, took a couple of practice swings, aiming for the fences.

Michael squirmed as the club whooshed through the air. "Peace in the valley, now."

"Relax, Michael." Danny was still swinging away. "Enjoy that feeling of doubt, that cold little tickle in your guts. I've been living with that feeling since those two cops showed up at my front door." He teed up a ball and tapped the club on the ground. "Come on. Grab a club and step up to the plate."

"No funny stuff," said Michael.

Danny squinted at his ball. He bent and tossed it to Michael and replaced it with another. "Where'd you get these beaters?" he said.

Michael rubbed his thumb over the cut in the cover of the ball. "Got a deal with a Mexican kid lives near the municipal course. He drops off a couple hundred every week at the front gate."

"Grounds keeper must love that." Danny topped

the ball. It blooped out about fifty yards.

"Free enterprise," said Michael. "Get closer to it. And don't pull back your shoulders."

Danny smacked a perfect drive, two hundred yards straight and true.

"Good. Now, try for some distance. The clump of three boulders out there is two hundred twenty-five yards. The big irregular one with the wave breaking over it is two hundred forty yards, and the tall one with the pelican sitting on it is two hundred sixty-five yards. See if you can hit that fucking bird."

"You go out there with a little rowboat and a measuring tape?" said Danny.

"Ever hear of trigonometry?" said Michael. "That's right, you're one of those social-science majors. Trust me, the pelican's two hundred sixty-five yards out."

"What else am I supposed to trust you on, Michael?" Danny pivoted on his left toe as he practiced his backswing. "Where is she, Michael? That's all I came for."

Michael sagged, the letter sweater drooping over his shoulders. "I don't know," he said finally. "I'm glad I don't."

"You were working together. If you don't know, who does?" He checked his grip.

"Listen to what you're saying," said Michael. "No one *works* with Lauren, you know that. She just calls when she wants something. Quit while you're ahead, bro."

"Fore!" yelled Danny as the ball streaked at the pelican.

CHAPTER 24

THIS TIME, DANNY THOUGHT for sure he was going to drown. Too tired to sleep after leaving Michael, he had gone swimming in the bay. He splashed out past the buoys, shuddering with the cold. There was no moon, only the stars and the faint lights from the houses on the shore. And those lights were going out, one by one. Michael was probably still standing on the edge of the sea, knickers billowing in the wind, drilling golf balls into the night. Danny knew just how he felt.

The cold filled Danny gradually, steadily, filled the vast emptiness inside him until he no longer felt the chill. He saw himself moving slower and slower, still making feeble motions as he sank into the murky depths.

Was it only three days ago that the cops had met him on the stairs? Three days. He had hardly slept since. After Lauren left him, the days had drifted by untouched, barely noticed.

Danny pushed off the hull of the schooner anchored down the channel and started back, his overhand crawl giving rhythm and reason to his breathing. All he had to do was keep breathing.

On his way to Yucatán, after the divorce, he had visited his grandmother in New Jersey. She was tiny and sharp-eyed, a woman who had worn no color but black since his grandfather had died twenty years before. She made him lasagna and asked when he and Lauren were going to have some babies. She couldn't wait forever. Danny just poked at the food with his fork. Finally, he told her what had happened.

"Oh, carissimo"—she heaped sweet sausage onto his untouched plate, clucking like it didn't surprise her in the slightest—"she broke your heart." She said there wasn't a day that went by that she didn't hear Grandpa coming in the back door after work. She and Danny sat there in her kitchen while the afternoon darkened, neither of them wanting to put on a light. She told him stories about her life with "that man," the two of them holding hands until it was time to go. He smelled baby powder and Ivory Soap when they hugged, her cheeks still as soft and smooth as a young girl's.

The tide was running fast against him tonight, pushing him out to sea. It forced him to quicken his stroke, to deepen his breathing as he pulled himself forward. He felt tired; his legs were heavy, his kick weak and out of synch.

Danny treaded water for a moment, getting his bearings. The lights on the shore were no closer than the distant outline of the schooner. If he headed back to the ship, at least he'd be going with the current—he could always crawl out on the far side, walk back around the bay. Going forward was a risk. Even the short time he thought about it carried him farther from shore.

He could feel the heat pouring out of him into the water. It made him think of Lauren's living room and the man whose life had streamed down his legs and onto the coffee table. Tohlson. Michael had said that was his name. Danny could still see the hieroglyphs on the walls, Tohlson's last words, written in blood. But it wasn't Tohlson who did the writing. It was Lauren.

She had killed him. Michael had kept calling it the accident. Danny said dropping a glass of milk on a tile floor was an accident. Not this. To him a death could mark you forever, send you spinning off with nothing to grab on to. There was a point after Danny's life fell apart where he took a certain comfort in knowing that nothing more could be taken from him. He was wrong. Lauren had killed Tohlson. What was worse was that Danny still loved her. Go figure.

He struck out for the lights, grunting with every stroke, barely kicking now, saving his strength for the arm pull. He was going back. The icy water broke over his goggles. His foot cramped and his shoulders ached. He was swimming sloppily now, swallowing water because he couldn't keep his head up. He clenched his teeth and kept on.

He wasn't going to quit. He wasn't going to die.

Not yet. Not here. He could imagine Holt standing over his body where it had floated back to shore, trying to think of something she could charge him with: Littering?

By the time he reached the shallows, his whole body was numb. He stumbled on the rocky bottom, crawling forward on his hands and knees. There were traffic sounds in the distance. Horn beeps. Someone was in a hurry to get somewhere. He rested his cheek on the cool sand, eyes closed, coughing up saltwater.

"I wondered if you were going to make it," Lauren said.

Danny looked up and saw her standing on the beach, holding his towel out to him.

CHAPTER 25

CUBANITO RAN THE TIP of his tongue over his lower lip, winced where it had been split open like a ripe tomato. His shirt was soaked. It stuck to him. The Baby Hueys had stuffed him behind the seats of their cheap little Corvette so he couldn't move, couldn't even see where they were going.

Cubanito had laughed when he saw them—not one but *two* Baby Hueys, all puffed out. Their legs rubbed when they walked. Baby Huey, just like in the comic books at the federal bucket at Atlanta. Baby Huey, the giant baby with the strength of Superman and the mind of a peanut.

Shame burned Cubanito's cheeks when he remembered how easily they had taken him in front of the liquor store, barely grunting at his blows and curses. They had carted him off like a sack of cornmeal, the bottles of white port broken on the sidewalk behind them. After all of his brave talk to Danny about street manners, it was he who had grown soft and stupid.

Now it was Eddie's turn to laugh. The Baby Hueys were payback for what Danny did to the Samoan, payback for the look Eddie's wife got when Cubanito slid a finger up her nose. Have your fun, Eddie. Later, he would show Eddie what payback *really* was.

His tongue tickled over what was left of his front teeth. The Baby Hueys had knocked out three of them, snapped them off at the root. Such pretty teeth too, shiny white porcelain caps to cover the stumps the sugarcane mash at the Isle of Pines prison had left him with. He sighed. The teeth had given him a smile that flashed in the night like a yawning cat.

Even more than the loss of his teeth, Cubanito regretted splashing blood down the front of his shirt. It was black, with tiny pearl buttons and a picture of Ricky Ricardo hand painted on the front. A gift from Danny when they first became friends. Not for a holiday or his birthday or anything. It was Cubanito's lucky shirt, and now it was ruined.

In the front seat, the Baby Hueys argued about amino acids and superset pyramids and bee pollen and somebody named Uncle Arthur. Baby Huey Boyd and Baby Huey Junior. Half the time they sounded like rocket scientists and half the time they sounded like retards.

The car stopped. Baby Huey Boyd dragged Cubanito out by the ear while Baby Huey Junior unlocked the door of the Hercules Iron Spa. He told

Cubanito the owner gave them a key so they could work out anytime they wanted. "Shut up, Junior," said Baby Huey Boyd.

Cubanito blinked as the fluorescent overheads sputtered on, reflecting off the full-length-mirrored walls. He had never seen so many mirrors, not even in the Miami whorehouse where he had celebrated his first marijuana deal in the U.S. It was just a one-pound score, but he had never felt so happy or so proud. "Today I am an American," he had announced as he unzipped his pants for the skinny conchita who had too much hair on her arms.

The Hercules Iron Spa was filled with padded benches, racks of dumbbells, and a rubbery carpet that squished underfoot. A row of barbells leaned against one wall and big iron plates were stacked next to the benches. It looked to Cubanito like a room full of giant Tinkertoys for the Baby Hueys.

Baby Huey Boyd threw him down and locked the door. It was the only door in the room, right under a hand-painted sign that said: THIS IS YOUR GYM, REPLACE ALL WEIGHTS!

The Baby Hueys took off their floppy jackets and trousers and slapped a chalk bag on their hands, raising clouds of white dust. They were wearing matching little-bitty black shorts and tank tops with gold trim.

Their silly clothes made Cubanito laugh, but he pretended it was a cough after seeing the look on Baby Huey Boyd's face. There had been some black guys in D-block at Atlanta that had pumped the iron for three or four hours a day. They had been huge too, but the Baby Hueys looked . . . different. Like they had more muscles than they were supposed to. Little muscles running into the big ones, and the big ones ready to split through their skin and roll out onto the floor.

Baby Huey Junior rooted around in the nylon bag he had carried in. He passed a leather weight-belt to his brother and cinched another one around his waist. Then Baby Huey Junior took a boom box out of the bag and dropped in a cassette.

Eyes closed, Baby Huey Boyd sat on a bench with his hands on his knees, deep breathing. He laid back, hoisted the barbell off the rack overhead, and snapped it up and down as the music bounced off the walls.

The music was the same as when the helicopters blew the gook village to shit in *Apocalypse Now*. It was Cubanito's favorite part of the movie. If these guys hated communists too, things might work out okay.

CHAPTER 26

DANNY SPRAWLED on his hands and knees in the shallows, still gasping from the swim, watching Lauren. She stood at the tide line in an unzipped leather jacket and short leather skirt, backlit by the yellow streetlights. The short blond spikes of her hair glowed in the golden light.

He got to his feet, shivered as water trickled from his scalp, zigzagged down his torso, and back into the bay. He didn't take his eyes off her.

Lauren held out his towel for him, but he stayed where he was, teeth chattering, afraid that if he moved she'd disappear. Hypothermia had played tricks on him before, summoning ghosts; Jerry and Janice backstroking beside him under a sensimilla moon. Maybe he'd drowned out there and this one last glimpse of her was a St. Christopher medal he was supposed to carry through eternity.

She splashed through the shallows, wrapped him in the thick towel, and led him to shore. "You're here," he said as she rubbed him dry, his skin tingling with her brisk movements. "You're really here." She worked her way down his legs, bent over, one knee in the sand. "I was afraid something had happened to you," he said. She giggled, the sound skipping across the bay.

Danny tried to walk, but his legs were wobbly and he stumbled against her. It was so quiet. He pulled away, suddenly alert. "Why are you here?" He glanced at the nearby houses, curtains pulled, sleepers tucked in. "Why now?" She slipped under the towel, draped herself around him. He felt her nipples stiffen against his chest. "Why?" he insisted.

"Because I need you," she whispered into his ear. Her hand on the back of his neck was as warm as fresh tears.

The feel of her soft skin started him shaking again; he clamped his teeth shut to stop himself.

She reached into her jacket, brought forth a plump orange. A mocking smile tugged at the corners of her mouth as she peeled it, dropping the skin onto the sand. She broke off a section and ran it across his lower lip, teasing him, then slipped it into her own mouth, bit off the end, and sucked it dry. Her smile was broader now, utterly confident. Why fight it? her expression said. What good will it do you? She tore off another section, offered it to him, closer now, still closer. He parted his lips and she slid it in, watching as his chattering teeth tore into the fruit.

The orange was still warm from where it had nestled against her hip. Warm and sweet. With just a faint bitter aftertaste. Of course. Lauren loved a picnic. Danny could see her now, bent over their kitchen table, the wicker basket filled with wine and crusty french rolls. Lauren injecting oranges with a hypodermic syringe: ecstasy and acid.

Juice ran down Danny's chin as he chewed. Her hot tongue danced across his face, cat kisses cleaning him. A section for her. Another for him. Feeding each other now, sharing the wickedness, piece by piece. Juice streamed down their arms.

Her full lips parted his mouth, tickling him with her tongue. He tried to talk, but she kissed him again. Her need filled him, sweet, pink, and beyond resistance, bitter at the edges. He closed his eyes, falling back, giving in.

The water lapped at the shore as they danced on the sand, belly to belly, heart to heart, wrapped in memory. Just the two of them. Like always. Faint sound of music from across the bay, distorted and sad from the distance. Lauren hummed softly along with it until Danny couldn't tell where the song came from or when it had begun.

A car screeched around the corner and Danny flinched, caught for an instant in the glare of the headlights, before the darkness covered them again. Lauren kept humming, never missing a beat.

Danny remembered headlights and rain and Lauren rubbing against him: the two of them soaked, crammed into a phone booth on the way back from Mt. Shasta because the car had broken down, the great white mountain looming out of the night as a summer storm crashed around them. Lauren unbut-

toned her blouse while he called for a tow, trying to keep his voice steady. They had gone at
it in the steamy phone booth, Lauren's bare back
pressed against the cool glass while he drove himself
into her, rain sheeting down the sides and across
the floor. Every few minutes, the booth would be
drenched by the headlights of long-distance truckers, down-shifting to slow themselves for the steep
grade ahead, the sound of their airhorns a wild
salute in the storm.

Danny blinked in the dark, staring up and down
the beach, trying to figure it out. "Where did all the
snow come from?" he said at last. She threw back her
head, laughing, her eyes so bright it hurt to look at
her. He still couldn't turn away. She shrugged out
of her jacket and tossed it down.

Snowflakes sparkled in the air like static, drifted
across the sand. Lauren was on her knees in front of
him, skirt hiked up. No silk panties these days. She
pulled at his swimsuit. He waved at the air, trying
to see her more clearly. The snowflakes spun. What
was *in* that orange? He felt Lauren's hair brush
against his thighs as her warm mouth closed around
the head of his cock. He heard himself cry out, the
sound so aching that at first he didn't recognize
his voice. She looked up at him and he blushed,
seeing himself in the middle of her smile. The snow
fell faster now, crackling, piling into drifts. He still
couldn't figure out where it was coming from.

It wasn't snow. He checked the sky and knew.
It was stars. The stars were falling, silver constel-
lations sifting down—Perseus, Orion, Ursa Major.

All gone. If this kept up, the whole Milky Way was going to be strewn across the beach. His knees buckled as Lauren dug her nails in and tore at him. He jerked against her, the stars exploded all around them, then he was pulling her hair, gasping, the heat rushing out of him and down her throat.

Lauren stood up and drew the back of her hand across her mouth, her expression languid and sated. She unzipped her skirt, kicked it away, peeled off her blouse, and stretched. She was smooth and shiny, supple as mercury, bathed in stars.

Danny swayed, beyond exhaustion. He gazed at her while she pretended not to notice. She was Itzamna, the Mayan goddess of morning mists and subterranean lakes—haughty and fluid. Drowned men were sacred to the goddess; she let them braid lilies in her hair with their mossy fingers.

"I missed you." Danny hated himself for saying it. He wanted to keep something out of her grasp.

"I know." She sighed, giving him a gentle, salty kiss.

Danny lifted her off her feet and swung her in lazy circles, his hands cupping her ass. He laughter was throaty and free as he worked his fingers into her. He twirled her faster, still fingering her, the sand spinning around them, a compass out of control, until they collapsed onto her jacket.

He entered her slowly. She urged him on with bites and pinches, trying to force him deeper, but he held himself back, going slow, losing himself. The two of them were back in Yucatán, swimming in a limestone pool, the water dappled by sunlight perforating the jungle overhead. Lauren dove under and Danny followed into the pale green depths, down to where the sunlight shaded into darker green. Lauren looked back and beckoned him on. Danny hesitated. The water shimmered and turned to blood.

Lauren groaned and Danny was back on the beach, her legs hooked around the small of his back, holding him all the way inside her. He covered her mouth with his own so that he didn't have to hear her triumph. It didn't work. As she started to come, she bit his lower lip, clamping down. He swatted at her, howling, batting the side of her head, but she hung on.

When she was through, she let him go; he rolled off and lay panting beside her. Her heart beat so loudly he thought it was his own. The sky was barren and black.

"What did you do?" Danny was shivering again, already knowing the answer.

Lauren shrugged. It was a casual movement, like she had come back from shopping and seen a parking ticket on her windshield.

"I was at your beach house," he said.

She touched the tear at the edge of his eye, sent it rolling down his cheek.

He slapped her hand away. "I was *there*." He wanted to turn away but couldn't, transfixed by the blood-splashed walls, the awful hieroglyphs she had scrawled.

Lauren scrambled on top of him, her cold eyes glaring through his startled expression. "Go on, tell me a story," she said, pressing her forearm into his windpipe.

He pushed against her, but she leaned into his throat with all her weight, cutting off his air. How did she get so strong? There was a pressure in his temples, a steady tightening that made his arms feel heavy, so heavy that it wasn't worth the effort to lift them.

"Tell. Me. A. Story."

Her eyes were so wide and blue that he thought for a moment it was daybreak and he was looking up at the morning sky. He wanted to tell her. His cock was getting thick and hard again. It was so strange that he wanted to tell her that, too. Maybe that would make her stop. But the only thing that came out of his mouth were faint strangling sounds.

He saw his hands reach for her, fighting back, but they acted by themselves. She shook her hair, preening, wild and capricious. It was so dark now that all he could see was her cruel mouth hovering over him. Maybe he was going blind. He felt her grab his erection and squeeze it in her fist. He knew who she was now: Ixtab, goddess of ropes and snares.

"Such a good Catholic boy." She took her forearm off his throat, reared back, and eased him inside her, taking short little gasps as she inched down his length. "Like someone is up there keeping score."

I'm keeping score, thought Danny. He was breathing through a pinhole, but it was enough. It was plenty. There was a glow at the edges of his vision, getting brighter. That's how he knew his eyes were open. He could hear her humming as she swiveled on him. It was a happy, contented sound, a marker buoy in the sea of the night.

The stars were back. Danny could see them twinkling behind her as she rocked on him, back and forth, back and forth, swinging her head with delight. He placed his hands on her hips, shifting himself deeper. She cried out, but he kept his mouth shut.

CHAPTER 27

LLOYD HELD THE RECIEVER to his ear while he watched Boyd practice his posing routine to the German opera music on their cassette player. Boyd moved slowly, gracefully, a perfect pink statue in the empty gym, the kettle drums booming around him. Boyd reared back and flexed his biceps at the mirrored wall, fanning out his lats. The muscles along the sides of his chest stood out in sheets. Like he had wings. Both he and Boyd had awesome lats, the *V* back that judges liked and that made their slim waists appear even narrower.

Spiderman answered the phone on the second ring.

"We got this Cubanito guy," announced Lloyd, still keeping his eyes on Boyd. "Tell Uncle Arthur."

"Good boy." Spiderman made it sound like he was talking to some old lady's poodle.

"He hasn't told us anything yet." Lloyd shook a dozen 500-milligram vitamin E capsules into his hand. "The little guy just keeps asking about somebody named Eddie." He picked up the capsules one by one, snapped them between his thumb and forefinger, squirting the oil in the back of his throat. "Who's Eddie?"

"I'm sure I don't know." Spiderman's mouth was talking to Lloyd, but the rest of him was someplace else.

Boyd dropped to one knee, a full hamstring-lunge, the muscles at the back of his leg bulging with veins as the German lady on the tape shrieked and the cymbals crashed. Lloyd shook his head. The two of them had the same problem with symmetry. Their legs were good, but compared to their massive torsos, they looked a little unbalanced.

The little guy stared at Boyd with his mouth open. He must have had allergies, because he kept sticking that inhaler in his nose and sniffling. When he did, his head jerked back. People who didn't take care of themselves got all kinds of fevers and diseases. He and Boyd had never even had a cold. Lloyd felt sorry for sick people, because they always looked sad and had a sour smell to them. Boyd said sick people deserved everything they got.

"So what should we do with him?" Lloyd asked Spiderman.

"That's entirely up to you."

"Wait a minute," said Lloyd. "You said he might know where this Danny was. You said they were friends."

"That's correct."

Yeah, that's correct. What a gilbert. "So what

should we *do* with him?" said Lloyd. "Me and Boyd can make him tell."

"Dr. Reese and I are no longer interested in Mr. Sanchez," said Spiderman. "I've got the situation under control."

"What about us?" Lloyd could hardly hear Spiderman, what with the lady singing. Boyd had his hands behind his neck, flashing his pecs. There was a soft sheen to his body, the flat muscles of his chest twitching with the intensity of his posing routine. They were going to kick butt at the contest, even if their symmetry was slightly off. No doubt about it. Lloyd snapped another capsule, missing his mouth so vitamin E oil dripped off his chin. He snapped another. "What do we do with him?"

"I really don't care. Just be a good boy and don't give him your address or home phone number."

"You think you're funny, Spiderman?" Lloyd realized he was talking to a dial tone. He banged the phone into the wall, cracking the plaster.

"Well?" said Boyd.

"Spiderman doesn't need to see him now," said Lloyd, nodding at the little guy. They had just been wasting their time. Like they didn't have anything better to do.

Boyd stopped posing. "I knew it! He was just trying to get us out of the way." Boyd's eyes got so small that the little guy started to shake. Boyd walked over, tore off the little guy's bloody shirt, and leaned his face into him. "This is your lucky day, greaseball."

Boyd dragged him to the Olympic bench press. The bench was thinly padded leather, the bar and plates chromed steel. When you worked out, you could see your reflection in the bar as you lifted it overhead. It was great motivation.

The little guy was real broad in the chest, and his biceps had decent muscle bellies. Way too much body fat, though. He could have been acceptable with the right program. Not competitive, but acceptable.

Boyd lay down on the bench and cranked off a couple of quick sets. He got up, not even breathing hard. "Your turn," he said to the little guy.

The little guy took a few more sniffs off his inhaler. He probably ate too many dairy products. Animal protein was mucus-forming and led to problems like halitosis and cancer and diabetes. The guy was killing himself with his fork.

The little guy lifted the barbell off the uprights. He groaned, brought it down, and slowly pushed it back onto the uprights.

"Not bad," said Boyd. "Throw on a quarter, Junior."

Lloyd picked up a twenty-five pound plate and slid it on one end of the barbell while Boyd did the same to the other end. That made an even three hundred pounds.

"I give you double anything Eddie's paying," gasped the little guy. "Name your price, man. No shit."

"We don't know any Eddie." Lloyd explained. "We told you. You're just not paying attention." The little guy wouldn't last five minutes in the jungle. No wonder Uncle Arthur didn't want to see him. Mr. Boar would just tear him up.

"You think you're cute"—Boyd's face was all twisted—"you and this Danny. Like we got nothing better to do than chase you two all over."

"Who?" said Cubanito. "Danny who?"

"No one cares what you know, anymore." Boyd ground his teeth. "You don't matter. Neither does he."

"You two ever think about investing in a McDonalds?" said the little guy. He looked scared. He probably never worked out once in his whole life. "Little franchise in a good location could make you some big-time money. You fuckers could eat for free."

"We don't eat meat, greaseball," said Boyd.

"That's okay." The little guy tried to get up. "We got nuggets. Chicken nuggets, man."

Boyd knocked him back down. "Pump some iron."

"Go ahead." Lloyd nodded. He patted the little guy on the shoulder and gave him a lift off the uprights. "You'll look better and feel better about yourself."

The barbell wobbled its way down and thudded onto the little guy's chest. He grunted, arched his back, and strained at the bar.

"Push! Push! Push!" Lloyd cheered him on, helping him lift it back up. "Go! Go! Go!" The barbell clanked onto the uprights, the bar bending with the weight of the plates. "Good job." Lloyd winked at him. "Can do, can do," the little guy answered back in this breathy singsong voice. He was all right.

"Another couple of quarters," said Boyd.

"I don't know . . . " Lloyd looked at his brother. "I think he's maxed out. Maybe we could set up a workout schedule—" Boyd slammed another twenty-five pound plate onto the bar. "We're not *training* him, stupid."

"Oh." Lloyd hesitated, then slid a plate onto the other end.

The little guy's head looked like a red balloon with a face painted on it. "You fuckers," he moaned. "Fucking Baby Hueys." His head flopped from side to side. "Big fucking babies. That's all you are, man." Sweat poured from him and dripped off the bench, He was floating in his own stink.

"You gotta concentrate," Lloyd whispered. "It's just you and the weight. You can't let it beat you."

The little guy mumbled something about Madonna. Lloyd thought it was a funny time to be thinking about some slutty singer. Maybe he was getting tired of hearing the German lady on the cassette deck. Lloyd gave him another lift off, but the little guy just wasn't trying. There was a wet popping sound as the weight hit his chest. Lloyd had to lift it back into place all by himself.

"Another couple of quarters," said Boyd. Lloyd looked at his brother, shrugged, and slipped on another twenty-five pound plate.

"Por favor, hombres," whispered the little guy. "Por favor." There was blood coming out of his nose and his eyes were rolled back.

"You can do it, little guy." Lloyd lifted the barbell for him, held it right out there. "Grab hold."

He wrapped the little guy's fingers around the shiny steel bar. "Come on, think STRONG!" Lloyd let the barbell go.

The little guy screamed like a girl.

CHAPTER 28

DANNY OPENED HIS EYES, saw a little kid in a Snoopy T-shirt poking him with a stick. He got quickly to his feet and scrambled for his bathing suit while the little kid's shocked mother dragged him away, looking back over her shoulder at Danny.

Danny blinked in the early morning glare off the bay, sand stuck to one side of his face where he had fallen asleep on the beach. He dimly remembered Lauren whispering goodbye at first light.

She had caught him by surprise last night, caught him off balance and out of breath. It was a page from one of her lectures on corporate psychology: Your initial foray should anticipate the competition's response. That way, they were always one move behind.

His sweats lay crumpled against the seawall, soggy and caked with grit. Danny put them on anyway, ignoring the startled looks from the people driving past on their way to the office.

He hurt. His back was scraped from the sand, and there was a deep cut on his leg where he had rolled onto a shell. Danny slowly walked the two blocks to his building, remembering the softness of Lauren's skin, the heat of her breath against his neck. He ran a hand through his hair and curls of brown seaweed fell down. The tide had come in on them last night.

Lauren hadn't gotten everything she wanted last night. Otherwise she wouldn't have arranged to meet him tonight. Some swanky restaurant on the *Queen Mary*. It should have been on the *Titanic*: a shivering embrace on the foredeck, foghorns blaring into the darkness, icebergs on the horizon, and the compass spinning like a top.

Eilene stepped out of her door as Danny started up the stairs. He hesitated.

"Don't worry, I won't bite." Eilene's smile was tired but bright. She wore a clean white blouse and neatly pressed Guess? jeans. "Want me to make you some coffee?" She brushed sand off his cheek.

"Thanks anyway," said Danny.

"I guess you heard about my coffee." It was the first time Danny had seen her laugh since Blaine left.

"You look beautiful, Eilene."

Eilene waved him off, trying to hide her pleasure. "I must have gained ten pounds in the last couple of weeks," she said. "Hey, is that a hickey on your neck? I didn't know guardian angels fooled around."

"What makes you think we were fooling?"

"I'm jealous.". Eilene kissed him on his clean cheek. "I gotta go. Blaine called this morning." She flushed. "He's coming home!"

"Wonderful."

"Act like you mean it." Eilene pouted. "Blaine just needs me to wire him some money for an airline ticket. It's going to be all right, you'll see." She smoothed her hair. "Do my eyes look puffy? Blaine says I look too old in the morning."

"Blaine should get his vision checked," said Danny.

Her eyes gleamed. "You're sweet." She squeezed his hand. "I can't talk now. If Blaine finds a job, he might change his mind." She walked away, suddenly turned and came back.

"My head is spinning so fast I almost forgot," she said. "Early this morning I heard somebody going up the stairs to your apartment. I thought maybe it was those beefcakes in the Hawaiian shirts, the ones from yesterday. But when I peeked out, there was nobody there. You sure you're not in some kind of trouble?"

"Thanks for the information," said Danny. He thought about it as she disappeared down the street. No visitors for almost a year, now suddenly he was Mr. Popularity. He climbed slowly up to his apartment, half expecting someone to leap out from his landing. Steiner. Cubanito. Freddy Krueger.

Danny stopped in front of his door. There were faint scratches on the deadbolt. He leaned his ear against it and listened. The only thing he could hear was his own heartbeat. Pounding away. He looked around. Cars moved slowly down the street, and televisions buzzed from the nearby houses. Nothing out of the ordinary here. He still hesitated before putting his hand on the doorknob.

He unlocked the door and pushed it open. The room was filled with shadows. Shadows under his desk and behind the armchair, shadows in the bedroom nook. That's what he got for keeping the drapes pulled. Make a note: Leave a light on next time you leave. A searchlight. Elvis stared at him from the velvet painting on the far wall. Is it safe, bubba? The refrigerator suddenly hummed, and Danny jumped.

There was something different about the room, a heaviness to the air: The apartment was at the bottom of a deep well. He had to make a conscious effort to breathe. Someone had been there, had come in and sucked the life out of the place.

He moved silently across the room, his eyes on the half-open bathroom door, listening so hard he could hear the dripping faucet in the bathtub. It couldn't be the two guys in the Hawaiian shirts, not if they were as big as Eilene said they were. There wasn't room enough for them in the tiny bathroom.

He picked up the diving trophy from the mantel and hefted it. It should have been a baseball bat or a hockey stick. Story of his life: He had lettered in the wrong sport. Why was he breathing so loudly?

Danny kicked open the bathroom door, brandishing the trophy. Empty. He checked behind the shower curtain to be sure, then sat down on the toilet seat. Laughter bubbled up inside him. It stopped as abruptly as it began when he noticed his razor lying blade-up on the sink. He never left it that way. Never.

CHAPTER 29

HOLT SAT ON STEINER'S hospital bed and took his hand. He woke with a start, smiled when he saw who it was. "I'm not supposed to stay long," she said.

"How's it going, Jane?" Steiner's eyes were sunken, but his grip was strong. "Geez, you look like a million bucks."

She nodded to the heart monitor next to Steiner's bed. "If that was a polygraph, you'd blow a fuse." Holt wore his favorite outfit, a mid-length white dress with a scoop neck and red piping. He said it made her look like Betty Grable. An exhausted Betty Grable maybe. Nothing could hide the double shifts, and she was having trouble sleeping, too. Every time she closed her eyes, she saw the coil of copper wire wrapped around the stump of Tohlson's genitals, a bright mouth between his dead white thighs.

Steiner jiggled the thin blue wires that sprouted from his gown, connecting the elcctrodes on his chest to the monitor. "They're not even warm," he protested.

The monitor gave a digital readout of Steiner's heart rate and blood pressure. Three tiny pens scratched wavering lines along a spool of red graph paper, recording more precise information about his condition. It *did* look like a polygraph machine.

Steiner pressed a switch and gears whirred, slowly tilting the back of the bed forward until he was sitting up. The color came back to his cheeks, waves of pink washing away the gray pallor. "Captain still riding you about breaking the case open?"

She stiffened and began fluffing his pillow.

"That's what I thought," said Steiner. "I know you think everything's got to be by the book, but that book don't fit every situation. You limit yourself to proper channels, nothing's going to get done."

"The captain was very accommodating." Holt punched the pillow flat. "He just said that unless I came up with something solid in the next forty-eight hours, he was giving the job to Ryan and Plesa."

"Those two." Steiner shook his head. "Every case is an easy grounder to them. They'll just round up a loner who'll confess to anything, including the Kennedy assassination. We're lucky to get another forty-eight hours. The captain don't like any mysteries stinking up his watch."

The captain had strolled by their desks every afternoon since they had been on the case, right before the end of their first shift, when they were typing their daily reports and thinking about dinner. He'd stand there, hands in his vest pockets, rocking back and forth. "Anything you want to tell me, Karl?" he'd say finally, ignoring Holt. Karl would look up like he had just noticed the captain, grin, and say, "Everything's hunky-dory, Cap, hunky-d. The bad guys're shaking in their boots."

The department *was* under a lot of pressure. So far the local papers had been kept out of it, but a couple of the beat reporters knew something big had happened. The captain was maintaining a strict no-comment, investigation-in-progress profile to their questions, but it was just a matter of time until one of Lauren Kiel's neighbors or someone at the coroner's office talked.

Holt wished she had Karl's easy confidence. This morning she broke a shoelace on her new black Reeboks and hurled it against the wall before she even realized it. Newport Beach was affluent, educated, and white, a quiet, button-down community with three Ferrari dealerships and no public transportation. The supermarkets were stocked with Black Forest truffles and Dom Perignon, and commodities fraud was more common than murder. Newport Beach didn't like messy homicides, and an unsolved homicide was the messiest kind of all. A high-profile case like this could make Holt's career. Or break it.

The captain wouldn't dare shunt Holt to traffic control or anything like that. He knew what a sex-discrimination suit would do to *his* personnel folder. No, he'd stick her in the community-relations unit, where her "sensitivity and intelligence would be invaluable, an asset to the department." Holt would spend her days giving Just Say No lectures to bored high school students who got their dope from their parents' medicine cabinets. And there she'd stay.

A bouquet of scraggly daisies stuck out of the blue plastic water pitcher on Steiner's nightstand, their stems bent and twisted. Holt picked up the greeting card that leaned against the pitcher. Outside, the card showed a photograph of a big-breasted woman in an unbuttoned police uniform. Inside, the woman wore just a garter belt and stockings, her police cap jauntily tilted back. "Get Well or You're BUST-ED!" read the caption. It was signed by all the other detectives. No one had asked her. She knew they called her the Ice Queen behind her back. If they were prejudiced against women police officers, at least they respected her. They just didn't like her. She replaced the card and looked at Steiner. "Very imaginative."

Steiner grinned with embarrassment. "Molina brought it by early this morning." His breathing was more ragged now, the hospital gown hanging on him like laundry on a line. The silver leads to the heart monitor sprouted from the neckline, his chest raw where they had shaved him to make a clean contact.

Seeing him like this made Holt miss his bad jokes and jelly doughnuts, the sloppy reports and ugly neckties. He looked so vulnerable and feeble, lost in these starched white sheets.

She had seen Steiner subdue a two-hundred-fifty pound suspect on PCP. The man had stood in the middle of the street, completely naked, stabbing the air with a butcher knife and screaming about "little gooks in UFOs." Holt called for a backup with a taser-gun. SOP. Why risk injury when they could shock him into immobility? Instead, Steiner just waded in, dodged the butcher knife, and threw a chokehold on the suspect.

"Did you really take in DiMedici?" said Steiner. "One of the ambulance attendants said you had him cuffed."

"Of course I arrested him. What did you expect?" She picked one of the daisies out of the pitcher, pulled off a petal. "He broke into a posted crime scene, Karl. Docsn't that matter?"

"Take it easy," said Steiner. "Sure it matters. But you got to admit he came through. I was down for the count, and the swimmer was right there with that CPR. Bet he was a lifeguard at the Y once upon a time."

"He's not a lifeguard anymore. He's a dope dealer."

"Ancient history," said Steiner. "Yesterday, he saved my life."

Daisy petals lay scattered across the bed. Holt felt herself flush as she swept them into her hand and dropped them into the wastebasket. The monitor pens scratched away, recording every squeeze of Steiner's heart.

"Jane, you got nothing to be ashamed of. He just beat you to it."

"It's not that." She picked up his water glass. "Here. Drink."

Steiner took a few sips through the straw and laid

his head back on the pillow, watching the ceiling with his watery blue eyes. "You know," he said, "I had a partner get shot on a domestic disturbance call once. The wife was waving a Saturday night special and it went off." Steiner's tired voice could have been counting the holes in the acoustic tile. "Let me tell you, I wasn't no Dirty Harry that day. My partner was gurgling on the floor and I just stood there like my legs were planted in concrete. I wanted to do something. I kept yelling at myself to do something, but all I did was stare at the mess he was making. The wife was the one who pressed her hand over the hole in his belly. If it was up to me, he'd have bled to death."

Holt's eyes shimmered with tears. "I'm sorry," she whispered. "You needed me, and I let you down."

"Hush."

Holt stared at her lap. "I'm so ashamed." She was not going to cry. Things were bad enough.

"People make mistakes," said Steiner. "You made one. The swimmer's made a few himself. Let me tell you, Jane. There's all of us done things we wouldn't want our mothers to know about."

"There's a difference between jaywalking and selling narcotics." Holt cleared her throat and sat up straight. "You cross the line with a felony. You don't come back."

"I wish it were that simple." Steiner sighed. "If it were, I'd sleep better at night, because then I'd know how to separate the good guys from the bad guys."

"I don't want to argue with you." Holt got up and

checked herself in the mirror, ran a brush through her thick red hair. Her hair was shiny and healthy, with a slight natural curl and not one split end. It was her one vanity. She used a special French shampoo and rinse, gave herself a warm-oil treatment every week. She got it cut and styled at a penthouse salon where the staff wore raw silk and no one would have believed what she did for a living.

"Let's just agree that Mr. DiMedici's no longer the primary suspect on this case," said Holt. She could feel Steiner watching her brush her hair. He told her once that they had been partnered because he was too old to make a play for her, but he could still admire the view. Coming from Karl, she didn't mind.

"You're a fine-looking woman, Jane," said Steiner. "I know, I know," he said when she gave him her prim-and-proper look. "But I wanted to say it. Somebody's got to tell you."

"What makes you think nobody tells me?" Holt teased him.

"Because they're all afraid of you. You make the boys at the station nervous."

"Sometimes they make me nervous," Holt said, gesturing at the get-well card.

"All I'm saying is that things look different when you're flat on your back." She grinned, and *he* blushed for a change. "That's not what I mean," he said. "Lying here, hooked up like this . . . well, it changes your priorities."

Holt sat back on the bed so that he didn't have to strain his voice.

"You and me, we got the most important job in the world," said Steiner. "But it's not everything there is. My wife walked out the day after our tenth anniversary. Took the kids back to Ohio and left me a note taped to the refrigerator. Funny thing was, she still left me dinner. Corned beef and cabbage. My favorite. Overcooked it as usual, but what the heck, it's the thought." Steiner's eyelids fluttered and he looked away. "I told myself I was better off. But you know, after her, no matter who I slept with, the bed always seemed empty."

"I missed my son's high school graduation," he said. "My daughter didn't even bother inviting me to hers. Five grandkids, and I never went to a Disney movie with any of them. Seemed like there was never enough time to visit. There was always some case, some big important case that came in the way." Steiner squeezed her hand so hard she almost cried out. "You got to *make* time for people, Jane. You got to grab on to people who count and not let them go."

"I won't let go of you, Karl," Holt said softly.

"Don't let Ryan and Plesa take our case. I want to finish with a clean slate, just like I came in. If I could get out of this bed, nothing would stop me from closing this one out. Nothing. Because I know that whoever did it is out there laughing at us. Don't let it happen. Don't let them take our case."

"Don't worry." Holt glanced at the monitor, but all the gauges were steady and unchanged. "I'll check in with you two or three times a day. You'll get more updates than the captain."

Steiner glanced around like he thought someone might be hiding in the room. "I'm scared of dying. I been in a dozen shoot-outs, wounded twice in the line of duty, and never worried before. But I lie here and all I think about is that machine going off and doctors running in saying I'm dead and I can't move or talk or tell them that I'm not. Is that stupid?"

"Not at all." Holt had never noticed the liver spots on his big hands.

"I'll tell you a secret, Jane. I've always been afraid of the dark."

"Me too, Karl." She held him tight. "That's why they let us carry guns."

A few minutes later, the nurse peeked in to see what the laughter was all about.

CHAPTER 30

DANNY STOOD IN THE doorway of Grace's, the smell of bacon and coffee and french toast rolling around him. His stomach groaned. Lauren had brought back his appetite. Among other things. He could devour the world.

Grace bellowed at someone over the sizzle of frying eggs and hash browns, the hum of conversation. The diner was a breakfast-and-lunch-only hangout with red vinyl booths along the wall and a twelve-stool counter. No checks. No credit cards. Grace said plastic money was part of 666.

The waitresses ferried plates of omelettes and hot cinnamon rolls to the booths, swiveling their way through the cluster of small round tables. Carol wore a frilly short yellow sundress today; it made her chubby knees look even chubbier. She saw Danny and waved. Denise had on the usual: short shorts and a sleeveless white T-shirt. No bra, no panties. Last year she bought a new midnight-black Porsche. The license plate read TIPS.

Danny found a spot at the counter, winced as he sat down. He was still sore from last night. Sometime during their time on the beach, Lauren had giggled and told him he was out of practice. He was surprised that she hadn't left a formal review scrawled in the sand. Give him the benefit of her professional advice. Something about goal-sharing and creative visualization.

Emilio wiped the counter clean and poured Danny a glass of water. Danny thanked his back.

Thrasher scooted over and sat down next to Danny. The long-haired kid leaned his battered skateboard under the counter. His grin was crooked, his eyes glassy. Thrasher drummed his fingers on the Formica, waiting for Danny to order. Danny told him to move over one stool. Thrasher looked hurt but did it anyway. Looking hurt wasn't nearly enough this morning. The kid stank of airplane glue from the sock soaked with Testors he kept in his hip pocket.

Sometimes Danny was convinced he was the only person on the planet who wasn't already messed up on something or looking to score so he *could* be messed up on something. He had told that to Cubanito after being bailed out and Cubanito had looked at him with shock. "Don't spread that attitude around, man," Cubanito said. "I go fucking broke."

Right after his shower, Danny had called Cubanito to tell him to stop looking for Lauren. But Cubanito hadn't answered his page.

Danny had come a long way from the academic

world. One sidestep at a time. He would have had tenure by now, would have been working on a paunch, complaining about the sloppy thinking habits of the undergraduates. Cubanito was supposed to be working in a car wash, driving a rusted-out Chevy and determined to win the lottery.

They were an unlikely pair, but there was common ground. They were true to their word. They stood by their friends, even when the odds were lousy. That was enough.

Hand-printed signs taped against the counter mirror of Grace's blared: "Jesus could kick your ass!" and "The Miracle is always right!" and "Don't be a strangler to God!"

The first time Danny had eaten there, a college kid with a little tennis player on his pink polo shirt told Grace that she had made a mistake, that she had misspelled *stranger*. He printed it out for her in big letters on a napkin. She threw him out. Just came around the counter and pushed him out the door. "Dumbshit," she yelled. "Take your wiseguy business to the Pancake House already!" Danny had been coming back for breakfast ever since.

The café attracted a mixed clientele of surfers and skateboarders, unhurried businessmen and chatty matrons in french-cut leotards who stopped by Grace's after their advanced-aerobics classes.

The café was the last of its kind in Belmont Shore, a neighborhood joint. The portions were large, the food was good, and Grace was rude. The café didn't advertise or sponsor a float in the Christmas parade or give cutesy names to the omelettes on the menu. The café flourished because Grace had had the good sense to buy the building before property values soared. She said God helped those who got in on the ground floor. She was right.

Grace came over and looked at Danny. "A refugee you are. Mr. Skin 'n' Bones." Her voice was metal on metal. She laid a double order of buttered wheat toast in front of him. "What am I to do with you?" She put her hands on her hips. There was plenty of room. She was an iron-haired grandmother from Düsseldorf, solid and thick and heavy as blood sausage.

Danny laid his head on the counter in obeisance. Grains of sand trickled from his scalp onto the counter. He needed more shower time.

Grace swept the counter clean. "Tschuch," she clucked, "*still* you swim alone at night? Like a frogman, you are, a saboteur. Sometimes you're getting a cramp and I lose a customer. You never heard the buddy system?"

"God is my buddy as well as my copilot, Grace," Danny said as she poured him a cup of coffee.

"See what good that does you," she scolded Danny, and slapped Thrasher's hand, which was scuttling toward the stack of toast.

Grace had married an American staff sergeant stationed in Germany after World War Two. When he was rotated back to Texas, she had changed her name from Gretchen to Grace and joined the local fundamentalist church, the Assembly of the Fiery Redeemer. The church collected old clothes for starving children in Africa and printed tracts warning Christians to buy guns and gold in preparation for a racial holocaust.

Taped beside the cash register was the 3-D postcard Danny had mailed her from Tijuana—a blue-eyed Jesus with soft blond hair and a crown of thorns. Pink blood trickled down Jesus' forehead, but his smile didn't feel any pain.

Thrasher palmed the top piece of wheat toast, piled on strawberry preserves, and gobbled it down, his tiny eyes darting from side to side. He was wearing black high tops and baggy black shorts covered with a skull-and-bone pattern. No shirt. His upper arms were a blue macrame of dragons and vampire bats and bug-eyed demon tatoos.

Danny drank his coffee while Thrasher palmed another piece of toast. It was a game they had been playing since Danny became a regular. Grace let Thrasher sit on the stools, but she refused to feed him. She had to let him in. He was her youngest son.

Grace refilled Danny's empty coffee cup and set down a cinnamon roll. "Go on, eat," she commanded.

The coffee was waking Danny up. He could feel every kink in his back. This morning, half asleep, Danny had turned over and seen Lauren down the beach, the public shower spraying rainbows off her body. Silent houses. Empty streets. Nothing else moving. She washed herself with the innocence of a child, perfectly at ease, then turned off the shower and shook her hair dry. She was pink and clean in the light. He had thought he was dreaming.

Danny pushed the remainder of the toast over to Thrasher and started in on the cinnamon roll. Grace set a glass of freshly squeezed orange juice in front of him and glared at the skateboarder. "Drink," she said to Danny, "before your gums bleed."

Danny wondered if Lauren had ever made love on a beach with Tohlson or any of the others. Just tore into each other and not cared who might see. Who might hear. Danny asked her about Tohlson, but she kissed him so gently, her eyelashes brushing his cheek. And he didn't care about Tohlson anymore. He felt like the old Danny again. Not afraid. Not alone. Not lost. She said she wanted the old Danny back again. So did he.

He whirled at the perfume smell. Eilene sat down next to him. "I'm glad you're still here," she said. "Sorry I was in such a hurry before." She stared at him, a tiny crease in her forehead. "You look different."

"Different how?" said Danny.

"I don't know. Happier, maybe." Eilene ran a finger-tip along the inside of his wrist. "You look the way I feel." She smiled. "I guess we're lucky."

Danny finished his orange juice, crushing the tiny beads of orange pulp between his teeth, filling his mouth with their tartness. "So, did you send Blaine your money?"

"Don't say it like that. He spent all his money trying to break into the New York modeling scene, and when he decided to come back, he didn't have any money left. It's hard to find a job in New York."

"I bet."

"Well, it is. Everyone is so competitive, and it's hard for Blaine to make friends." Eilene flagged down Grace. "Miss, I'd like black coffee, dry wheat toast, and a poached egg, please."

"No poached egg," said Grace. She topped up Danny's coffee cup and set one out for Eilene.

"I don't understand," said Eilene.

"No. Poach. Egg." Grace's thick red lipstick cracked with her exaggerated enunciation. "Fry or scramble?"

"Just toast." Eilene sniffed. "Honestly," she said to Danny as Grace chugged off, "I don't know why you eat here."

"It's the ambience."

"Did you ever find out who came by last night?" said Eilene. "Was there a note?"

Danny shook his head. In the mirror, he could see a tall, skinny man sitting alone in the corner booth. With his gray suit and polka-dot blue tie he looked like a big gawky bird. One of those poor goonies that could never get airborne. Denise leaned over the man with a coffeepot, but he waved her away.

Eilene sipped her coffee, made a face. "Miss," she called to Grace. "Do you have any Sweet 'n' Low?" Grace barreled past without a word.

"So, when does Blaine's plane get in?" Danny said distractedly, still watching the man in the mirror.

"Blaine owes people some money." Eilene pushed the coffee cup as far away from her as possible. "He's very responsible about paying his debts."

"Right," said Danny. The man in the mirror was

eating french fries. He picked one up, squeezed a strip of ketchup along its length, and nibbled on it until it was gone. Then he picked up another and did exactly the same thing. "Don't turn around," said Danny. "Check out the skinny guy in the mirror. Watch how he eats. It's hilarious."

Eilene watched the man for a moment. "What a terrible suit. Fits him like Pee-Wee Herman," she said.

Grace came back with a plate overflowing with an omelette for Danny. Mushrooms, green onion, ham, cheese, and crumpled bacon. She added a side of hash browns and a thick piece of apple strudel. "Don't argue," she said to him.

Danny drove his fork into the strudel. The blond Jesus smiled back at him, serene in his immortality. "I wouldn't think of it, Grace."

"Maybe when Blaine gets back I'll throw a surprise party for him," said Eilene. "I can pick up a few trays of sushi and that Cru Negro champagne he likes." She ticked off the items in the air. "And some 'ludes. I just wish he had more friends. Most people don't like Blaine because he's so good-looking. He makes them nervous. You'll come, won't you?"

"Sure. Maybe Blaine's gotten uglier since he's been in New York."

Eilene leaned her head against his shoulder. "You're just teasing. I told Blaine that you've been real sweet to me. I think you two could be friends."

In the mirror, Denise set two plates of pancakes in front of the skinny guy. He emptied the syrup bottle over them. Life was a surprise party, all right.

*   *   *

At the Huntington Beach municipal park, still sluggish from breakfast, Danny stretched as he got out of his car. Little kids pumped away on the swings while their pretty young mothers watched. Three bored park workers squatted outside the restrooms smoking cigarettes. As Danny walked past, one of them flicked his butt into the water fountain.

Danny cut across the grass and into the trees, taking the narrow dirt path that wound around the perimeter. It was cool and dim under the canopy of trees, the air smelling of leaves and wet newspaper. He took a sharp left at the lightning-blasted pine tree, then crawled through the bushes until he came to a tiny clearing. He tore at the earth with a gardening trowel, digging down until he pulled out a heat-sealed plastic envelope of money—twenty thousand dollars in hundreds. Nonsequential serial numbers. The last of the money. Money stashed during his dealing days. Rainy-day money for a monsoon life.

There was also a widemouthed thermos jug. He unscrewed the lid and pulled out a snub-nosed .357 magnum revolver. He spun the chamber, sighted, and checked the action. Perfect. Two years underground and not a trace of corrosion on the chrome finish. He should look so good.

Danny could hear cheers go up in the distance. There was a softball game on the other side of the park. Someone had belted a homer. Or struck out.

Back at the parking lot, Danny called Cubanito from the phone booth, watching the pretty young mothers while he waited for Cubanito to answer his page.

One of the little boys fell off the swing and his mother rushed over, bent down, and kissed his scraped knee, dried his tears. She was an athletic blonde wearing white shorts you could almost see through. He wondered if her husband knew how perfect she was. Did he work in an office and call her during the day, just to hear her voice? He and Lauren should have had children. It might have made a difference.

Danny checked with Cubanito's service. The operator said he hadn't called in for messages since the night before. She thought it was strange, too. Danny tried Michael. No answer. No answering machine, either. Michael hated to miss a call. The telephone was his lifeline. Danny thought about that. He was glad he had the gun.

CHAPTER 31

MESSAGE PENDING FLASHED as soon as Detective Holt logged on to her computer. She stabbed the message key, her stomach already tense.

"If you are unable to determine the most likely suspect in the beachfront homicide, perhaps you could at least suggest a cover story I can present to the intrepid members of the fourth estate. Detective, either do your job, or make way for someone who can."

Before she spiked the captain's message to computer hell, Holt made a hard copy for her files. It was unlikely that she could build a harassment charge—the captain was too canny for that—but she believed in the value of complete records.

Sunlight slanted through the Levelor blinds of the fifth-floor detectives squad room, laid a neat pattern on the thick teal-blue wool carpet. Holt could see sailboats tacking lazily across Newport Bay.

Small, upscale, and efficient, the Newport PD was called "the prototype of the modern police department" by the *American Journal of Criminology*, and the country club by other Southern California law officers. The ten detectives in the department rotated by their assignments, covering everything from armed robbery to homicide. After decades as a suburban outpost, the Newport Beach PD was now regarded as a stepping-stone to upper management in law enforcement.

Chief Evans had successfully lobbied through a bond issue to construct a new administration building. Federal grants paid for the computer system and the helicopters. The department was in line for a five-hundred-thousand-dollar portable laser system that could pull fingerprints off a Kleenex. The tradeoff was that the detectives were pressured to close out cases quickly, without following up on leads that might stall the investigation. Detectives who didn't maintain a healthy conviction ratio risked a negative performance evaluation.

Newport Beach police detectives did not curse. They did not smoke or sport facial hair. They wore dark suits and rep ties and called suspects sir and Ms. The detectives had college degrees. They didn't care who won the World Series or the Super Bowl; they played racquetball, and their children competed in the local soccer league. Desktops were neat and had a maximum of one personal photograph in a standard-issue metal frame. The squad room reminded Holt of the brokerage office where her father was a senior partner. Steiner said if he hadn't been so close to retirement, he would have transferred out.

Steiner's desk was right next to hers, an auto-
graphed picture of Joe DiMaggio facing a wallet-size
Marilyn Monroe. Papers and manila folders were
stacked haphazardly and a handful of pencils stuck
out of a grimy OAKLAND RAIDERS mug. Her first day,
Holt saw Steiner remove the pencils and fill the mug
with coffee, then pour in a couple of inches of white
sugar and stir with one of the pencils.

Holt dunked the teabag in her mug of hot water
as she diagrammed the details of the case on a legal
pad. This morning she was drinking peppermint-
chamomile, which the package said was supposed to
calm and soothe jangled nerves. Time for a refund.
She squeezed out the bag, sealed it in a Baggie, and
dropped it into the wastebasket. Steiner teased her
about being so fastidious, but she didn't like making
a mess for the janitor.

The yellow pad was no help. Under the name
Lauren Kiel she listed "no apparent motive," "no
unassisted means of killing," and "missing." Danny
DiMedici's jealousy and history of violence pro-
vided motive, and his physical strength was suf-
ficient to overpower Dr. Tohlson and haul him
up to the ceiling. But Steiner was right. DiMedici
wasn't innocent, but he didn't kill Tohlson. The
only breakthrough they had had in the case was
finding the body, and that was the result of an
anonymous tip. Maybe the captain had a point.

There was still the brother, Michael Kiel. Holt
had run a credit check with TRW, which confirmed
that he was a legitimate businessman, very successful, never even late with a payment. She still had a

feeling about him. Mr. Kiel had sat in his freezing little room answering their questions, a joint dangling from his lips, sat there on the edge of nowhere, surrounded by his medals.

On the other side of the room, Ryan and Plesa processed a suspect, a rabbity skinhead with acne scars and a tough expression that was rapidly deteriorating into acute contrition. Probably an inlander from Santa Ana or Tustin caught boosting auto tape decks in the Heights, thinking he was inconspicuous as long as he didn't make eye contact. Plesa typed the arrest report into the computer with two fingers, jab-jab-jab, while Ryan sat next to the suspect, his pale, puffy hand resting on the kid's shoulder. In five minutes the kid would be bawling for his mother. Ten, tops.

Two desks down, Nichols hunched over a stack of mug books with Mrs. Pierce-Addington, one of the local doyennes, a tiny, fragile widow whose sparse hair was brightly hennaed and crimped flapper-fashion. It looked like she was wearing a shower cap made of orange cellophane. The diamonds on her blue-veined fingers flashed as she separated the pages, turning them slowly, carefully, not wanting to miss a thing.

Mrs. Pierce-Addington hobbled in regularly twice a month to stare at the faces in the books. Coarse faces, heavy-lidded and ugly, choirboy faces with smooth skin and depraved smiles, brutal faces with ragged scars and flattened noses. Holt had helped her only once, but she still remembered the old woman's heavy rosewater perfume and the obscene way her lips worked as she turned the pages, eyes glittering with some private delight.

The autopsy report on Tohlson had found that his tissues were saturated with a variety of illegal and prescription drugs: marijuana, cocaine, morphine, Percodan, Valium. Plus other substances the pharmacological tests were unable to identify.

According to Dr. Reese, Tohlson had access to a variety of drugs in the context of his research. Although there were supposed to be strict records kept, Reese admitted that Tohlson might have pilfered drugs without being detected. Holt had already notified the state board to check into Reese Pharmaceuticals and its handling of controlled substances.

Not that it would do any good. Due to budget cuts, there were only twenty-eight field agents to police the entire state. The clerk who took Holt's report said that last year they had over 2,300 complaints, mostly about inner-city MDs writing scrips for diet pills to anyone who could pay the thirty-five-dollar office fee. The backlog of cases was three years and growing.

Holt dug in her purse for her Rolaids, getting angrier as she searched. Finally, she snapped it shut, opened Steiner's top drawer, and pulled out an economy-size bottle of Pepto-Bismol. She fed herself two spoonfuls, wincing at the taste. When she had started with the department, Holt was startled to see Steiner belt it down straight from the bottle and smack his lips with approval. The other detectives were more discreet. They sloshed three fingers of the sweet pink medicine into paper cups before the 8 A.M. briefing, crunched through rolls of antacids like they were Certs. Their breath smelled of chalk. They blamed it on fast food and slow court schedules.

Steiner didn't equivocate or make excuses. He said that in the old days, when the job was more bare knuckles than diplomacy, every detective stashed a quart of rye in his desk. Now, a cop needed Tagamet. Frustration was the strongest acid in the world, he said. It could eat right through your soul.

Holt told Steiner he would be better off taking up jogging or swimming, even offered to show him some relaxation exercises. He just smiled. Three days into the Tohlson case, she started raiding his top drawer. He smiled even more broadly, said she may have graduated from the academy at the top of her class, but now she was a real cop.

She was a real cop, all right. Tell that to the captain.

The phone on Steiner's desk rang three times. A few moments later hers went off. She got it on the first ring. "Detective Holt."

The man's voice was gruff and clipped. "I wanted Steiner."

"Detective Steiner isn't in. What can I do for you?" Holt reached for her notepad.

"Negative. My information's for Karl."

"Who is speaking?" Silence. "Karl is my partner. If you have anything to say, you can say it to me." Silence. "Hello?"

"You the society babe he talked about?"

Holt decided not to hang up. "Yes."

"I want this kept in the strictest confidence, Detective. I did this as a favor to Karl. Is that understood."

The point snapped off Holt's pencil. "Who are you?"

"A colonel in the United States military, which is all you need to know. Karl asked me to check into the service record of a PFC Tohlson, Harold Tohlson."

Holt silently cursed Steiner. Those records were privileged. She looked around the squad room. "Was this an official request?"

"Fine, Detective. Please tell Karl that I called."

"Wait!" She saw Plesa glance over at her. "Colonel?" she said softly.

"Yes?"

"I'm sorry, Colonel." Holt cradled the receiver against her ear, fed herself another spoon of antacid. Using sealed information in a court of law was strictly forbidden. Even knowingly asking for such information was a violation of federal statutes. She wiped the spoon clean with a napkin.

"Well?"

Holt turned away from the rest of the room, bending over the phone as if that could shield her from what she was doing. "Any help you could give us would be greatly appreciated." Holt didn't recognize her own voice. "It's just that I'm a little nervous about bending the law."

"Oh, it's not *bending* the law, Detective." He

chuckled. "Regulations are quite specific about the release of such records."

Holt waited for herself to do the right thing. And waited in vain. "I understand." The words fell out of her mouth like rotten teeth.

"Well, for starters, your PFC Tohlson is a head case," breezed the colonel. "*Was* a head case, from what Karl told me. Good riddance. Tohlson should have been bounced dishonorable, but some bleeding heart put him down for an administrative discharge. The army's loss was your gain. Like they say, all the fruits and nuts roll to California." The colonel's laughter was grating and unapologetic.

"Colonel, could you please tell me the exact nature of PFC Tohlson's problem?"

"Like to, but the file just stated that he had been found in a compromising situation. No queer stuff, mind you, he was found by himself. There was some suggestion of a suicide attempt, but Tohlson denied it. Whatever he was doing, it just wasn't kosher."

"That's it?"

"The man was a psycho. Even in California, I can't see you wasting the taxpayers' money trying to catch whoever put him out of his misery."

"I'll tell Karl you called, Colonel."

"I *didn't* call, Detective."

Holt listened to the dial tone for ten seconds before putting down the phone. Alive or dead, Dr. Tohlson's right to privacy had been violated. It was a small offense, but she took no comfort in that. She was sworn to uphold the law. Not some of them some of the time, but all of them all of the time.

Steiner said she acted like the law was a minefield waiting to blow up in her face. Said he was happy just to keep the peace.

Holt stared at the yellow pad on her desk. She had drawn a succession of boxes across the page, filling them in until there was no room left inside.

She looked around. The squad room looked the same as before the phone call, but she knew something was different.

CHAPTER 32

FROM THE CREST of the road, Danny could see a new, white Range Rover parked in front of Michael's. The Mustang rumbled as he idled, watching. The front door was open. Danny let the Mustang roll back down the slope, out of sight. Michael would never leave the door open. He didn't waste air-conditioning or anything else. Danny turned the car around on the narrow road, then switched off the ignition but left the keys in place.

He slid the magnum from the folded newspaper on the passenger seat, unloaded, and dry-fired it again, just to make sure. The action was smooth, precise. It was quiet in the car with the windows rolled up and the engine off. The hollow-points made little snick-snick sounds as he dropped them back into the chambers, metallic whispers in the silence.

Danny scrambled to the top of the rise and checked the house. There was no way to approach it unseen, but going cross-country could minimize his exposure. The brambles hooked his jeans as he moved across the hard-packed sand, keeping low. Michael's jeep was parked out back, thick with dust.

There was never any thought of leaving Michael behind. Danny might as well try to abandon his shadow. It was recognition that marked them, bound them together. Recognition of who they were, what they had shared. Danny had tried to separate himself. They had all tried. You could hide things underground, bury them deep, but they were always there, waiting for you to need them.

A pebbly lizard scuttled over to where he lay and stopped a few inches from his face. Shiny black eyes watched Danny, the lizard's throat gently inflating and deflating. Danny stared back, barely breathing. He felt light and buoyant. Searching for Lauren had changed him, stirred up old feelings, old strengths, and given him a direction—forward. Driving golf balls into the surf with Michael had helped. So had shoptalking with Cubanito. Even the Samoan was part of it. Taking arms against a sea of troubles.

Lauren had marked him. Marked him the first time they met, and collected on it last night. She knew him. That gave her certain privileges, certain advantages. But he knew her, too. Time was compressing into a dense moment, an instant around which the rest of their lives would revolve.

Michael Kiel's photo album bothered her, but Holt couldn't stop turning the pages.

Danny and Lauren on a sailboat, Danny with a

ridiculous feathery British admiralty hat tilted back on his head, Lauren topless, saluting. Michael in full camouflage makeup, proudly holding up a dripping bluefin. Danny and Michael drunk, arms around each other, toasting the camera with jeroboams of champagne. Danny and Lauren lying on the teak deck, holding hands, ankles entwined.

The next section of the album was devoted to the big wedding. Danny in a tuxedo, handsome and happy. Lauren in a designer white french-lace wedding gown. She had the figure and the face for it, but her eyes were too knowing for the innocent bride.

Holt glanced up and saw Danny poised in the doorway, pointing a shiny gun at her. She blinked. For an instant she thought it was her imagination, a fantasy evoked from the romance of the photographs.

Danny straightened up, surprised. The gun dropped to his side. His Levi's jacket was dusty and the knees of his jeans were grass-stained. "Where's Michael?"

"I don't know." Holt carefully set the album on the coffee table next to her purse. She was still wearing Steiner's favorite outfit, the white dress with the red piping. Her slip rustled as she balanced on the edge of the sofa, trying not to stare at the gun in his hand.

"You don't belong here," Danny said, his angry profile moving side to side in the doorway, as though he couldn't make up his mind.

Holt casually picked up her purse and fiddled inside, pretending to search for a Kleenex. She

found her revolver, aimed it at his chest from inside
the bag and waited to see what he would do. She
had never fired her weapon in the line of duty, but
she had no doubts about her survival instincts.

"What are you doing here?" he demanded, his
voice louder.

Still keeping her hand in her purse, Holt eased
back the hammer of the revolver, coughing to cover
the cocking sound. Before he could raise his gun and
fire, she could put three rounds into his chest. A
tight pattern, too. The rangemaster at the academy
had said that when a man decided to kill you, his
eyes would slightly squint. "I could ask you the same
thing, Mr. DiMedici."

"Don't give me that, lady. Michael's my friend
and I wouldn't walk into his place uninvited. You
have a special dispensation I don't know about?"

"I left the door open," said Holt. It sounded like
a lame excuse, even to her. "I didn't want to startle
Mr. Kiel when he returned."

Danny slapped the dust off his jeans, stalked
inside, and over to the three TV sets lined against
the wall. He laid the gun down on top of the
nineteen-inch model. The TVs were turned to different channels, but all of their pictures were rolling,
steadily flip-flopping. He reached behind the first
set, adjusting the vertical hold. Holt had found the
flickering TVs irritating too, but she had left them
alone. She had felt guilty enough just being inside.

She watched his back as he fine-tuned the other
sets. Holt slowly uncocked the hammer of her gun.

Danny turned at the tiny metallic sound, glanced

at the purse, then up at her eyes. "Me?" He seemed genuinely hurt. "You're still worried about me? Lady, if I wanted to shoot you, it would have happened a long time ago."

"It's not lady," said Holt, enunciating every word. "It's Detective Holt."

"Are you going to shoot me, Detective Holt?"

"I wasn't cocking my weapon, Mr. DiMedici, I was backing it off. You're the one who walked in armed and dangerous. Now that we've cleared that up, do you know where Michael is?"

"No. Which means something's wrong." Danny stopped in front of the two computers. The scroll-lock keys had been hit so that columns of numbers raced down the screens—fractions, pluses, minuses. A waterfall of prices moving too fast to be understood let alone acted upon. He tapped some keys and the numbers slowed their pace. "Michael's found his spot and you're sitting in it. For him, it's just back and forth to the front gate for supplies, and maybe a quick circuit of the pumping stations once a month to record the output levels. That's it. His jeep is still here and Michael isn't. So something's wrong."

"I see." The case was floating out of Holt's grasp now, disintegrating like a wet newspaper.

"By the way, Detective," Danny said lightly. "Do you have a warrant to be in Michael's house?"

Holt couldn't get away with anything. Maybe that's why she believed so strongly in law and order.

She had knocked on the door and circled the house, looking for Michael Kiel. When she tried the front door again, it swung open. She didn't even have Steiner to blame. She had done it all on her own.

"Sounds like criminal trespass to me," said Danny. "I'm an expert on that charge. That's what you busted me for. You'll probably have to hock your earrings to make bail. I'm really disappointed. You were going to make our world safe from the threat of overdue library books, and now here we are, a couple of outlaws clogging up the courts."

Holt was a second-degree black belt and a volunteer instructor at the Women's Self-Defense Center. She was not a violent individual, but if Mr. DiMedici wasn't careful, she was going to side-kick that smirk right off his face.

"Could we declare a truce, Mr. DiMedici? You've proved your point. If you'd like to file charges with internal affairs, I won't dispute it."

"Somehow, Detective Holt, I can't picture myself dropping a dime on you. We're not on the same side. Nothing's going to change that. But we're not on opposing sides, either."

It was true. There was right and wrong, and there was Danny somewhere else, not part of either, waiting to decide. Steiner had known it all along. It had taken her a little longer. Maybe it was the pained expression on his face when he heard her uncock the pistol. He was offended that she really thought he could harm her.

"I hope you're having better luck locating your ex-wife than I am," said Holt.

Danny didn't say anything, just watched her with

that same half smile. In spite of herself, Holt found herself liking him. Trusting him. Her mother had always told her to keep silent rather than be forced into a lie. Lying was easy. Stillness required character.

He was different now. Holt could tell from his voice, from the way he moved. Confident. Not arrogant, the way he had been in his apartment. He wasn't flailing around or putting up a tough front. He was holding his ground.

"At least tell me where Michael Kiel fits in to this investigation," said Holt. "He's your friend. Why not act like it?"

Danny moved to the coffee table and stood over the open photo album. "I haven't seen these in a long time."

He gazed at the wedding pictures with such a wistful expression that Holt was embarrassed. She wanted to turn away but couldn't take her eyes off him, drawn by the intensity of his longing. His long, tapered fingers glided over the pages, barely touching them. Danny looked up at her, and she felt caught by his eyes.

"I'm sorry about going through the album before. I know it's personal property, but I couldn't stop myself. You all looked so happy."

"We were."

"Your ex-wife is a stunning woman," said Holt. "It's more than being beautiful. No matter who's in the picture, they seem to revolve around her. Even you."

"Have you ever been in love?"

Holt opened her mouth. Closed it. Did Brad count? They still exchanged Christmas cards, but she couldn't even remember what he looked like naked. "No." She nodded at the album. "Not like that."

He smiled at Holt and abruptly closed the album. "Michael's the keeper of the flame—Lauren's Ph.D. thesis, my Smithsonian monograph on the Mayans, every postcard, photograph, and letter. He thinks it keeps us all together. A family portrait. Even if we're not a family anymore."

"My mother does the same thing," said Holt. "She's got all my equestrian medals mounted over the mantelpiece. Right next to the marksmanship awards from the police academy."

"Where does she keep the deb ball photo? You know the one. You're wearing something pale blue and strapless. Grandmère's pearls around your neck and a freckly WASP on your arm."

Holt looked surprised. "It was pale yellow." She shook her head. She hadn't even told Steiner about being a debutante. "It's hanging above my father's desk in the library. He said that was the last time he really understood me."

The two of them sat there on the couch, their knees touching. The room was so quiet Holt could hear the waves crashing on the beach. They were entering unexplored terrain, and neither of them wanted to move too fast.

"So how *is* Karl, anyway?" Danny said at last.

"He's going to be fine. I wanted to thank you for that, for what you did."

"First time I ever kissed a cop. Tell Karl I want a date as soon as he gets better."

"It's the eroticism of the badge." Holt laughed and ran her fingers through her hair. "Works every time."

"I know what you mean." Danny's eyes dropped to the closed photo album and he cleared his throat. "Did you see Lurp when you drove up?"

"Lurp?"

"Michael's dog, a big black Lab. Kind of cute. Kind of stupid." He got up and went out on the front porch. "Lurp!" he called. "Here, boy!"

"Maybe Michael took him for a walk," said Holt, joining him. "That would explain everything."

"No." Danny walked toward the face of the bluff and stopped at the edge. The waves boiled over the rocks below. Clouds of mist rolled up the sides, tickling their faces.

Holt stood next to Danny, the wind whipping her dress up, trying to understand what they were looking for. "Do you think he jumped?" Her thick red hair swirled around her face, glinting in the afternoon light.

Danny started walking again, then bent and picked up something in the weeds. He held up a dog collar, cursing. The wind carried the words away before she could hear what he had said. They moved along the cliff line, walking faster now, intermittently glancing over the edge. Holt didn't ask him any more questions.

They stopped at a scraggly eucalyptus tree that grew half over the edge, its trunk contorted by the constant wind. Danny hung on to the tree, looking down.

She didn't see it at first.

A large black dog dangled from a length of wire twisted around the base of the tree. Holt could see the dog's eyes bulging out, blood smeared across his muzzle, a foam of blood that had bubbled out his nose and dried. The wire was looped around his neck, a slipknot drawn so tight that it cut through the short fur and exposed raw flesh. It looked like he was wearing a pink collar. The poor thing must have struggled for a long time, the wire noose getting tighter and tighter as he fought. There were deep gouges torn from the sandy face of the cliff where he had tried to scratch his way up.

Danny straddled the tree. He braced himself against the trunk but slid toward the edge as he began to pull the dog up. Holt walked over and stood behind him, leaning into his shoulders, holding him down.

"It's just a damn dog," Danny said, his dark eyes wet. "I don't need any help."

Holt stayed right where she was.

The back of Danny's head pressed against Holt as he slowly dragged the dog back up the cliff face, hand over hand. She could feel the hard muscles in his shoulders and arms as she pushed down on him, keeping him from slipping over the edge. The wind billowed her dress as they worked. Danny turned his head to wipe away the sweat and grazed her thighs with his cheek. They both pretended not to notice.

CHAPTER 33

THIS MIKE PECKERHEAD made Lloyd mad. And Boyd had that look like he was showing himself slasher movies in his head every time he saw the guy. Mike peckerhead had let Spiderman snatch him so easy that Uncle Arthur decided the twins were lazy and stupid. Like it was their fault.

They had *tried* finding Mike peckerhead's dopey house a couple days ago and gotten lost in the oil field, driving around all confused, like rats in Uncle Arthur's maze game where he kept moving the cheese out of reach. Each time Lloyd bottomed out the Corvette on the twisty road, Boyd screamed at him, finally getting so frustrated he leaped out of the car, snapped off the antenna, and flailed the windshield until it cracked. They didn't talk the whole way back to Uncle Arthur's.

Spiderman cheated. He distracted them, sent them off to pick up that little greaser, Cubanito, then went for Mike peckerhead himself. Spiderman didn't care that it was pitch-dark out there in the middle of nowhere. He sneaked up on Mike peckerhead, wearing a pair of those DEA night goggles that made him look like the Fly, then sprayed knockout juice in the guy's air conditioner. Big deal. He and Boyd could have done it too, but Spiderman didn't pass around his toys. Not since they got sand in his parabolic microphone and then washed it off in the ocean.

The worst thing about Mike peckerhead was that Uncle Arthur liked him. You'd have thought they were old pals. Raggedy-ass Mike peckerhead telling Uncle Arthur war stories about living in the jungle for months, not taking a bath either, and eating bugs that probably didn't have enough B vitamins. Uncle Arthur laughed his real laugh, too. He told Mike peckerhead about these nasty little booby traps the African bushman made, even drawing them out to show him. Uncle Arthur was probably going to adopt him and make Lloyd and Boyd call him Uncle Mike peckerhead.

Through the thick glass window, the twins could see Uncle Arthur and Mike peckerhead in the secure lab, the one with the stacks of petri dishes and all the shiny ductwork that sucked away the bad germs. They wore the baggy white contamination suits with gloves and clear plastic hoods, like spacemen with air hoses running down their backs. Uncle Arthur leaned over the fat binocular microscope on the lab table, hood to hood with Mike peckerhead, explaining something to him. Even from where he was standing, Lloyd could tell that Uncle Arthur was all puffed up and proud. Lloyd hated the secure lab. The jumpsuits were tight on him, the air tasted funny, and the lab was filled with equipment he didn't understand.

"Hey, Junior." Boyd tapped Lloyd on the back. He held up one of Uncle Arthur's bell jars. The fetus inside stared back. "How 'bout a little milkshake?" Boyd jiggled the jar. The fetus bounced around inside, its tiny head making soft sounds against the glass.

Uncle Arthur's jars always made Lloyd sad. He didn't know why.

Boyd shook the bell jar to a froth, holding it high overhead. Uncle Arthur and Mike peckerhead were still bent over the microscope, Uncle Arthur with a stainless steel needle probe in his hand. Boyd shook the bell jar at the lab window, barely able to restrain himself. The formaldehyde was turning pink.

"Don't." Lloyd spat. "We'll get in trouble."

The bell jar shattered in Boyd's grip, spraying them both with glass and bits of rubbery flesh.

"Uh-uh." Boyd's hands were bleeding, and pink glop dripped from his short blond hair.

Uncle Arthur glared at them from the secure lab. Mike peckerhead just stood there, his mouth hanging open. The lab window must have been really strong. Otherwise, it would have melted from the look Uncle Arthur was giving them.

The phone rang. Lloyd grabbed it, turning himself slightly so he wouldn't have to see Uncle Arthur. "Hello."

"I'd like to speak to Michael Kiel," a woman said.

"He's busy," said Lloyd.

"This is Lauren Kiel."

"Wow." Lloyd meant it. He waved the phone at Uncle Arthur and switched on the intercom extension in both the outer lab and the secure lab. "Here's Uncle Arthur."

"Dr. Reese?" said the woman.

"Miss Kiel, how nice to hear from you."

"Hi, Lauren," said Mike peckerhead. "Thanks for calling back." He had left a message on her service, giving Uncle Arthur's phone number.

"Michael," she said. "Are you all right?"

"So far so good." Mike peckerhead glanced at Uncle Arthur. "Lauren? Would you call Danny and tell him to drive out to my place and feed Lurp? Dog chow's under the porch."

"Sure."

"He likes to have a little warm beer poured on top," said Mike peckerhead. "It softens it up."

Boyd walked over to the lab, smacked the glass, and left a bloody handprint. "Come on out and play," he said to Mike peckerhead.

Uncle Arthur waved Boyd away. "Miss Kiel, since we each have something that the other wants, I'd like to discuss a trade." She didn't say anything. Just static on the line. "Miss Kiel? I've become very fond of your brother. He's more than a smart businessman. I can work with him. And if you knew me better, you'd realize what a compliment that is."

"I'm sure he's glowing with pride, Dr. Reese."

"Indeed. Still, much as I value his friendship, I must insist on the return of my property. Both as a medical doctor committed to alleviating suffering and as an injured party demanding justice."

"I sympathize, Doctor. Perhaps, we can negotiate a solution."

"That's very kind of you. Miss Kiel, I'm using a safe phone, and Michael has assured me that you're just as cautious. So perhaps we can speak plainly. You have Dr. Tohlson's notes on our experiments. Those computer disks are my property. *My* property, Miss Kiel. I'd like your assurance that they're undamaged and that they haven't been put on the market."

"An admission like that could only exacerbate any legal problems I might be facing concerning Dr. Tohlson's unfortunate accident."

"Lauren," Mike peckerhead interrupted. "Just for the sake of argument, let's say you have the disks." His eyes darted from side to side, like the greaser's when Lloyd gave him the last lift off with the barbell. "Why don't we give Dr. Reese an opportunity to present his offer?" Lloyd had kind of liked Cubanito. The little guy was scared and sweaty, but the way he still sang the can-do song, even at the end, was real Rambo. This Mike peckerhead was sweating now, but he wasn't singing. He was on his own as far as Lloyd was concerned.

"Fine, Michael. I'm waiting for your offer, Dr. Reese."

"I'd like to reunite you with your brother." Uncle Arthur stabbed the needle probe against the black marble lab table, snapping it in half. "I'm a great believer in family."

"Yes, you certainly must," she laughed. "I remember your two nephews very well."

What the heck did that mean?

"Return the notes, and I'll return your brother. I can also see to it that someone else is indicted for Tohlson's murder. Your ex-husband is the most likely candidate."

"Oh, Dr. Reese, that's so reassuring. I feel strongly, however, that some sort of cash settlement is indicated, in addition."

Uncle Arthur crooked his finger, and Lloyd scooted back to the desk in the far corner of the outer lab. Uncle Arthur kept the Polaroids in an envelope in the top drawer. He let the twins look at them as much as they wanted, but they weren't allowed to take them out of the room.

"When you last saw Dr. Tohlson," said Uncle Arthur, "was he in full possession of his genitals?" Uncle Arthur was smiling again, but Mike peckerhead didn't look so good. Maybe he was starting to realize it wasn't so easy being Uncle Arthur's friend.

"I beg your pardon?" she said.

Uncle Arthur waved Lloyd over. Lloyd riffed through the Polaroids, picking out the best ones.

"I'm afraid that the good doctor had a little . . . accident after you so abruptly left."

Mike peckerhead stood by the lab window, right next to Boyd's bloody handprint, watching as Lloyd held up the Polaroids to him, one after the other. Mike peckerhead sagged against the glass, eyes closed.

"Michael," said Uncle Arthur. "Would you please attest to the doctor's condition? I'm not sure she could hear you. Perhaps you wouldn't mind repeating yourself, considering the importance to all concerned."

Mike peckerhead hung on to the table, his legs going bouncy-bouncy-bouncy. "They castrated him." He sounded like somebody crumpled his voice up and tossed it in a wastebasket.

"I wish I could take credit for the idea," said Uncle Arthur, "but the kudos belong to McVey. Do you remember him? McVey's a very creative fellow, a man who pushes the limit of his authority. But then I allow my key personnel a certain autonomy. It's the price you pay when you hire good people. I must confess, when McVey showed me what he had done to Tohlson's body, I was annoyed. I felt he had overstepped himself. Now, I see the wisdom of his action. The police just want to charge someone with the killing, Miss Kiel. I can assure you, they do not care who gets credit. Nor do I."

"I'm listening."

"Yes, I'm sure you are. All the police have is circumstantial evidence and a few obvious suspects." Uncle Arthur put his arm around Mike peckerhead's shoulders. The guy tried to pull away, but Uncle Arthur hung on. "Don't worry, Mike. I like you just the way you are."

"Your point, Dr. Reese?"

"All I have to do is say the word and Tohlson's balls end up in Mr. DiMedici's freezer, right next to the ground sirloin. Pretty incriminating, don't you think? It's a fine freezer, Miss Kiel, plenty of room. McVey already checked it out. Checked out the closets, too. The police can be very thorough once their noses are pointed in the proper direction. Why not make it easy on them? Make it easy on all of us."

It sounded like Miss Kiel was humming to herself.

"You should be able to concoct a plausible story for your disappearance," said Uncle Arthur. "I'm afraid Mr. DiMedici will have a more difficult time of it. I'm sure you can see the police report now: the jealous ex-husband; the new lover; a violent confrontation. You flee for your life, terrified, hysterical." Silence. "Miss Kiel?"

"I'm thinking."

"Don't." Mike peckerhead's face was white and blotchy. "Not for me, Lauren."

Uncle Arthur patted Mike peckerhead on the back. "It's a little bit bigger than that. Right, Miss Kiel? No heroes under the microscope, are there?"

"No heroes anywhere," she said. "This does add a new factor to the equation."

"I thought it would. Yes, I rather thought it would. But then you're used to thinking on your feet, aren't you? 'Mastering a Shifting Business Climate.' That was the title of one of your lectures, wasn't it?"

"I'll call you at this number tonight or tomorrow morning," she said. "I'll want to speak with Michael at that time, too."

"Don't keep me in suspense, Miss Kiel, *pretty*

please." Uncle Arthur cackled wildly. "Please, Miss Kiel, *pretty please?*"

It was amazing. Uncle Arthur sounded just like Dr. Tohlson had when he was begging Miss Kiel to stop hurting him. Lloyd and Boyd had listened with the parabolic microphone until they got disgusted, then turned on the tape recorder and went for a walk on the beach. It had been like that the whole weekend. Dr. Tohlson would whine, "Pretty please," and Miss Kiel would laugh and let him go. Then they'd start up again later. Bore-ing. The tape recordings were lousy, all pops and hisses. Uncle Arthur's imitation was better than the real thing.

"*Pretty please?*"

The dial tone buzzed. Uncle Arthur winked at the twins through the glass and gave a high five to Boyd's bloody handprint that shook the glass.

CHAPTER 34

SOMEONE WAS FOLLOWING HIM. Danny felt it at the back of his head, like standing beside an aquarium, turning around and seeing the trigger fish staring. He veered onto the freeway entrance ramp, punched the Mustang, and cut across three lanes of traffic, his neck slapping against the headrest. He got off in three exits, barreled down the back alleys of the darkened industrial district, then pulled behind a concrete abutment and waited for ten minutes with his lights off, engine idling. Nothing.

Danny hit the freeway going in the opposite direction, driving to where the *Queen Mary* was docked in Long Beach harbor, his eyes flicking between the road and the rearview. If they were still with him, they were too good to shake.

Some leisure-industry corporation had bought the *Queen Mary*, sailed it into the harbor, and turned what had once been the grandest luxury liner in the world into a British-theme shopping mall. Red triple-decker buses shuttled tourists to scenic spots in the harbor, and even the yawning, surf-blond parking lot attendant said, "Thanks, guv," when he took Danny's five dollars. The lower decks were a jumble of fish-and-chips take-out joints, T-shirt shops selling shirts picturing Queen Elizabeth with a mohawk, and upscale stores where you could buy handknit sweaters and alpaca scarves.

Lauren had said she'd meet him on the upper deck, outside the Mayfair Pub. It was the most expensive restaurant on the *Queen Mary*, an imitation London chop house, mahogany-paneled and dark. The Mayfair specialized in good service, overcooked food, and walls lined with oil paintings of ugly, wan-faced men in ruffled collars.

"Lovely suit," said Lauren from behind him, "but the gun ruins the line." Danny turned, reflexively patting the bulge in his right pocket. "Aren't you supposed to be wearing a shoulder holster or something?" she said, her mouth moist and mocking in the subdued light.

"I loaned mine to James Bond." Danny remembered Cubanito showing off a spring-loaded quick-draw holster. "Think fast, sucker!" Cubanito had said, reaching into his jacket. Danny had taken him to the emergency room with flash burns in the armpit.

Lauren took his arm as they walked toward the reservations desk, kissed him on the lower lip, a lingering kiss that threatened to become a bite. The other people waiting cleared their throats and looked at their shoes.

The maître d' of the Mayfair ran his bony finger down the list of reservations, dismissing the couple standing in front of him with a sniff. "Forty-five minutes." He was a stumpy man with stained incisors and a nasal pukka accent. Liverpool pretending to Regency Park. He snapped to attention as Danny and Lauren approached, inclined his head at her. Danny didn't blame him.

Lauren wore a black silk sheath cut well off her shoulders, so the graceful delicacy of her neck and back were accented. A diamond necklace brushed the tops of her rounded breasts. Her hair was a blond bob tonight, perfect curls framing her high cheekbones.

"Table for two," oozed the maître d'. "Right this way, madam."

Danny and Lauren followed the maître d' on a winding route through the room. The men sneaked glances at Lauren, covering their interest by sipping drinks or turning to cough. The other women weren't fooled. Danny could hear the sharp metallic clinking of forks on china plates, a staccato accompaniment to their passing. Lauren hummed softly to herself, taking her time.

The black dress rustled as she walked, hot and electric, the side slit playing peekaboo with her long, smooth legs. He had bought the necklace for her on their first anniversary, thirty-six matched two-carat blue-white diamonds. It took the jewelry clerk ten minutes to count his way through the neat stacks of currency Danny dropped onto the counter. The clerk pursed his lips as his fingers flew. When he finished, he counted it again.

The maître d' stood beside a window table overlooking the harbor and pulled out Lauren's chair for her. Danny sat so that he could see the whole room, close enough to her that they wouldn't be overheard. "You own this place?"

Lauren fixed him with her arctic blue eyes. "Every way but financially."

"Sir Winston Prime Rib? White Cliffs of Dover Sole?" Danny read from the leather-backed menu, shaking his head. "Lady Godiva Veal Chops?" He tossed the menu aside. "Very chic."

"That's why I selected it." Candlelight flickered across Lauren's face. "We'll never run into anyone we know here. Besides, they shoot fireworks off the stern at nine P.M. and I know how you like skyrockets."

The waiter brought champagne and a silver ice bucket. He had perfect posture and four chins, uncorking the bottle with a practiced twist. At least he wasn't giddy with false enthusiasm over the specials and didn't feel the need to introduce himself. Danny mentally doubled the man's tip, ordered a dozen oysters for an appetizer and a couple of very rare steaks.

Danny waited until the waiter hustled away, then took Lauren's hand. "I've got bad news."

Lauren picked up her crystal champagne flute. "Michael's disappeared." She took a sip.

"Okay," said Danny, annoyed. "As usual you're a couple of steps ahead of me. If you know Michael's gone, you must also know where he is."

Lauren fingered the diamonds at the base of her throat. "He's been . . . picked up. It's his own fault." She tossed her head. "I told him to go away for a while, but you know Michael."

Danny knocked her hand away from the diamonds. "Look at me. Last night on the beach, the stars came out. You want an affidavit, I'll sign it. But it's twenty-four hours later and we've both got our clothes on. Where's Michael?"

She stuck her tongue out at him. For that instant she was sixteen again. Sweet sixteen. She was at a slumber party, sitting cross-legged on a canopy bed in a shorty nightie, smoking clove cigarettes with her girlfriends and telling penis jokes.

"I'm still waiting for an answer."

"Michael's being held by Tohlson's former employer, Dr. Arthur Reese," she said. "They were working on a project together and Tohlson kept his notes on computer disks. Dr. Reese thinks I've got them."

"Which, of course, you do."

"As a matter of fact, I do." Lauren's hand arced through the candle flame, making the light dance. "Tohlson was a world-class researcher. A man with severe personality disorders but a brilliant scientist. Anyway"—she shrugged—"Dr. Reese wants to exchange Michael for Tohlson's computer disks."

Danny followed Lauren's gaze out of the window at the charter boat *Bonita* churning alongside. It was brightly lit and overloaded, a party boat tonight, filled with sales executives pretending to be fishermen and deckhands who had to bait their hooks for them. Pennants flapped in the wind as the *Bonita* headed toward deep water, waves crashing over the bow. The bluefish were running, great schools of them, all muscle and teeth, with scales like straight razors and never more dangerous than when they were gaffed. Danny could see the novice anglers lurching across the crowded deck in their new nylon jackets, drinks in hand, toasting the *Queen Mary*.

Danny imagined the charter boat floating dead in the water at daybreak, deserted, fishing poles snapped in two, teeth marks on the bulwarks. Score one for Moby Dick.

"Do it," he said, turning away from the window. "Make the trade. Give him the computer disks, and get Michael out of there."

"Tomorrow," said Lauren. "If you come with me." Danny nodded assent. "Good," said Lauren. "Oh, by the way, Michael asked for you to feed Lurp."

"Lurp's not hungry anymore." Danny's voice cracked. He saw the dog as a puppy, all feet and ears, tucked into the warmth of his jacket as he drove out to Michael's. Saw him again as he had looked a few hours ago, a bag of black hair being dragged up the side of the cliff. Danny remembered the feel of Holt's strong hands on his shoulders steadying him. He had been wrong about her. Add it to the list.

Lauren watched his face and nodded. "I see." She glanced around the room, then seemed embarrassed that he had caught her. The waiter arrived, oysters on the half-shell fanned out on a bed of crushed ice and lemon wedges. Lauren picked up an oyster with her long fingers, the gnarly shell contrasting with her flawless skin. "Aren't you hungry?"

Danny shook his head.

"This kidnapping business is ridiculous," said Lauren. "Dr. Reese could have simply told Michael what he wanted and what he was willing to pay for the disks. He could afford it. There was no need to be so melodramatic."

"Maybe he liked Tohlson. Maybe he doesn't believe in paying for something he already owns. It happens. Emotions are such unpredictable things."

"Not for the professional." Lauren fiddled with another oyster.

"What kind of professional are you? Your whole operation's out of control. Michael's been snatched. And Tohlson. . . . How's Tohlson supposed to feed you inside information now—channeling?"

"That was an . . . accident."

"Didn't Michael tell you? I was at your house. I saw the mess you made."

Lauren's eyes glinted in the candlelight.

"I *saw* what you did."

"What makes you think I did it?" Lauren pouted. "It could have been anyone. It could have been you. You're the expert on killing. Not me."

Danny wanted to slap her.

"Look, we were engaged in mutual role-playing that night," she said. "Don't expect an apology."

"I guess apologies don't suit you," Danny said. She licked the oyster liquor from her lips, then saw him watching and laughed at the expression on his face.

The first time they made love, she had reached between her legs and tasted him with the same eager curiosity. He had laid his head on her belly, exhausted, felt the rise and fall of her breathing while she stroked his hair. He told her a story, her first story.

"I thought you were gone," she said. Her eyes were wet. "I thought I had lost you forever."

"You lost me?" Danny said incredulously. "Who left who?"

"You don't know." She sighed. "You were so different after the farmhouse. Full of doubts and equivocations, just like the rest of them, like the nothing people. I'd wake up in the middle of the night and find you curled up next to me crying in your sleep."

"A killing leaves a hole in things," he said, reaching over and taking her hand.

"I want the old Danny back," she said. Her fingernails dug into him. "I want the Danny who doesn't question his actions, doesn't explain himself."

"You're scared." The realization shocked him. "That's it, isn't it?"

"I thought you'd be able to handle this," said Lauren. Her necklace trembled, the diamonds flashing with color torn from the candlelight.

"I don't blame you for being scared," said Danny, "*I'm* scared. You're in over your head, and everyone close is getting pulled in, too."

Lauren's face hardened. "Then walk away," she said quietly.

His eyes slid down to her breasts. She always put a dab of perfume between them. He used to watch her from bed after they had made love, watch her sit at her vanity, still nude, and brush her hair. It was longer in those days, falling across her shoulders and down her back. She would cup her breasts, barely overflowing her hands, smiling at him in the mirror, knowing he was watching. Then she'd reapply the perfume with a slow caress of her index finger and come back to bed.

"I can't," he said quietly. "We have to get Michael back."

CHAPTER 35

DANNY AND LAUREN strolled along the upper deck of
the *Queen Mary*, the red and green lights blinking
atop the offshore oil platforms.

They were alone in the cool night air. Lauren laid
her head on his shoulder as they stood in front of the
plateglass window, looking into the main lounge,
listening to a torch song from the forties or fifties,
all saxes and clarinets. Middle-aged couples danced
in the smoky room, a mirror ball slowly revolving
overhead.

The dancers shuffled against each other, gray-
haired and awkward, chasing the rhythms of their
youth without much success. One couple was different. He wore a plaid jacket. She had too many
ruffles. They didn't care. They danced in perfect
harmony, his hand on her waist, hers resting on
his upper arm. They moved like they were the only
ones in the room, moved in a bubble of soft light.

I need your love so badly,
I love you oh so madly,
But I don't stand a ghost of a chance with you.

The saxophones came up, and Danny tucked his arms around Lauren. He had wished that someday they would be like the couple. Getting old together, the passion still there, so closely attuned that they could dance without music.

I thought at last I'd found you,
But other loves surround you,
I don't stand a ghost of a chance with you.

The couple beamed. They had been dancing together for decades. They were as smooth and polished as the spoons nestling in the wife's silver drawer. The man spun the woman under the mirror ball; they dipped and smiled at each other. Oh yeah, they still had it.

If you'd surrender, for a tender kiss or two,
You might discover, that I'm the lover,
Meant for you, and I'll be true.

Lauren looked at him. "What is it?"
"Nothing."
The couple bowed to each other as the song ended, walked back to their table holding hands.
"You were sighing," said Lauren.
"There's a lot to sigh about. We're standing outside watching the people inside having a good time."

Danny checked her reflection in the glass. "What I want to know is how *you* ended up running from the cops. That was supposed to be my job." She walked over and leaned against the railing, stared across the harbor. He followed.

"It's a long story."

"Long stories," said Danny. "That's my job, too. I've got to talk to my union."

Lauren turned to face him. "I did it for you. Satisfied?"

"You murdered Tohlson for me? It's a little early for my birthday."

"I'm cold," said Lauren, and Danny put his arms around her. "*Murder* is not the operative word," she said.

"He's dead, Lauren."

"You don't understand the mechanisms of paraphilia."

"I'll survive." Alongside the *Queen Mary*, Danny could see the aluminum geodesic dome housing the *Spruce Goose*, the gigantic wooden airplane designed by Howard Hughes. A tourist trap now. Hughes flew it only once, piloted it over the white caps on a bright, clear morning forty years ago, just to prove the point to a doubting press. Bigger than a Boeing 747, the *Goose* lay trapped forever, a dinosaur in a glacier, safe from the elements and the open sky.

"Tohlson liked being laced into a corset until he turned blue," said Lauren. "He liked being walked on a leash. Most of all, he wanted to be strung up and hung by the neck until he passed out. It's called autoerotic hanging in the professional literature.

Cutting off the blood supply to the brain evidently gives the most intense orgasm imaginable. I wish you could have seen his face."

"I saw the room," said Danny. "That was enough."

"We were so high that night." Lauren drifted with the memory, closing her eyes with pleasure. "Tohlson had wonderful dope. If it wasn't in stock, he cooked it up himself. Pharmaceutical coke. Acid. A ketamine derivative." The wind lifted her hair, raised goosebumps across her bare arms. "You ever do ketamine? No? You'd like it."

"Between the drugs and Tohlson's cooperation, you could cop to manslaughter," said Danny. "With your record and the right lawyer, you'd pull two or three years at a minimum-security country club, max. Maybe even probation."

"That's what Michael said." Lauren swayed to the faint music from the lounge. "Mr. Percentage Player."

"Michael's a smart guy," said Danny. The coastline stretched out beyond the harbor, a string of light and darkness meandering all the way to the tip of South America. He and Michael could stand at the edge of Tierra del Fuego and drive golf balls toward Antarctica. With a tailwind and a good roll, they could scare some penguins.

Lauren's voice dropped to a whisper. "Tohlson was trussed up like a chicken and talking baby talk. God save me from the ones who think they're bad little boys." She shook her head. "I took off my panties and stuffed them in his mouth to shut him up. He finally got hard." She giggled.

The sky over the harbor exploded red and purple, skyrockets bursting into streamers, a steady barrage that lit the night and bathed Lauren's face in red light, now yellow, now red again.

"I remember asking myself what it would take to bring you back," said Lauren wistfully. "And there was Tohlson, dangling from the ceiling, slowly twisting as he struggled. Because of the drugs, I was exploring a different moral and logical universe. I decided that if it was blood that took you away from me, then it was blood that would bring you back."

"We're drowning in blood. Don't you see?"

"You've got to consider context," Lauren said. "Didn't you teach me that? Now, you stand out here and think it's all plain and simple, but in that room, on that night, it made sense."

Danny looked down at the water and watched the reflection of the fireworks boiling overhead. Wilson stared back at him from the explosions, Wilson standing there in the farmhouse with his hands up, saying, "Don't do it, slick, you'll never forgive yourself." The fat man's sneer turning startled as Danny emptied the Mac-10 into his chest, making the hula girls dance on his Hawaiian shirt, a shimmy of right and wrong, good and bad. In that room, on that morning, it had made sense.

Lauren was right. They crossed a moral landscape without boundaries or markings. The maps didn't match the terrain, but there was nothing else to go by.

"That night"—she looked directly at Danny—"I was Ixtab, goddess of ropes and snares."

Danny nodded.

"I always think about you when I'm blasted out of my skull," said Lauren. "You taught me about Ixtab. Archaeology three-oh-one, Sacred Sites of the Classic Maya. Our summer expedition to Copán. I can still see you in the ceremonial chamber, torches flickering on the walls. You were so dramatic."

A skyrocket flashed across the night. Before the darkness returned, Danny thought he saw a gangly shape pressed against the upper deck. He reached for his gun.

"What is it?" said Lauren.

Another flash, this time yellow, a volley of roman candles drifting slowly, illuminating the scene for seconds before fading into black. There was nothing there. "Go on," said Danny. He kept his hand on the gun, waiting for the next skyrocket.

"Is everything okay?" said Lauren.

"No," said Danny. "But that never stopped us before."

Lauren tossed her head. "You wore little khaki shorts and lectured the class on Ixtab, the most powerful goddess in the Mayan pantheon, Ixtab, the one true lover of the young corn god. You said that the Mayans sacrificed a male child to her to ensure a good harvest, said they hung him and bled him drop by drop while he slowly strangled. You said it was an honor for him." She brushed his cheek with her lips.

Danny wished he were surprised. Ignorance was the best excuse he had for being here, and even that didn't hold up. He had known when he stood in

Lauren's living room what had happened. Blackened blood crunching underfoot, splatters across the walls. He just didn't know why.

"Ancient history," Danny choked out. He felt his heart plummet through him and into the black water below. "You killed Tohlson for nothing. You killed *us*."

"But you are back." Lauren kissed him hard, tore the breath from him. "The real Danny. My Danny," she sobbed, the happiness overwhelming her.

The real Danny. She was right. He had changed in just the last few days. The terrible part was that she had changed, too.

"I've missed you so," she murmured into his chest while he stroked her hair, unable to stop himself. "All the ones in between . . . important men with important plans." Her fingers clawed at him. "They didn't fool me, not for a minute."

"Hush," he said, her hair soft and sweet against his cheek.

"You know," she said gently, "at the end, when he had reached decathexis and knew he was dying, Tohlson started to cry." She looked up at Danny. "He cried blood. Big red tears running down his cheeks." She laid her head back against him. "He was so tired of living. Don't feel sorry for him."

"I feel sorry for us."

The old couple was back under the mirror ball, dancing closer now, a lace handkerchief between their clasped hands. Danny envied them. He and Lauren weren't going to grow old together. They had had their chance and lost it. Danny held her. He didn't know what else to do.

They danced together on the upper deck, cheek to cheek, hardly moving.

"Once upon a time," Danny whispered in her ear and she sobbed and nuzzled him closer, "once upon a time, a man went for a midnight swim and got caught in a current that took him far out to sea, a riptide that carried him round and round so that he didn't know where he was anymore. The stars were gone. He couldn't see lights on the shore. In the darkness, he heard the voice of the woman he loved calling him. And he swam toward the voice. After what seemed like hours, he stopped. Treading water, trying to get his wind back, he waited. He heard her voice again, urging him forward. He didn't know if he was headed toward shore or further out to sea, but he followed her voice."

Skyrockets erupted in a climax of red and yellow and blue, the grande finale, roman candles trailing sparks into the sea.

"Mmmm, that was a good one." Lauren was warm against his neck as the sky went black again. A foghorn sounded in the distance. Danny squeezed her even tighter against the night.

CHAPTER 36

LAUREN STRETCHED HER LEGS and laid her high heels on the dash of the white Jaguar sedan. She had to bunch the tight black cocktail dress to do it. The tips of her heels dug into the leather as she pivoted on them, aiming her toes first at Danny, then out the side window at the lights rushing past, then back at Danny, keeping time to her own rhythm.

She cracked the window, felt the night air tickle her thighs, and hummed softly to herself, remembering the cool breeze off the ocean and Tohlson's body swinging from the ceiling. She had stood in the doorway of the beach house, blood sprayed across her face, her skin tight in the moonlight. Far down the beach, she heard two men yelling at each other.

She stayed in the doorway, wondering if McVey was out there, waiting for her to take a shower, turn out all the lights. She trembled on the edge of panic, so close to being caught that she hung on to the curtains, the fabric bunching in her fists. McVey didn't show. She was almost disappointed.

"What are you thinking about?" said Danny.

Lauren looked over at him and smiled. "Just how much I love you."

The passing headlights played across Danny's handsome features, lit his long eyelashes and strong jaw. He was tired, fatigue etched into his face, but there was no slack to him. He was all there, every bit of him. He glanced over at Lauren, then back at the highway, guiding them through the traffic with barely perceptible movements of his body.

Lauren watched the night sky through the sun-roof. "When this whole business is over, why don't we take a trip to Europe? We could blast down the autobahn in one of those big Mercedes 560SLs with smoked glass."

"Let's see how the next twenty-four hours go."

She pressed herself into the leather seat. "No speed limit on the autobahn, Danny. It's every man for himself." On the edge of the horizon, a shooting star flashed and died.

The townhouse was in Irvine, inland from Newport Beach, a gated complex with a man-made lake and manicured trees. Like everything else he owned, Michael had bought it sight unseen, carrying it on the books of one of his shell corporations.

Danny and Lauren pulled up to the double garage of the townhouse, and she keyed the five-digit security number on the remote. He drummed his fingers on the steering wheel as the heavy garage door slowly opened. "No one knows about this place," she said as the garage door opened. "Or the Jaguar, either." He pulled in and turned off the car. "Cash in the dresser. Three different passports in the nightstand. Golf clubs in the closet. Michael was always expecting an emergency."

Danny just paced around Tohlson's ugly beige BMW parked in the other side of the garage. She had to take the BMW from her beach house, since, as usual, he had blocked the driveway. She drove the back roads to the townhouse, drove barefoot, drenched with blood.

Danny opened the door of the BMW and gingerly stuck his head in, wrinkled his nose as the ammonia smell hit.

"Cleaned up pretty well, didn't it?" she called. Most of the mess was on the BMW's sheepskin seat covers and driver's-side custom floor mat. Yesterday she had sat crosslegged in the loft, eating a bowl of fresh raspberries while she watched the garbage truck haul away the black Hefty bags.

Every light in the townhouse was on when they walked in: the overheads, floor lamps, table lamps, even the gooseneck next to the couch.

"I don't like being alone in the dark, okay?" Lauren said in response to the knowing look he gave her. She kicked off her shoes and headed for the bathroom, her dress dropping onto the living room floor, the diamond necklace tossed onto the dress. She felt his eyes sliding over her hips.

She had just eased into the bubble bath when he came in, put the lid down on the toilet, and sat next to the tub. "You never called out from this line, did you?" he said. "Never received one here from Michael?"

"Don't be foolish." The soap made sudsy sounds up and down her outstretched legs. She still did a ballet barre one hour a day, every day. "Every call is scrambled through an intermediary service and relayed on. Michael thinks of everything."

"Yeah, well, everything Michael thought of wasn't enough to save himself; the line of joints on his coffee table wasn't even disturbed. Early this morning someone was in my apartment. I can't prove it, but it happened."

She added more hot water as he talked, turning the tap with her toe. She needed a pedicure.

"Turn yourself in," pronounced Danny. You'd have thought it was up to him. "Cop to involuntary manslaughter. Knowing you, you'll get a suspended sentence, teach inner city kids to read or something."

She soaped her breasts, her eyes half closed.

"Listen to me." Danny leaned closer. "This exchange thing you're planning isn't some blue-chip merger where everybody sits around a walnut table with a prospectus and takes turns speaking. Are you listening? We haven't got a backup. It's just you and me and Michael stuck in the middle."

A strand of iridescent bubbles looped across her breasts, rimming her pink nipples at the water line. She dripped a handful of warm water down her throat, washing the soapy necklace away. "I've got another orange in the refrigerator," she teased, remembering last night and the juice running everywhere. Danny shook his head, and she knew he meant it. "Well then, why don't you climb in and do my back?"

"I'm out of practice."

"Don't underestimate yourself."

He walked out, quietly closing the door behind him. She settled deeper into the tub and closed her eyes, the water lapping at the back of her head. She *had* missed him. All the ones since Danny had been too easy, eager to tell her everything, desperate to prove what big, important men they were.

Tohlson was the worst. He'd lie there in bed waving his bony wrists, bleating about how his research was going to rewrite the textbooks and win him a Nobel Prize. Lauren was the one who suggested he would be better off leaving Reese Pharmaceuticals and setting up his own facility. She could raise the money. As much as he needed. All he had to do was provide the details of his experiments, complete work-ups that she could present to her investors. Poor Tohlson. He should have tatooed a target on his heart.

Lauren had gotten carried away back at the beach house. She'd be the first to admit that. Michael had just wanted the computer disks. She didn't need to kill Tohlson. That was clearly excessive. It was just that once she started, the act took on a momentum all its own.

"Why would you do that?" Michael had said when she called to tell him about Tohlson, his voice so soft and sad she could hardly hear him. "Why? Things were going so well."

When Lauren got out of the tub, most of the lights in the townhouse were off. She walked into the bedroom, patting herself dry. Danny was curled up in bed, his back to her. She didn't like that at all.

She dropped the towel and slid into bed. "You're not sleeping, are you?" she whispered into his ear. "I thought after last night . . . I thought we could begin all over." He didn't say a word. "You always hold a little bit of yourself back from me." She pouted. "Just enough to keep me interested." She touched his cheek and he pulled away. "You're upset."

"I'm not upset." His dark eyes drove into her. "It's a lot worse than that."

"Tohlson got me high. Why does everyone blame me? Michael is the same way."

Danny shook his head. "I've been high. I never punched holes in a guy until he bled to death."

"You're tired," she snapped, getting out of bed. When he didn't say anything, she went into the living room and stood in front of the picture window, still nude, watching the rain howl across the artificial lake.

After a while, she looked in on Danny. He was already asleep, one leg pulled up under him. Lost in his own dreams. She thought about the morning she awoke to find him laughing in their bedroom doorway, his arms filled with purple orchids and hundred-dollar bills. Before she could say a word, he flung them into the air. The two of them made love, crushing the perfumed blossoms while hundreds of Ben Franklins watched.

More than anything, Lauren wanted Danny to look at her the way he had with the flowers raining down, wanted to feel his kisses hot against her neck as he entered her. She wished he had gotten religion or something. It would be easier to turn him. And a lot more fun. What he had gotten was a lot worse than religion.

She walked to the computer, engaged the modem, and dialed Michael's, listening to the intermediate number beep-beep as it relayed into his computer system. She keyed his access code and began scrolling through the financial directory. She had been searching his data banks since he disappeared, trying to locate his bank accounts. *Their* bank accounts. It wasn't that he tried to hide things from her, but he was constantly shifting money around, front company to front company, country to country. There was no way for her to keep up. Last year alone they had made over a quarter-million dollars just on currency fluctuations, their money shifting from Swiss francs to yen to dollars to pounds and back to dollars again.

She found their Liechtenstein account, but that had less than a hundred thousand dollars. Both corporations in the Cayman Islands were drained. Michael had said something about needing all their resources to take advantage of an expected dramatic rise in the price of some strategic metal found in central Africa, palladium or rhodium. He would have split the money into a dozen parcels to avoid taxes or potential problems with the SEC.

Lauren snapped off the screen with a flip of her

finger. She needed Michael back. No two ways about it. She turned away from the computer with a sigh, picked up the cellular phone, and strolled back to the picture window. The rain had tapered off.

Dr. Reese didn't sound surprised to hear from her.

"Ms. Kiel," said Reese. "You're calling on business, I trust."

"I think we can arrange a trade, Dr. Reese."

"I'm listening."

"You can have Tohlson's disks—"

"My disks."

"Just release Michael and wire transfer forty million dollars to our numbered account on the Isle of Man." She heard the clink of ice cubes and Reese chuckle. "That really isn't an outrageous request, Doctor. Tohlson told me your European subsidiary generates that much profit every year." Reese stopped laughing.

"That's it?" he barked.

"You know better than that." The wind rippled the dark surface of the lake, ran from one end to the other like a sheet slowly being pulled up. "There's the matter of Danny."

"I already—"

"No. Implicating him in Tohlson's . . . death isn't enough. I don't want him anywhere near a witness stand." She glanced toward the bedroom.

Silence on the line. "I suppose that can be arranged," Reese said slowly.

Lauren stood so close to the window that her bare breasts grazed the cool glass. "Not arranged, Dr.

Reese. I want to see you do it personally. Then we'll be even. When the police discover Danny's body, they'll search his apartment and find Tohlson's penis in the freezer. I'll certainly testify to his violent temper and jealous rages. I have certain connections with the district attorney's office; they'll be only too happy to pass out commendations and dismiss his death as a drug-related homicide."

"I'm impressed," said Reese. "But why settle for forty million dollars?"

She looked at the phone in her hand.

"The problem with any sort of extralegal bargain is the matter of trust," explained Reese. "Once I wire the money to your account, what leverage do I have? Once you hand over the computer disks, what leverage do you have?"

The swans had retreated from the lake, hidden themselves under the white gazebos sprinkled across the lawn. The swans and gazebos were supposed to make the complex feel like a country estate.

"Are you still there? I'm willing to turn over a hefty minority share of Reese Pharmaceuticals to you and your brother."

"Such generosity, Doctor. Why should I believe you?"

"Money is quite overrated, Miss Kiel. When you get to be my age, you'll understand that. What counts is working with people you like, special people. Your talents are quite evident, and I've grown very fond of your brother in just the short time we've spent together. You have no idea how difficult it is to find someone who really understands."

At the edge of the lake, Lauren could see clumps of soggy white feathers.

"Besides," said Dr. Reese. "I assume you've already copied the disks. If you're a partner, you're not likely to resell them to my competitors. *Our* competitors."

"That's a very interesting offer," she said. "I'll certainly consider it. Danny and I will meet you tomorrow, to trade the disks for the money and Michael. I'll call you in the morning to give you the specific location."

"How very cautious of you."

"Remember, I insist that you kill Danny yourself."

"You're a very exceptional woman."

"I'll bring the first five disks to seal the bargain. And if you have any second thoughts, you should know that my presence is required to retrieve the rest of them." She hung up, watching the lake with a satisfied expression. Her heart was pounding. She went back to bed, wrapped her arms and legs around Danny, clinging to him.

"What is it?" he asked, still half asleep.

"I was thinking how much I love you." She closed her eyes so tightly they burned with tears. "And how little good it's done either of us."

CHAPTER 37

DANNY KEPT HIS EYES on the twisting road, holding the Jaguar right at the speed limit. The air was fresh after last night's rain. It was the kind of morning that made him want to keep driving and never stop, just let the wind wash away all his cares.

Instead, they were on their way to a trade-off that was probably going to turn into the shoot-out at the OK Corral. And there wasn't a thing he could do about it.

"Not many men turn me down." Lauren tilted the rearview mirror, checked her lipstick.

"I'm an endangered species, all right. If I'm not careful, they're going to put me on a postage stamp."

"You're always careful, Danny." She smiled at her reflection.

Danny readjusted the mirror. He liked knowing what was gaining on him.

They drove down Pacific Coast Highway, heading south into the empty coastline between Newport

Beach and Laguna Beach; it was rocky, rugged and untouched, the last fifteen miles of undeveloped waterfront in Southern California. Plans to subdivide the area, called the Golden Wedge by the developers, had already been filed, but slow-growth groups were fighting a holding action, protecting the jackrabbits and sagebrush from minimalls and automatic sprinkler systems.

The road narrowed, rose, and fell, the shoulder dropping away to a rocky ravine littered with crushed cans and broken bottles. A long-haired kid stood beside a battered VW van parked in a turnoff, dejectedly pulling off an orange tiger-striped wetsuit. The ocean was glassy this morning; even the surfers were going to class.

Lauren had arranged to make the trade at the Date Shack, a deserted roadside stand stuck in the middle of nowhere. Danny told her that a more public place was safer, but she wanted things kept private.

"Did you tell Reese to come alone?" asked Danny.

"He'll have his security chief with him, Frank McVey. Maybe his two stupid nephews. That's it."

"That's plenty," said Danny. "Four against one."

"Don't I count?" said Lauren.

Danny turned into the gas station, kicking up pebbles and dust. The sullen teenage attendant ambled over wearing a greasy MEGADEATH tank top and camouflage pants. "Fill it up," said Danny. The kid pushed his headphones off, left them dangling around his neck, blaring a metal guitar solo. "Fill it, please," repeated Danny. The kid shuffled to the pump.

"Gotta pee," said Lauren.

In the rearview, Danny saw the kid's eyes following her ass. She wore tight black jeans and cowboy boots, a white T-shirt with the sleeves rolled up, and no bra. When she disappeared into the restroom, he picked up the cellular phone and dialed Holt's home number. If he called the station she might answer, and he needed time. Just in case things actually worked out. Her answering machine came on: "This is Jane Holt, please leave a message. You have as much time as you need."

That's what you think, Jane. "Hello," Danny said. "This is your favorite felon. I wanted you to know that Arthur Reese is up to his eyebrows in the Tohlson murder. He had Michael snatched, too. If I don't get back to you by tonight, come looking for the pieces near the Date Shack on PCH." Lauren stepped out of the restroom. "Ten-four, Jane." He hung up.

"That's fourteen twenty-five," said the kid, watching Lauren get in. Danny handed him a ten and a five. The kid stuffed the bills into his pocket, put his headphones back on, and walked away.

"Who were you talking to?" Lauren said lightly.

"Cubanito's service." The Jaguar kicked up dust as Danny accelerated back onto the road. "He's not answering."

"Count your blessings." The wind whipped Lauren's hair.

A few miles later they passed a turnoff to the

beach, and Danny slowed and pulled into the gravel surrounding the Date Shack. The stand was set on a promontory high above the beach, just four stumps that had been stools and a faded red Formica counter. Sun-bleached picnic tables were scattered behind the stand, a rusty chain-link fence zigzagged along the edge of the drop-off to the beach.

Lauren got out and stretched.

Danny was hot and overdressed in the suit from last night, feeling foolish in his fancy alligator loafers. He didn't like the shoes, but they had been a gift from Lauren and he had worn them to the *Queen Mary* with the same sentiment that made her wear the diamond necklace. He stood by the car, one hand in his pocket, taking comfort in the weight of the gun as he looked back down the road.

"Bring the disks," Lauren called over her shoulder. Danny caught up with her at the most distant picnic table, the stand hiding it from the road. He put the picnic cooler containing the disks under the shade of the table. She leaned against the fence, looking out to sea. "It's going to be a great day," she said, shading her eyes from the sun.

"For somebody." Danny shrugged off his jacket and laid it on the picnic bench, keeping the gun within reach.

Lauren turned to him. "What are you angry about? You've been mad at me since last night, and I don't know why."

Danny stalked over to look down the road,

checked his watch, and came back and stood next to her. Gulls keened overhead. The water was deep blue close to shore but slate-gray farther out, colder too. "I just don't want to be laid out in these fucking pimp shoes." He watched the ocean.

"What are you worried about?" said Lauren.

Danny nodded to the white van that was pulling onto the gravel. "Your friends are here."

"Kiss me." Lauren reached for him, still dancing. She ran her tongue across her lips. "Kiss me for luck."

Danny shrugged her off. "I've got all the luck I can handle."

CHAPTER 38

THE DOOR OF THE WHITE van swung open and this short geezer hopped out from behind the steering wheel, wearing a khaki bush jacket and twill pants, a cigarette bouncing between his lips. Had to be Dr. Reese. Or Jungle Jim. He strode to the front of the van, spotted Danny and Lauren, and flicked the butt in their direction.

Lauren sat on the picnic table, her back to the water; the wind stirred her hair as she caressed the line of her jaw with her fingertip. Danny stood next to her, his shirt soaked with sweat, the pistol at arm's length, tucked against the back of his right leg.

The breeze off the ocean carried the faint smell of salt and seaweed. Then he got a whiff of Lauren's perfume, just a touch and it was gone. Maybe he should have kissed her when he had the chance.

Reese banged on the side of the van, then stalked over to the picnic table, carrying a briefcase. He looked like the town badass in a cowboy movie, the chesty runt who straightened horseshoes with his molars and brained the hero with it when his back was turned.

Lauren acted like she had just noticed him. "Doctor, so nice you could make it." She indicated the picnic table with a wave.

Reese sat across from her, opened the briefcase, and exposed a portable computer. He glanced back at the van. "My nephews fell asleep on the ride over."

At the sliding-door sound, they all turned. A couple of blond behemoths climbed out of the van, still yawning, the vehicle rocking with the weight of them. They were dressed in baggy knee-length white shorts and identical Hawaiian shirts.

Danny rubbed the scar curved across his abdomen as he watched those bright silky shirts flapping in the wind. He saw Wilson's startled face back at the farmhouse, the hula dancers on his shirt splattered with blood. The Mayans believed the god of death showed himself many times to a man before snatching him up, a series of visitations designed to prepare each man for his fate. For some men death appeared as a jaguar, for others a squawking parrot or an ear of corn with black kernels. For Danny, death was Don Ho.

"What are you laughing at?" Reese said.

"You'll find out," said Danny. He pressed the pistol into Reese's spine and patted him down, trying to keep his gun hand from trembling. Control was a kite string humming through his fingers. If it slipped through, there was no getting it back.

"I'm disappointed in you," Reese said to Lauren. "You said no guns, and here you brought a shaky one."

Danny whacked Reese's head with the pistol butt, knocked him forward. Reese grunted, and Danny smacked him again. Reese twisted, cursing, but Danny held him down with one hand, jammed the gun against the base of his skull as the twins raced toward them. "Say good night, Gracie," whispered Danny, thumbing back the hammer.

"Boys!" Reese raised his hands. The twins stopped, unsure of themselves. Reese spoke calmly, though the tips of his ears were livid. "Listen to me. I want you to sit down, both of you. Just sit down." He sounded as if he was talking someone off a ledge. The twins sat.

Danny moved back next to Lauren, stood covering both Reese and the road. His hands weren't trembling anymore. "Tell the beef brothers to toss off their weapons."

"You think I'd trust the boys with guns?" laughed Reese. His pale crab eyes followed Danny. They should have been on stalks. "I like a man who's not afraid to show his claws." He dabbed the back of his head and grimaced. "And not afraid to use them, either. When you're outnumbered, you *have* to hit fast and hit hard." Reese indicated the twins with a flick of his wrist. "I do the same thing myself. Have to. You let these boys get up a head of steam, it's going to take a freight train to stop them."

"I don't need to stop them," Danny said evenly. "I just need to stop you."

"Right you are," said Reese. "Right as rain."

"Where's Michael?" said Danny. "The van?"

"He'll be along," said Reese.

"Let's get down to business," said Lauren.

Reese turned on the portable computer. A soft hum, and the liquid-crystal-display screen winked on. He took the floppy disk that Lauren handed him and slipped it into the computer. His gnarly fingers flew over the keyboard. "Ah," he breathed as the document came up, his eyes dancing across the screen as he scrolled through the report.

Danny didn't belong here. He was window dressing, as useless as the twins sitting there on their haunches, mouths dropped open, not comprehending a thing. He moved away from the table and leaned against the rusty chain-link fence.

"Oh, don't go," Reese called to him, not looking up from Tohlson's notes. "I'm beginning to enjoy your company. Takes a real man to step into this kind of situation. But here you are, right in the middle of it."

Danny felt the hair on his neck lift. He tightened his grip on the pistol.

A large truck roared down the road. They all jerked their heads and waited until it disappeared around a curve before speaking.

"Do we have a deal, Doctor?" said Lauren.

Reese pulled on his lip, lost in thought. "Tohlson evidently went off on a tangent," he murmured. "He thought the answer lay in the fibrous matrix, protein molecules that connect all the cells . . ."

"Doctor?"

"Oh yes," Reese said absently. "Worth every bit of it. And I hope you've given serious consideration to my proposition, Ms. Kiel."

Lauren glanced over at Danny, stared right through him. Her eyes were as empty and clear as arctic ice. There had been a time when he would kiss her and the ice would soften and melt, when the hardness in her would give way in a rush. If he kissed her now, his bones would shatter with the cold.

Danny turned at the faint sounds from the beach. Michael was down there. There was a man standing next to him. The man laid his hand on Michael's shoulder, and Michael collapsed onto the sand. The breeze carried his cries to Danny.

"Hey!" Danny shouted down to them.

Lauren and Reese hurried over to the fence.

"Do something, Reese," said Danny.

As Michael got to his feet, the man in the blue suit grabbed his wrist. Michael screamed.

"Looks like McVey is exceeding his authority again," clucked Reese. "He was just supposed to bring Michael around for your inspection, and instead, here he is showing off."

Danny grabbed Reese by the jacket, pressed the gun against his cheek so hard it left a ring of white skin radiating around the barrel. He tried the whisper again. "Call him off."

"McVey?" Reese's bushy eyebrows flew up. "Not hardly." The gun in his face didn't register at all; it might as well have been made of licorice.

The sun burned through the thin clouds, the

light making Reese blink. He slowly pushed the
gun away with his index finger. "You think you
know what's up?" He snickered at Danny. "You
don't know anything."

Lauren leaned against the fence, watching the
two of them with a glittering intensity.

Suddenly, Danny vaulted the fence, dirt and
pebbles rolling down the steep slope. He slid down
the bluff, hanging on to the bushes that grew out
from the sides. His alligator shoes slipped on the sea
grass, but he kept on, one hand holding the gun, the
other trying to brake his fall.

"Do it!" Lauren shook Reese, her face tight with
rage. "Kill him!"

Reese watched Danny's descent with interest.
"Plenty of time for that. All the time in the
world."

Danny was almost at the bottom, skidding in a
barely controlled slalom.

"Look at him go." Reese whistled. "Agile as a
Himalayan goat."

"You said you'd kill him. It has to be you."

"Boyd," said Reese. Boyd raced for the briefcase.
Lloyd spat over the edge of the drop-off, watched
it bounce and fall.

"McVey drove by your ex-husband's place late
last night, but there was a problem," said Reese.
He popped out the false bottom of the briefcase.
A dismantled rifle nestled in the foam insert. "A
policewoman was sitting in her car watching the
apartment." He screwed the rifle barrel into the
stock. "But don't worry. We'll stick Tohlson's organ

in the freezer, a little pink Popsicle for the police. There's plenty of time."

"I wish things had been different," said Lauren, looking at Danny so far below. "Everything would have been perfect."

Reese sighed so deeply it seemed to resonate through all of them. "We all have our regrets," he said, snapping on the telescopic sight. "I wouldn't know where to begin."

CHAPTER 39

DANNY TUMBLED THE last few yards down the bluff. He got slowly to his feet, hands scratched, his ears still ringing with the sound of Lauren's voice. One of his shoes was gone; he kicked off the other one. Danny looked up and saw Lauren, Reese, and the twins far above, silently peering down over the fence.

The beach was a long, broad inlet walled in by the cliffs. Michael was on his hands and knees at the water's edge, wearing madras Bermudas and a T-shirt. McVey stood beside him. He looked like a man walking a brightly colored dog.

Danny wiped the gun clean on his pants, blowing out the grit. It seemed like he had been scared forever. Scared Lauren was never coming back to him. Scared even more when she did. Now he was steady. He glanced up again, but Lauren was too far away for him to read the expression on her face. He started toward Michael.

McVey impassively watched Danny approach. Up close, he was more scarecrow than man. Michael stayed on his knees, head down.

"Get away from him," said Danny.

"Oh, I'm afraid that's out of the question, Mr. DiMedici." McVey's voice was flat and bland, the hum of a radio transmission when the signal has been lost. "I'm just a drone. A good little drone following orders, doing what I'm told."

"Following orders?" said Danny. "Reese said you weren't supposed to hurt Michael."

McVey ran a hand through his soft, wispy hair. An embarrassed smile twitched at the corners of his mouth.

Michael looked at Danny, eyelids drooping with pain. "Don't waste your time, bro."

"Shhhhhh," said McVey.

"You shouldn't have come." Michael started to rise. "Lauren set you up."

Danny kept watch on McVey. "I came for you, Michael, not for her."

"How very noble of you." McVey planted his foot in the center of Michael's back and drove him down. "We're not so different, you and I," he said to Danny. "Miss Kiel made fools of both of us, but that is ever the way with men of honor. We are easily betrayed."

"You head one way, and we'll head the other," Danny said gently. "Why make things worse than they already are?"

"Things are just fine," said McVey, measuring out the words.

Danny pointed the gun at him. "I'll use this."

McVey considered it for a moment, then shook his head. "I rather doubt that. Shooting an unarmed man isn't nearly as easy as most people think. A killing in the heat of the moment is one thing. Anyone can do that. Anyone. But in the bright sunlight? After such polite conversation?" Contempt veiled his face. "No. Killing without anger takes a certain . . . discipline. Do you have such discipline, Mr. DiMedici?"

"You'd be surprised."

McVey moistened his lips with the tip of his tongue. "I don't think so. I've seen your apartment. I've seen the disorder of your life."

Michael spit out sand. "Shoot the son of a bitch."

The wind was rising, slapping the waves against the shore. McVey jerked Michael to his feet, pulled him near. Michael swung on McVey, but there was no strength left in him. A gull shrieked past in a blur of wings. McVey draped his hand across the base of Michael's neck and Michael moaned, his body falling limp. "Whoops," said McVey. "I did it again."

Danny fired the gun past McVey's ear.

McVey took a step backward into the water. He looked down at his soaked shoes and soggy pants cuffs as if he had just noticed the ocean.

Michael crawled up onto the sand. Danny took a step toward him.

McVey looked wistfully out to sea, still ankle-deep in the water. "Tide's coming in." He said it so wearily that Danny stopped. "Time and tide, love and duty, and here we stand, good soldiers on the edge of the world, trying to make things right, without any hope of success."

"What are you waiting for?" Lauren said to Reese.

Reese sighted through the rifle's scope. "I love this. You have no idea, none at all."

McVey patted his suit jacket, held up his empty hands to show Danny. "Getting a chocolate. That's all." He slowly took a candy kiss from his inside pocket, unwrapped the foil, and offered it to Danny. He waited for a moment, then popped it into his mouth.

Danny reached for Michael, glanced up to see McVey whipping a gun out of his jacket, then firing once into Michael's back. Danny shot McVey twice in the center of the chest, knocking him backward into the water, but even as he fell, McVey fired again.

Danny found himself sprawled on the beach. He felt around for his gun, but it was lost. There was a roaring so loud that he thought Lauren was next to him, humming her little song, but it was just blood trickling down his scalp, running into his ear. It was an easy mistake.

He staggered over to where Michael lay and cradled him close. There was blood everywhere. The two of them were soaked. Tears ran down Danny's cheeks and dropped onto his hands.

"Hey, you're the one in trouble." Michael's grin was broken beyond repair. "No way you're ever going to convince Lauren I didn't tell you where all the money went."

Danny rocked him in his arms.

"I want to go home," Michael said dreamily. "Everything bad happens outside the perimeter."

"Don't go," pleaded Danny as the color drained out of Michael's face. "Stay here." He stared at the blood spreading onto the sand like a pink rose. "Michael?" he said, knowing he was already gone.

"Step away from him, Mr. DiMedici," said McVey. He stood in the shallows, dripping wet, gun aimed at Danny.

Danny eased Michael's head onto the sand and smoothed back his hair.

"Stand up," said McVey. "You deserve to get it on your feet." He grunted in pain. "My suit is double-woven Kevlar fabric," he said, straining to maintain his level intonation. "It'll stop a magnum round, but there's not much you can do about the impact. Pity." He touched his chest and winced. "I do believe you've broken some of my ribs, Mr. DiMedici." He had that wistful smile again. It looked like it was painted on a skull. "I do so abhor discomfort of any kind." The smile evaporated. Only the skull remained. "I asked you to stand up, Mr. DiMedici."

Danny got slowly to his feet. He looked out to sea, the horizon stretching out to infinity.

"About a hundred and fifty yards, I figure," Reese said to Lauren, pulling the rifle sling taut. "McVey gets the first one, for disobeying orders. I *liked* Michael. Don't worry; Mr. DiMedici doesn't appear to be going anywhere."

Lauren hung on to the chain-link fence, her knuckles white.

"I've got the muzzle velocity for the shot," said Reese. "It's the wind gusts I'm worried about." He took a deep breath, let half of it out. The cross hairs locked onto McVey's head as Reese waited for the wind to die. He slowly squeezed the trigger.

Danny heard a crackling sound and looked over at McVey. Where had he gotten that extra eye? The black one in the center of his forehead. How could Danny not have noticed that before? McVey slid into the water, collapsing so abruptly that it seemed every bone in his body had dissolved.

The cross hairs wavered slightly at the back of Danny's head as Reese shifted position. "Come on," Reese said. "Turn around so I can see the look in your eyes at the moment of impact."

At the crunch of gravel, Reese backed off the trigger, turned to see a white Range Rover skidding across the parking lot, Jane Holt behind the wheel.

"Do something," said Lauren to Reese, waving at the dust that billowed around them.

The car door flew open. "Detective." Reese smiled, lowering the rifle. "I'm glad you're here."

Danny collapsed beside Michael, watched the clouds float past, big fluffy ones, turning slowly in the breeze. The big cloud directly overhead looked like a horse, a white stallion charging across the sky. Danny wanted to ride him, hang on to the wispy mane, but the horse was falling away now, falling behind, falling into pieces as Danny watched.

A woman was crouched over him, so near that her long red hair brushed his cheek. What was Jane Holt doing here? One of them was crying, but he couldn't tell who. He wanted to ask her, but his mouth wasn't working. He closed his eyes. He would ask her later.

CHAPTER 40

THE SLEEPY-EYED RESIDENT checked the CAT-scan results, muttered something to Danny about how lucky he was, and waved Jane Holt in from the hallway. "You don't have to do this," she said to Danny. "You have the right to have a lawyer present."

"You're good enough, Jane." He was propped up in the hospital bed, his head swathed in bandages.

"Jane, is it?" Sniffed the lanky man in blue pinstripes who bustled in after her, a monogrammed leather clutch under his arm. "How very friendly." A sweating court reporter followed, carrying a steno machine.

Holt sat in the chair next to Danny's bed, crossing and uncrossing her long legs. She had on the same gray tailored suit she wore when she had surprised him at his apartment that first night.

"I still don't understand why you feel the need to be present during Mr. DiMedici's deposition,

Detective," said the pinstriped man from the far side of the room.

The door swung open and Karl Steiner rolled in. "Gangway," he said, the electric hum of the wheelchair rising and falling as he parallel-parked at the foot of the bed. "Howdy, neighbor!" he said, thumping Danny's leg. Steiner was on the fifth floor, but this was the first time he had made it down to visit. His voice was the same familiar bellow, but the smile was unconvincing. Mirth trickled across his puffy face but didn't sink in.

"Nice wheels, Karl." Danny returned the wink.

"I hate to interrupt your little reunion," said the pinstriped man, "but I'm Assistant District Attorney Phipps, Mr. DiMedici, and we have business to take care of." He pulled a sheaf of yellow legal pads from his folder, aligning them into a neat stack with a rap of his hand.

The court reporter sat down, balancing the steno machine on his knees as he swore Danny in. Phipps laid the groundwork, spelling out his name, having Danny do the same while the court reporter tapped away.

"Detective Holt has turned over a phone tape in which you accuse Dr. Arthur Reese of involvement in the murder of Dr. Harold Tohlson."

"Reese didn't kill Tohlson," said Danny. "He just covered it up."

"Hmmm." Phipps leafed through another legal pad. "Yes, that's right." He sounded bored, not even bothering to look at Danny. "You told Detective Holt that Lauren Kiel committed the murder after stealing certain research information. Part of a pattern of industrial espionage she was engaged in."

Danny glanced at Holt. "That's what I said."

"Do you have any substantiation for your charges, Mr. DiMedici? Anything at all. Take your time."

"Ask Lauren," said Danny.

"I've already deposed Ms. Kiel." Phipps stared out the window at the construction project down the street. A jackhammer started up in the distance. Phipps wet his lips. "She says Dr. Tohlson was alive when she left her beach house, repulsed by his aberrant sexual demands. While she doesn't know who did kill him, certain . . . physical evidence found in Mr. McVey's office, in his refrigerator to be exact, make him the primary suspect."

"She killed Tohlson," Danny said evenly.

"You're a psychic, are you, Mr. DiMedici?" A steam shovel tore into the side of the hill, dredging out boulders and thick white roots. "Do you place that before or after narcotics dealer on your résumé?"

Danny touched his forehead, encountered the bandages, and put his hand down. "I know Lauren. That's enough." The court reporter tapped away.

"So, Mr. DiMedici, knowing Ms. Kiel as you do, believing her to be a killer"—Phipps moistened his index finger and rubbed at a scuffed spot on the toe of his shoe—"you decided to have sex with her on a public beach. That's what Ms. Kiel testified under oath."

A flush crept up Holt's neck.

"She said she came to you for help," continued

Phipps. "She said she knew the police wanted to question her, but she was confused, terrified that she might have been the intended victim of whoever killed Tohlson. She came to you, the one man she trusted. You tricked her into taking drugs and took advantage. Is that what happened?"

Steiner had helped himself to a glass of water from the bedside pitcher. "You got a real nice bedside manner, Phipps," he said, "reminds me of the nurse gave me an enema last week." Ice tinkled.

"I'm sorry, Mr. DiMedici"—Phipps didn't miss a beat—"what was your answer? Would you like the court reporter to read back the question?"

"It was a mistake. I can't defend it." Danny was talking to Holt now. "But that doesn't change what she did to Tohlson. Or what happened to Michael."

"Yes," said Phipps, dragging out the word. "Michael Kiel. You don't dispute that Mr. Kiel was killed by Frank McVey, do you? That McVey also shot you?" Danny shook his head. "Please answer verbally, Mr. DiMedici."

"No. I don't dispute that."

"Hmmm." Phipps tapped his pursed lips. "Let me make sure I understand. Ms. Kiel never threatened you, never harmed you in any way. Is that correct?"

"That's right, but—"

"And Dr. Reese didn't harm you in any way either. In fact, Dr. Reese shot McVey to save your life, didn't he?"

"You're missing the point," said Danny.

Phipps slowly exhaled. "The point, Mr. DiMedici, is that initially you were the only person carrying a gun on the one occasion you actually met Dr. Reese. True?"

"Don't say a word," Holt said to Danny. "Possession of a handgun by a convicted felon is a serious crime. You know better, Phipps."

"You're in the wrong profession, Detective. You should be a defense attorney."

"Aren't you done?" said Holt. "You've gone through the motions, now you can scurry back to the DA and tell him that there's no grounds to pursue the investigation. Then the DA and the chief can go on TV and tell the cameras that the case is solved, that the system works."

"You seem a bit overwrought, Detective." A thin smile from Phipps. He closed the pad, zipped his folder, and stood up. "Thank you, Mr. DiMedici. Your deposition will be given to the district attorney. He'll decide whether to file charges."

"He's telling the truth," Holt said angrily. "You should have already indicted—"

"If you have a problem with our handling of this matter, take it up with your superiors."

"I have," said Holt.

"Then that settles it, doesn't it?" said Phipps, walking brusquely out. The court reporter followed.

The three of them sat there. Danny wanted to say something, but he was distracted by the way Holt's stockings rustled when she crossed her legs. She couldn't get comfortable. Neither could he. Finally Steiner cleared his throat. "Well, it's time for my nap, and I'm sure you two kids got plenty to talk about." Holt held the door open for him. "See?" he said to her, jerking his head toward Danny. "I told you he was one of the good guys."

Danny waited for the door to close. "Is he going to be okay?" he said.

"Depends on what you mean by 'okay.' " She looked away. "He's . . . not coming back to work, though."

"Thanks for finding out about Cubanito," Danny said before the silence could take hold. Holt had located Cubanito in a south county hospital's intensive care unit, with crushed ribs and a ruptured spleen. One of his lungs had been removed. But he was alive. "That meant a lot to me." He toyed with the sheet, pulling it into peaks, then smoothing it out until it was perfectly flat again. "Lauren's going to walk, isn't she?"

"I don't know."

"Yes, you do. She's going to walk. Reese too. Everybody wins but us, right?"

Their eyes met. "Don't count on it," she said. "I don't care what the DA decides. You and I both know what she did."

"She likes it even better that way," said Danny.

Holt nodded. "She's quite a woman, your ex-wife. I questioned her myself; she was ever so helpful, with a perfect little catch in her voice when she talked about you, how concerned she was for you. She had an answer for everything."

"Ask her what she sees when she turns out the light," said Danny.

Holt leaned closer. "I don't need to ask her anything. She didn't fool me for a moment." Her elbows rested on the bed, all that dark auburn hair of hers tumbling forward, brushing the sheets. "How did she manage to fool you? I sat across from her in Interrogation . . . " She shook her head, tried to dismiss the thought but failed. "I know it's none of my business—"

"It is your business." They let that hang in the air for a moment.

"She was different when I first met her," said Danny. He could see Lauren, sitting on a beach at sunset in a loose cotton dress, digging her toes into the sand as the sky grew darker. "Maybe I was different too." There was a tightness in his chest. Holt reached over and blotted his forehead with a tissue. "I started dealing gradually," he said, "it wasn't an overnight thing where you wake up and start moving quarter-ton loads of sensimilla. It happens one step at a time. Good times and handshake deals and picking up the check. And one day people are dead, and you've got too much money, and there's no way to make it right."

"Yes," Holt said, her voice dropping to a whisper, "one slip is all it takes sometimes." He could barely hear her. "But Karl says, 'A cop who don't make exceptions is no better than a meter maid.' " She looked at him, her green eyes flecked with darker green. Playful now. "If I don't stop associating with you and Karl," she said, "I'm going to get in trouble."

Danny took her hand. It fit easily into his. "When someone leaves you," he said, carefully lining up the words, "someone you love . . . there's a part of you that's always waiting for them to come back. Well, Lauren did come back. But she was different. I remember looking at her on the *Queen Mary* and knowing it was over between us. I was wrong about her. Haven't you ever been wrong about someone, Jane?"

"Yes." She squeezed his hand, her eyes bright. "Once upon a time."

CHAPTER 41

BOYD WAS HOGGING EVERYTHING, as usual. He had the binoculars dangling from his neck, the extra canteens strapped around his waist, and their rations in a backpack. But when he tried to red-light the rifle, Lloyd put his foot down.

"Uncle *Arthur*," said Lloyd, "you said we were supposed to take turns."

Arthur Reese looked up from where he was bent over the trail. "Damnit, Boyd, share it with your brother. That's what this is about."

Uncle Arthur's bush jacket was streaked with sweat, and tiredness creased his face like cracks in the earth. He had slept the whole way on the helicopter ride to San Gennaro Island. Even now, when he had yelled at Boyd, his voice was slow, without any real heart. He sounded beat. Which was the scariest thing Lloyd had ever heard.

"Take a break, boys," said Uncle Arthur, getting slowly to his feet. He walked over to one of the raggedy-ass eucalyptus trees that dotted the island and sat down, his back against the tree trunk, his rifle across his knees. Lloyd brought him a canteen. Uncle Arthur grunted, took a drink, and held it in his mouth for a few seconds before swallowing.

Boyd had torn branches off a sapling, twisted himself a leafy hat. He sat right in the middle of the trail, guzzling at a canteen, not even trying to conserve water. The rifle was propped up under his arm so it pointed straight at Uncle Arthur.

"Lloyd!" shouted Uncle Arthur. "Take that rifle away from your idiot brother." He shook his head in disgust. Seeing him angry made Lloyd feel better.

"Kissass," whispered Boyd as Lloyd took the weapon from him.

It was a neat gun, a pump-action 30.06 with a scope and everything. Uncle Arthur said it was his first rifle, from when he was a boy himself. He said the rifle had taught him everything he needed to know about life. The twins weren't going to college anyway. Lloyd put the rifle to his shoulder and whirled back down the path, sighting on birds and rocks and a big dragonfly.

A rocky, mountainous speck, privately owned and uninhabited, San Gennaro was one of the small channel islands off the coast of Santa Barbara. There were no buildings on it except for an abandoned World War II radar station. Too barren for agriculture or tourism, the island had been stocked with game during the 1920s—elk, deer, kit fox, and Russian black boars—and turned into a hunting preserve.

The elk and deer population had been decimated —they were too tall and easily sighted among the stunted vegetation. The tiny foxes, though blinded by the dense brush, managed to survive through their keen hearing and sense of smell, living on lizards and birds' eggs. The black boars, in contrast, were perfectly suited to the rugged terrain; they were omnivorous and low to the ground, their thick hide was impervious to nettles and foxtail. The abundance of roots and blackberries, the absence of predators, made the island a pig paradise.

Uncle Arthur and the twins had been hiking up and down the hills and gulleys since morning, following the game trails that crisscrossed the scrub, looking for signs. Boyd just wanted to go home and lift some serious iron. Uncle Arthur said patience was all part of the game. The funny thing was, Lloyd actually liked it on the island. The air was fresh, climbing up and down the hills was a good workout, and there were all these pretty wild flowers that smelled like organic honey. And no people.

Uncle Arthur talked with his eyes closed. "You're both going to have to learn to follow orders, to take on more responsibility. I'm depending on the two of you. You've got to be my strong right arm, now that McVey is gone."

"That was some shot you made, Uncle Arthur," said Lloyd, "Spiderman never knew what hit him." He aimed the rifle at a gawking crow, remembering McVey's face. "Pow! Dead center."

Uncle Arthur's eyes flew open. "Shut up, Lloyd."

"Yeah, shut up, Junior," said Boyd. "You just tell me what to do, I'll do it," he said to Uncle Arthur.

Uncle Arthur wiped his face with the sleeve of his jacket. "I know that. You're good boys. You just need a little seasoning." He rubbed his temples as he talked. "Hunting's the thing for you. Learn to depend on each other. Learn to depend on yourselves." He lifted his head, pinning them with the terrible bitterness of his gaze. "It's just us now. We're all there is."

The twins nodded at him, understanding nothing.

"Sir?" Lloyd hefted the rifle. "You sure this'll stop Mr. Boar?"

Uncle Arthur spat. "Look, you've got four one-hundred-eighty-grain slugs in the clip," he said for the tenth time that day, "and one in the chamber. One shot'll do it. One shot in the right place—right behind the shoulder. A heart shot." He waved a finger at them. "Remember. Things happen fast out here. Some boars'll duck and cover, some'll come right for your goodies." The twins glanced at each other. Uncle Arthur stood up and took off down the narrow path.

"This is stupid," Boyd said.

They started up a steep slope, the path slippery with dry weeds. It was Boyd's turn to carry the gun and he was acting up behind Uncle Arthur's back, marching stiffly, pretending to be a toy soldier. Boyd wasn't usually so disrespectful, but they both had noticed the change in Uncle Arthur since the shootout at the Date Shack. It wasn't that he was scared of the police; Uncle Arthur said as long as the three of them kept to the same story, everything would be all right. Every time either of the twins was questioned, Uncle Arthur made sure his lawyer was there, so he could tell them when not to answer.

The police weren't bothering Uncle Arthur. And it wasn't Spiderman; he was just hired help. Lloyd thought there was something more. He heard Uncle Arthur and that Lauren babe arguing on the phone a couple of nights ago, and Uncle Arthur was saying the notes were useless, and she kept wanting her money. They both used bad language, and afterward Uncle Arthur had bourbon breath.

Lloyd had picked a little bouquet of wild flowers. He kept picking more flowers, as he trotted behind Boyd, the bouquet getting bigger and bigger, a fist-size bundle of blue and yellow blossoms. He wished he had someone to give them to.

Uncle Arthur bent down on one knee, pointing something out to Boyd. "See," he said quietly, "see how deep the gorges are? This fella's going to weigh in at over five hundred pounds, a real monster. How'd you like to have his head in your bedroom? Huh, boys? That'd give you some sweet dreams."

Boyd stared at the ragged slashes in the hard packed earth where the boar had rooted for food. A fallen tree lay shattered, the decayed wood torn apart in the search for insects.

"Mr. Boar's not just smart," Uncle Arthur said, still kneeling, crushing clods of dirt between his fingers, "he's got a mean streak. I've seen a boar open up a man's belly, run off, then turn and give the man another toss. He could have gotten clean away, but just couldn't pass up an opportunity." Uncle Arthur laughed. "That's the big fella whose head's on my office wall." Uncle Arthur put his arm around Boyd. "Your first kill."

Boyd looked sick.

Lloyd wandered over for a better look.

Uncle Arthur smacked the flowers out of his hand. "Pay attention," he hissed.

There was a crashing in the bushes off to the right. They froze. Uncle Arthur made hand signals for Boyd to get into position. Boyd moved slowly, crouched and raised the rifle toward the sound. The tip of the rifle shook.

Far down the path a huge head covered with coarse black hair poked out of the brush. The breeze carried the sharp smell to them. The boar snorted, lifting its head; it looked oily in the afternoon sunlight, with short tufted ears and a broad, muscled body.

The boar trotted down the path toward them; so big that its flanks brushed the bushes on either side of the trail. Forty yards away it stopped, its head twitching from side to side, one pair of tusks jutting straight up from its top jaw, another curved out from its lower.

"Shoot," whispered Uncle Arthur.

Boyd fired. Rocks flew ten feet past the boar. He pumped in another round, fired again. The boar raced into the underbush. Boyd fired again. And again. And again. The clip was empty but he kept pulling back the bolt and pulling the trigger until Uncle Arthur took the gun from him and smacked him across the face with it. Uncle Arthur tossed the empty gun to Lloyd and handed Boyd his own rifle. "Here," he said to Boyd. "You aren't going home until you kill something."

"It was looking at me, Uncle Arthur," Boyd sobbed, "I could see it looking right at me and it knew, it knew."

Uncle Arthur kicked Boyd in the butt, pushed him down the trail the way they had come. "Scoot! He'll be coming out down that way." He glanced back at Lloyd. "Reload that weapon. One of you is going to do something right!"

"Yes, sir!"

Lloyd followed behind Uncle Arthur and Boyd, pushing bullets into the clip as he ran, jacking one into the chamber. Just like he had been taught. He was so busy he tripped on an outcropping of shale and skidded forward, howling with pain. He got up, still holding the rifle, his face and elbows scraped raw. Uncle Arthur and Boyd waited ahead, watching the underbrush. Suddenly the boar burst out of the bushes right in front of Lloyd, squealing, its eyes ablaze with hate.

Lloyd didn't even have time to think; he swung the rifle at the boar as it came at him, swung it as hard as he could, breaking the rifle over that ugly, shaggy head. The beast caught him in the leg, and tossed him aside. He heard Uncle Arthur telling Boyd to shoot, then the boar thrashing in the scrub. Lloyd looked down and saw his right leg had been torn from knee to hip. He could see every shade of pink in his body. It didn't hurt. Not even a little bit. Lloyd lay back on the ground.

Uncle Arthur leaned over him, wrapping a neckerchief around his wounded leg. Lloyd could hardly believe how quickly the old man's hands moved, tying the cloth tight, elevating the leg. "Boyd!" Uncle Arthur shouted. Boyd stayed where he was, the rifle hanging from one hand like he didn't even know it was there.

The ground under Lloyd felt wet. He wanted to tell Uncle Arthur that he was okay, but it was so nice to see how concerned he was. Like Uncle Arthur said, family was all any of us got.

The boar poked his head out of the brush. "Take it easy," Uncle Arthur gently said. Lloyd couldn't tell if he was talking to him or to the boar. Uncle Arthur carefully slid over to the broken rifle and picked it up. The boar snorted and took a step toward them. It was breathing hard, watching, its leathery snout puffing in and out. Uncle Arthur tapped the dirt out of the barrel, and braced the shattered stock against a big rock. He aimed the gun right at the boar, but Lloyd could see it was bent.

"Boyd." Uncle Arthur didn't raise his voice. "Take your shot. Now."

Squealing, dirt flying, the boar charged straight for Uncle Arthur. "Shoot!" he screamed. Lloyd looked up and to his astonishment saw Boyd running away. Lloyd closed his eyes, smelled the rotting-mushroom stink of the boar. He heard Uncle Arthur fire the bent rifle. Eyes clenched, Lloyd imagined himself at the bodybuilding competition, doing his posing routine alone, all by himself onstage while applause rained down upon him.

CHAPTER 42

THE NIGHT WAS COLD but the bay was colder still, so cold that Danny was barely beyond the reflection of the street-lights before he turned back to shore. He swam through rainbows of light, the surface of the water rippling in his phosphorescent wake.

He toweled off and bundled into his fleecy sweats. This was his first swim since he had gotten out of the hospital, his return to the icy currents that had sustained him for so long. On those dark swims he had pushed himself beyond endurance, until the cold had reached his bottomless longing for Lauren. Now when she called, asking what Michael had told him on the beach, wanting to know where her money was, Danny just hung up on her. He was going to have to get used to swimming in sunshine. If his teeth hadn't been chattering, Danny would have smiled.

It felt good to walk the beach, to feel the sand under his bare feet, smell the salty air. He looked up. The stars twinkled firmly in their places, riveted to the sky.

He headed back to his apartment, passed slowly through the peaceful streets, taking his time. Eilene's curtains were pulled, the room dark. He paused at the top of his landing, looked back toward the beach one last time, and glimpsed his footsteps in the sand filling with moonlight.